DICKSON UNIVERSITY BOOK TWO

max

New York Times & USA Today Bestselling Author

monroe

AUTHOR NOTE

Welcome to Blake and Lexi's world—a place where opposites don't just attract, they collide in the most delicious, laugh-out-loud, "I can't put this book down" kind of way.

Lexi Winslow is brilliant, snarky, and has a tendency to overthink everything—in fact, she's probably already analyzing this sentence and readying herself to break it down in a self-made app. But Blake Boden is magnetic, confident, and has a way of making people forget their carefully laid plans—even perfectionists like Lexi.

Together, their story is…*everything*.

Prepare yourself for THE BEST banter, just the right amount of steam, and the kind of binge-read you won't be able to put down. Trust us, we should know. This book kept us up way, way, *way* past our bedtimes for several weeks straight.

Playing Games has quickly become one of our favorite books we've ever written. Lexi Winslow and Blake Boden are so special to us, and we feel incredibly honored that we finally get to share them with you. Something about their chemistry feels like magic.

And, as a bonus, some really great check-ins with our favorite characters from Dickson University book 1, Learning Curve, and the Winslows and Billionaire Bad Boys will keep you smiling from ear to ear. If you don't know those people, don't fret—this book stands truly alone if you want it to. ☺

Happy Reading.

XOXO,

Max & Monroe

DEDICATION

This book is for anyone who's ever tried to overanalyze love (read: all of us at one time or another).

To the spreadsheet-makers, the overthinkers, and the ones who triple-check everything (including their feelings). And to the wildcards, the rule-breakers, and the ones who always forget to text back.

Love isn't about making perfect sense.

Love is about finding someone who sees your quirks and calls them magic.

Playing

GAMES

INTRO

Sometimes, when you have a genius IQ of 146 in a sea of average 100s, you start to think you can't be wrong.

You know better, you know more, you have the *data* to back yourself up, and the possibility of falling victim to unsound theorization is so low, it's barely a possibility.

But then there are moments that define us—little slivers of time that change the way we think about ourselves and our existence. It happens in science, too, of course, when some small piece of information shifts the course of your experiment entirely when you least expect it. But when it happens in life, the swift and all-encompassing fist to the gut is even more debilitating.

Because, as it turns out, geniuses *can* be wrong. *I* can be wrong. So wrong, in fact, I nearly crash and burn altogether.

"Hey, Lex, I have a question," my little brother Wes Jr. says, his tone way too innocent for the certified smartass I know him to be. I listen, but I don't look up yet. I can't.

I'm in the middle of running a test on an AI-coded app I've developed for my second doctoral dissertation. My first PhD, in Mathematics, completed a year and a half ago, is an accomplishment to be proud of, but it also isn't enough to prepare me for what I want to do in the world of technology.

So here I am at the dinner table with my favorite food getting cold, knee-deep in my second PhD, this time in Computer Science. The spaghetti on my plate sits untouched, but my test run is almost complete—sixty seconds to go, if I can just finish without interruption.

My little brother is undeterred by the fact that I'm clearly busy, plowing ahead to drop *the* bomb.

"Will you have a funeral one day…or will we just have to visit your rotting corpse in the lab?"

My gaze jerks to his, a mischievous curve to his lips setting the tone, and my breath catches in my chest. His words should be inconsequential—to many people, they would be—but to me, they are earthshaking.

Because of my complex, neurodivergent chemical makeup, being caught off guard is almost akin to an extinction-level event. I'm a planner. A thinker. A certified head case of attention to detail confirmed by a neurologist and seven highly efficient screenings by the state of New York from the age of four onward.

When people speak, I expect to have an idea of what they're going to say, but nowhere on my radar did I see this incoming missile of attack.

"Seriously, Lex," my little brother adds. "Hazmat suits are expensive and hard to get. Just want to know if I need to start figuring out the dark web to get my hands on one."

"*Wes*," my mom chastises through a half sigh and a half laugh, while my stepdad fights the urge to burst into his own laughter.

My brother's bravado is bolstered by their amusement, so he stares, waiting for a response.

I roll my eyes, pause the test run on the app, set my phone on the table beside my plate, and pick up my fork again. "My doctoral dissertation on advancing technology with artificial intelligence-based code is due at the end of this summer. It's normal to be preoccupied with it," I argue sensibly, fighting the sting in my chest.

"Yeah. Maybe if you hadn't already finished your dissertation over two months ago—before your final semester even starts," Wes objects on a snort. "Now you're just obsessing."

"Wes, stop picking on Lexi," my stepdad says, attempting his best stern dad face. You'd think that being a billionaire and the owner of the New York Mavericks, one of the most successful professional football teams in the country, would make him a master at laying down the law—and maybe it does in business—but when it comes to my brother and me, Wes Lancaster Sr. is no firmer than microwave-softened butter.

When my mom met him, I was just a little girl, and from the start, he treated me like I was his own. My biological father, Nick Raines, wasn't around back then, so for a long time, Wes wasn't just *like* a dad to me—he *was* my dad.

Even now, at the age of twenty-five—with a biological father who *is* in the picture—I still address him as *Dad*.

"Yeah, Wes," my mom chimes in. "I'm sure there are quite a few things Lexi could find to tease *you* about."

"No way. I'm pure perfection," my little brother comments haughtily, like only a teenage boy can. "And I'm not picking on her, just inserting a few strands of reality into her perfect DNA." He looks over at me. "I know you like the lab, Lex, but there's more out there. I promise."

My smile is smug. "The thirteen-year-old expert on life. Trust me, Wes, I have more going on than coding and apps."

He snorts. "Ah, yes, you have complex mathematical equations and the whole difficult mental challenge of trying to solve all of the mysteries of the universe too."

I shake my head and look down at my plate, willing myself to keep my mouth shut. Just because my little brother is instigating doesn't mean I have to be reactionary. I have lots of things in my life that he doesn't know about—that practically no one knows about.

I run Dickson University's underground secret society, Computare Caterva, for one, and as soon as I finished my run of my dissertation test app, I was going to start planning for tomorrow night's event at Dragon Stadium. We've expanded to seventy-five members now—due in large part to Ace Kelly, a family friend and fellow Dickson student, who invites people as if secrecy is just a suggestion—and pulling off each gathering is getting harder and harder.

Not only that, but I've had boyfriends. I've had sex. I haven't experimented with drugs or alcohol, but that's more because of my fear of feeling out of control than anything else.

Milestone-wise, I'd say I'm just about on freaking schedule for a woman my age.

"You don't know everything that's going on in my life," I settle for arguing. "None of you does."

My mom's face saddens a little, though she does her best to cover it. She's been fighting for me since the moment I was born through a myriad of huge happenings, including my biological dad leaving when I was just a baby, my being diagnosed on the autism spectrum, and through a rigorous, accelerated academic schedule. And in return, I've given her little more emotional connection than a muskrat. And secrets. Lots of secrets.

Winnie Winslow Lancaster deserves better. Especially from her only daughter.

I don't want to be cold or self-involved or numb to others—all of which I could appear so easily without exercising diligence not to be. Intellectually, I'm advanced, but my social skills and understanding of emotions could always use work.

I clear my throat, picking at the napkin in my lap to distract myself from the burn of awareness in my lungs. "But maybe you're right, Wes. I'll take what you've said into consideration and try to expand my horizons."

"Really?" His face lights up, and even my parents' eyes lift with optimism.

Great. It's going to be hard to deny all their hopeful faces now.

"Really. I'll make an effort," I promise, though I'm not entirely sure what that means yet.

Maybe it starts with this dinner—keeping my head out of

academia long enough to genuinely connect with them. Maybe it's learning to say *yes* to things more often, even when it feels uncomfortable. Maybe it's being willing to change.

I don't have the answers, but for them, I'm willing to try to figure it out—even if it means being wrong a lot more often.

1

The lights are off, the halls eerily quiet as I tiptoe through Dickson University's Dragon Stadium. Each step echoes, even though I'm moving as softly as I can, and behind me, Julia Brooks and Ace Kelly follow hand in hand, completely oblivious—as usual—to how ridiculously perfect they are for each other.

They're both a year younger than me, soon-to-be sophomores, and when I first met Ace last fall, Julia wasn't far behind. Honestly, I thought they were a couple, and it didn't take long to figure out so did everyone else on campus. But they've insisted time and time again that they've been best friends since childhood, nothing more.

Still, the way they're constantly attached at the hip tells an entirely different story, and I'm always wondering when one of them is going to realize the truth.

The navy blue of the concrete walls makes the already dark space seem even darker, and I try to get a look at their faces to see how they're feeling about being here, but seeing anything clearly is impossible. I turn forward again, hustling through the maze of pathways that'll take us to the field.

At the beginning of the year, Ace, Julia, Finn Hayes, Scottie Bardeaux, and I became fast friends, getting into more than our fair share of excitement and trouble. Fights, firsts, parties, and laughter filled our time, until it all changed in April. When Scottie—our good friend and a star Dickson cheerleader—suffered a devastating spinal injury at a competition in Daytona, our group tightened even more, every ounce of our focus shifting to supporting her as she adjusted to the new reality of her paralysis.

For the past month, that focus has been our entire world.

But with spring semester winding down and Scottie adjusting remarkably well—thanks in large part to Finn's unwavering support—it finally feels like we can breathe again. Tonight, Finn and Scottie are spending time with their families, officially a couple again, as they're so obviously meant to be. That means Ace, Julia, and I finally feel okay to let loose for the first time in a while.

And there's no better place to do it than at a Computare Caterva event.

Dickson University's underground society is always a thrill—a secret mix of risk and adrenaline that guarantees a good time. But it's terrifying too. One wrong move could land us all in hot water with the university and then some, and I'd certainly have a hell of a lot to lose. A single misstep could cost me my football scholarship and send my future dreams of playing in the pros spiraling down the toilet.

Normally, I'm cautious about my actions, and when it comes to football eligibility, I always follow the rules. I don't drink, I don't do drugs, and knowing what I know now about Double C, I shouldn't be doing this.

But when the text came through two hours ago, telling us to meet at Dragon Stadium, I wasted no time reaching for my keys.

There's only one reason I'm not my usual rational self about this…and all the signs point to Lexi Winslow.

This is likely the last Double C event of the year, and with my crush, Lexi, running the show while inching closer to finishing her doctorate—and leaving Dickson University for good—I couldn't miss it. Even if being here is a risk, it's a chance I'm willing to take.

She's a few years older than me—twenty-five to my twenty-one—and I've been crushing on her beautiful, endlessly intriguing personality since the first time I laid eyes on her at the start of fall semester. I thought it was a stupid crush, but instead of fading, my feelings have only grown. Her stubbornness and complete avoidance of every advance I throw her way? That just makes me want her more.

After all, a good quarterback goes for the win at every possible opportunity, down to the last second, even when the odds aren't in his favor.

"Guys," I call back to Ace and Julia, who've stopped for a giggle in the middle of the hall that leads to the locker room. "Hurry up."

We have five minutes until we're supposed to be at the meetup location in the south end zone, and I know from experience that the walk from the locker room takes at least half of that. We used my code to get in the back entrance door, but I have no idea how the hell the rest of tonight's attendees are getting in.

Our athletic director implemented pretty strict stadium security two years ago, the year before I came to Dickson, after the team came to practice one Monday to find a goal post missing. Ironically, now that I know about Double C and the brilliant girl who runs it, I can't help but wonder if she had something to do with it.

If she ever decides to give me the time of day, I'll have to ask her.

"Blake, is this your locker?" Julia asks, her soft whisper turning into a trill of interest. "Can we look inside?"

I laugh. "There's nothing exciting in there, I promise."

"No sweaty game-day socks you refuse to change?" Ace hedges, waggling his eyebrows.

"No."

"What about a jock strap you've used since you started here?"

"What exactly is your obsession with poor hygiene practices, Ace?"

"I just figured you'd be superstitious."

"I'm too good to be superstitious."

"Hell yes, you are, you cocky son of a bitch," Ace replies, his mouth curved so high it threatens to brush his damn forehead as he loops an arm around my shoulders and jostles me side to side. I roll my eyes and laugh, waving Julia away from my locker.

"Come on, Jules. I'll show you my locker another time if you really want to see it."

Ace runs back to grab her hand and pull her forward again, and we're off to the races at a run to make it out to the field in time. I follow the curve of the golden dragon that's painted on the tunnel wall, grazing it with my fingers as I lead the way just like I have for every home football game this year. Without the roar of the waiting crowd at the tunnel's end, it feels a little different.

The delusional part of me thinks tonight's version is even better, and that's all because of one specific girl and a whole lot of unfounded optimism. Lexi Lou Winslow treats me like the scummy dirt on the bottom of her shoe, but tonight, if I have any say in it at all, that's going to change.

Golden blond hair shimmers in the moonlight atop the girl of my dreams' head as she scrolls through her phone, checking people in. I study her closely, willing my racing heart to calm down a little in the hopes that I won't come off as a total fucking dweeb.

It's not like I'm some virginal schoolboy, for shit's sake. At twenty-one years old, I've had more pussy than Garfield. Girls flock to me, throwing themselves at the Dragons' star quarterback every chance they get.

But Lexi Winslow is a whole other level of intimidating. She's brilliant and beautiful, and, so far, after an entire year of trying to get on her good side, she wants absolutely nothing to do with me.

I smile. *God, I love a challenge.*

There's a line in front of Lexi waiting to check in, but after a quick glance at my watch and a bump in the back from Ace, the three of us play cutsies with little to no remorse. There's a groan or two until a couple of people see it's me and use their elbows to shut up their friends.

There are perks to being the quarterback at a sports-obsessed university, star power being one of them. I wouldn't normally be the type to use it to my advantage, but when it comes to face time with Double C's fearless leader, I'm shameless.

"Hi, Lexi," I greet, my voice warm.

"Blake Boden," she says in return, just barely glancing up from her phone. "You're checked in."

I grin. "How are you tonight?"

Her hands pause at her phone before her gaze slowly lifts, and even though they're filled with annoyance, I'm thankful for the intimate view of her baby blues.

"Busy."

I smile. "Is that a subtle hint to leave you alone?"

"No."

"No?"

"It wasn't subtle."

She's so fucking incredible.

"Okay," I agree easily, ignoring Ace's obnoxious laugh behind me. "We'll catch up later, then."

Lexi quirks a defiant brow at me. "Will we, though?"

"I'm planning on it."

She purses her perfect lips at me. "Maybe you shouldn't hedge your bets."

"Gah, Lexi!" Ace cries, shoving me forward. "You're ruthless to this poor, talented man. Give him a break every once in a while!"

I shake my head, disagreeing. "No, no. It's okay. She'll come around to me eventually. She should do it on her time."

Lexi narrows her eyes slightly, studying me. "Cover charge is twenty dollars tonight. Winner takes the pot."

I pull a trio of twenties from my jeans pocket and hand them to her, waving off Ace when he pulls out money of his own. "I got it tonight, Ace."

I smile and wink before leaving Lexi to finish business without much of a fuss. I like that she's not trying to impress me or cowing to my wants and needs right off the bat. I like that she's an individual with high standards and uncompromising boundaries. It's a hell of a change from the women I'm used to and a breath of fresh air.

Since my freshman year of high school, when I made the varsity football team as starting quarterback to the chagrin of many up-perclassmen, I've been an object of female pursuit. Girls wanted to date me, kiss me—fuck me—anything to say they did and list it among their accomplishments with friends.

I took proper advantage of my popularity for a while, but after a few years, the same old shit starts to taste stale. I'm not just look-ing for a good time anymore; I'm looking for a long time.

And I know damn well, thanks to my parents' inspiring exam-ple of what a marriage full of resentment and bickering looks like, you don't pick just anyone.

"I'm so excited, I can feel a little tingle in my spine," Ace says, bouncing on his toes. It's an innocent statement—one none of us would have thought a single thing about a month ago—but immedi-ately, it casts a pall over us for our missing friends, Scottie and Finn. "Shit," Ace says, apology in his eyes, and Julia leans in to rub his arm.

"It's okay. You didn't mean anything by it."

"I know. I just… Fuck, I still can't believe any of that shit re-ally happened."

I nod. "Either of you talk to Finn or Scottie?"

"I did," Julia answers. "Earlier today. Things are good. Really good. Scottie is starting to sound like herself again."

"Yeah," Ace agrees. "Finn's stopped breaking shit in our dorm room too."

"Tonight feels weird without them," I remark. But at least she and Finn are officially on the mend. It took them a while to over-come all the hurdles in their way, but they're a strong unit now. I'm sure it won't be long before they're doing all this stupid shit with us again, even if the physical specifics for now-wheelchair-bound Scottie look a little different. Hell, knowing Finn and how much he loves that girl, he'd carry her ass around all night if he had to.

"Definitely," Julia agrees. "Maybe we can swing by—"

"Welcome, everyone!" Lexi greets, moving to stand in front of the group, a small light clipped to the collar of her pink T-shirt. Julia's message is cut short, but I have no trouble reading between the lines. Sometime in the next couple of days, we need to make sure we pay Scottie and Finn a visit. Which, no doubt about it, I agree, and I give Julia a thumbs-up to communicate it.

Lexi keeps talking, and I turn my attention to her with my usual avid devotion. "Tonight's activities have officially commenced. If you're waiting on other people from your group, they won't be making it. You're on your own."

Ace bounces on his toes behind me again, hanging off my back and practically choking me out. I let him do it for a minute, and then I set him to the side with a quick grip of his forearm.

"As you may know, Dickson's Dragon Stadium has a capacity of thirty thousand seats, positioned in alphabetical and numerical order. What you may not realize, however, is that sixty years ago, one of the graduating classes switched two of the seat numbers as their final prank, and they've never been switched back. The challenge tonight is to find them both while there's still time on the twenty-minute clock. Winner takes the pot. I assure you, though, it won't be easy, so do yourself a favor and keep your cockiness in your pants."

"I swear a whole persona comes over her when she's doing this shit," Ace whispers to Julia and me, laughing lightly. Even he's afraid to get caught chatting while she's talking, and given how crazy he is, that says something about Lexi Winslow. Both Ace and Julia have known her all their lives—their parents are close friends with her parents—so the intimidation factor shouldn't be a factor at all.

But it is, because Lexi Winslow isn't just any average girl. She's a whole other level of backbone, intelligence, and breathtaking beauty.

I smile. *Man, she's so perfect.*

"Keep the noise and other identifying factors to a minimum and break into your groups," my dream girl commands to the group. "As always, teams get paid as a team, and how you split it up isn't my problem."

She nods toward her sidekick Connor, who holds up a stop-watch and makes a show of starting it in front of all of us. The crowd scatters like a bunch of damn ants, giggles and chatter running a short course of excitement as they hurry for the stadium seats.

I reach out for Ace's shoulder, shoving him in the direction I think we should go first, and he reaches back for Julia's hand to pull her along at a run. "Let's start with the high-dollar seats in the VIP section. They'd either not care or shit themselves every time, so it's worth a shot. We'll either get a win or eliminate a section really quickly."

Ace picks up his pace as we're passing Lexi and Connor, and I let him and Julia take the lead and drag my feet. Lexi rolls her eyes as I approach, but I don't let that deter me.

"Did you need something, Boden?" she asks.

My smile grows cocky and my heart thrums in my chest as I lay it all on the line. "Only you."

She scoffs and Connor snorts, speaking for her while she stays silent. "You're playing out of your league on this one, Blake."

Both Connor and Lexi are a few years older than me, and from what I know, they've been friends for years. But Connor doesn't know jack shit about just how determined Blake Boden can be when he wants to win something.

"That's never stopped me before," I say, shrugging off his comment confidently. "No point in playing the game if you're not going to play to win."

Connor laughs, but I don't miss the way Lexi's eyes go wide for the briefest of moments before she schools her expression into her usual poker face.

It's not much, but it's just enough to keep my sights set on the prize—*her*.

2

Lexi

"**G**ood luck getting rid of that one, Lex. He's stuck to you like a leech," Connor remarks as Blake Boden finally runs off to join Ace and Julia in their search for the switched seat numbers.

I roll my eyes and shake my head. "He's a gamer. He likes to win things, and because I'm a challenge, he wants to win me. Simple. He'll get over it eventually."

Connor shakes his head on a chuckle. "He seemed pretty determined."

"Yeah, well, he was determined to take the Dragons to the championship last year, and he failed at that. So I assure you, a conclusion rooted in disappointment is possible for him."

Connor's laugh is stilted and a little weird—like it always is—but undeniably loud. It pulls Blake's attention from the far side of the field, and I wave a hand in front of Connor's face to shut him up. "Were you not at orientation? Keep it down, Connor, please."

"Is there a particular reason you're dead set against giving him a shot? Other than the fact that he's a football player?"

"That's enough of a reason, isn't it?" I scrunch up my nose as I challenge what I think is a clearly dumb question. Connor has known me since elementary school. When we were teenagers in high school, our friendship even blossomed into a coupledom—though, we weren't a romantic match. He should know me well enough to know that I don't get involved with football players.

Being the stepdaughter of the New York Mavericks' owner, I've been surrounded by them since I was a little girl. And I've seen and heard way too many things to not understand that football players are the opposite of an ideal mate for a girl like me.

If I'm honest, I'm not sure there's anyone out there who is an ideal partner for me. On paper, Connor should technically be one, but even that relationship went back to just friends before we started Dickson University as college freshmen.

"I don't know, Lex. You always got along so well with the Mavericks when we were kids." Connor shrugs. "And you haven't really dated since we did."

"Oh, come on." I roll my eyes, my laugh smug. "You can't believe that, can you? That I haven't truly dated someone since we were teenagers and using each other to study the mechanics of kissing?"

"Well, I haven't dated anyone since then." Connor blushes and turns his head. "And you're always occupied with the lab and school. I just assumed."

I sigh. "Relationships and physical attraction are a study in human behavior, Conn. I couldn't exactly consider any of my research conclusive without going further than a kiss."

"Understood." He's silent then, turning to face the stadium at large and putting his back to me.

I ponder over his state of mind. A year ago, I never would have considered that I might have hurt his feelings because, to me, the concept of emotion tied to other people's behavior is somewhat asinine. You can't control it, so to base your own well-being on it is risky, statistically speaking. But my little brother explained it to me last summer, when I accidentally sent my mom to her room crying after what was, to me, a simple interaction.

It might not be rational, but for better or worse, total forfeiture of emotional control is evidently a characteristic of neurotypical human behavior. And I'm trying to be better about taking that into consideration.

"I'm sorry, Conn, if the news came as a shock," I say, my voice quiet but as sincere as I can manage. "I didn't mean to spring that on you."

"It's fine." He shakes his head, turning briefly but declining to meet my eyes. Truth be told, neither one of us is the best at making direct visual contact. I sigh, and he pauses briefly before speaking again, his gaze still in the opposite direction. "I'm going to go double-check that the gate we came through is still unlocked."

"Okay." It's a pointless endeavor, seeing as I have the combination, but I don't deny him the task. Frankly, it'll be better for us both if he gets a little space. I don't like the gnawing feeling of awkwardness between us. We've known each other too long, and he's one of the only people I don't have to pretend with.

It'd be easy to be with him since he understands all my quirks, but there is absolutely zero physical attraction to him on my end, and I've done the research on how damaging dry sex is on the vaginal microbiome.

And a life full of UTIs, other infections, and no orgasms?

No, thank you.

Plus, it feels all kinds of wrong to be with someone you know isn't right for you. I might not be the best with emotional things, but I'm not impervious to the fact that something like that can be hurtful to the other party. And the last thing I want to do is hurt people, even if my mouth deviates from my purpose every now and then.

Connor's back retreats toward the far end of the field, disappearing into darkness just past the fifty-yard line. I look down at the stopwatch to check the time, noting that only half of it is left. Ace and Julia streak by, running hand in hand from one side of the field to the other, Blake Boden in their wake. I look down at my phone, feigning avid concentration, but the pulse of his presence as he comes to a stop in front of me is undeniable.

It's concussive, and I really wish I could nail down the physics of why that is. A hormone? His muscle density triggering an atmospheric shift?

I wish I freaking knew.

Whatever it is feels stupidly magnetic.

"Can I help you?" I ask, glancing up from my phone briefly and then looking back down. "By the looks of things, you haven't located the seats yet, and we're more than halfway through your time."

"I just noticed that you lost your sidekick. Maybe—"

"What in the hell is going on here?" a stern voice asks from behind us, spinning us both around right in the middle of Blake's sentence. A bright flashlight shines directly in our faces, and I hold up a hand to block the piercing power of it. When it finally clicks off, it takes ten seconds for my eyes to adjust back to the darkness. Blake's correction is quicker.

"Director Hughes," he says immediately, the volume of his voice heightened in an effort to alert me and everyone else to the seriousness of the situation. The athletic director catching us in here is about as *worst-case scenario* as it gets.

All the kids in the stands scatter and run, and I suck my lips into my mouth over how freaking guilty that makes us look right off the bat.

My throat feels clogged, and my cheeks feel hot as I fight to keep my carefully crafted Double C persona in place. It's a form of masking, of course—something I've gotten so good at over the years I hardly even realize all the times I'm doing it—because underneath, I am a basket case of embarrassment and disillusion.

This shouldn't be happening.

I covered all the bases. I made sure the stadium would be deserted and planned this for the night of the staff banquet so Coach Gordan, Coach Jimmen, and Coach Niles would be occupied. I checked and double-checked the shift change on the security patrol of the interior and turned off the cameras with my signal jammer.

I don't know how they figured out we were in here, and boy, does that grate on my nerves.

I'm not used to not knowing. Since I was six years old, I've known almost *everything*.

Clearing my throat, I steel my nerves against my growing

uncertainty and lift my chin with confidence I'm no longer feeling. "Good evening, Director Hughes. I'm so sorry you got pulled out here in the middle of the night." I laugh softly, shaking my head and willing a reason for being here to come to mind.

"I'm afraid it's my fault, sir," a male voice says, startling me from my side. Blake is still there, his best *Leave It to Beaver* smile in place, even though I half expected him to be gone or—if not in a cloud of desertion dust—silent. All the do-gooders I know would have dropped this in my lap and left me hanging in a heartbeat. "I left my backpack with my AirPods, computer, and some other notes and gear here after practice, and I enlisted some friends to come help me look for it so I can turn in my Engineering Dynamics final paper on time. Silly of me, I know, but I didn't back it up anywhere other than my laptop's hard drive, and it's due first thing tomorrow morning. I know how important it is to keep my GPA up so I have eligibility to play next year."

My stomach flips as our athletic director's eyes narrow, his hands settling on his hips in a posture of frustration. "You should have notified security, Blake. You don't just sneak in the stadium and start rooting around."

Blake nods. "Of course. I… Well, sir, I was a little embarrassed, as I'm sure you can imagine. But it won't happen again, and we'll get out of here now."

"Did you find the backpack?"

Blake shakes his head, dejected. He's playing the part of a damsel pretty well for someone who benches over two hundred pounds. "No, sir. I have a few more places to look on campus, though, before I give up all hope."

"Coach Gordan know about you leaving this to the last minute?"

Blake winces, hooking his thumbs into his pockets and shrugging in a form of visual *gee golly gosh*. "No, sir. He'd be pretty disappointed, so I'm trying to make it right. Can we just keep this between us for now? I promise, if I don't get the paper turned in on time, I'll tell him myself."

Director Hughes groans. "You're killing me, Boden."

Blake nods enthusiastically. "Yes, sir. I know."

Hughes takes one long, deep sigh but then, finally, nods. "Fine. But you need to gather up all your friends and get them out of here, pronto. And I swear, if I find any damage or problems in the light of day, I'm coming for your ass."

"Of course," Blake agrees. "I wouldn't expect anything less, sir."

"Jesus Christ, football players. You're all going to send me to an early grave."

"Again, sorry, sir. Truly. We'll get out of here now."

Blake grabs me by the elbow and starts to walk, dragging me along with him toward the players' tunnel he arrived through. He makes a big show of yelling out to the abandoned stadium in case any of the others are still here. "Come on, guys! I don't think my backpack's here! Let's go look at the pedestrian court!"

"How Director Hughes didn't know you were full of shit, I'll never know," I mutter under my breath as we make our way through the hall, the locker room, and out to the other side, where the darkness of navy-painted walls consumes us. Blake comes to a stop and I keep walking, but he reaches out and grabs me again, slowing me before I can get away.

"Hey. Where are you going?" he asks.

"I'm leaving. Just like you told him we would," I explain slowly, troubled by his struggle to understand.

He shakes his head and tightens his grip on my arm. "You can't just leave. You owe me."

"I *owe* you?" I narrow my eyes. "For what exactly?"

His smile is one hundred versions of cocky all combined into one. "For saving your ass."

"My ass doesn't need saving," I scoff. "It's not sentient. But even if it did, I'd have saved it myself."

"You know what, though?" He shakes his head, his blue eyes so bright in comparison to the dark navy walls of the hallway they almost glow. "It didn't look like it. It looked like you were floundering."

I frown. I loathe the idea of being anything other than self-sufficient. I planned, I prioritized, and still, I ended up getting caught. But I'm not an invalid. I know I would have figured a way out of it without Blake Boden's help.

"I was thinking," I retort sharply. "About to speak, believe or not, before you butted in."

"My dad always says 'about to' never got anyone anywhere."

Annoyingly, he's not wrong. The truth is, I was drowning in my thoughts, scrambling for a valid excuse to give Director Hughes for our very illegal presence in the stadium. And until Blake piped up with his *"I lost my backpack"* masterpiece, I didn't have a single plausible reason. I would have come up with one, though. I know I would've.

"Fine," I sigh, my shoulders sagging. "What exactly do I owe you, then?"

"Pizza."

His smile is so big it's borderline unnerving, and worse, it makes my mouth twitch like it wants to smile back. I don't, of course. Smiling in this situation makes zero logical sense.

"Pizza?" I repeat, brow furrowed. "You think I owe you *pizza?*"

"Yeah." He nods, full of irritating confidence. "And you're going to get it with me. Right now."

"*Now?*" I echo, horrified. My adrenaline is still spiking from our near run-in with trouble, and all I want is a warm bath and the soothing hum of my white noise machine. Pizza grease, a crowded restaurant, and whatever voodoo Blake Boden exerts on my nervous system sounds like a trifecta of bad ideas. "Can't we do this another time? I mean, I'll pay up, but…not *now.*"

"The semester ends Tuesday, Lexi. I know if I let you walk away tonight, I'll never see you again."

"I keep my word," I argue, slightly offended.

"I want to believe you. I do. But I don't." He shrugs, annoyingly unbothered. "So, you're coming with me now. It's paramount to the balance of the universe."

"Oh, right. The *Cosmic Balance Theory of Pizza*. I think I've heard of it, Mr. Theoretical Physicist."

"What's it going to hurt to believe it's true? Just for tonight?"

I narrow my eyes. "This wasn't in my plans."

"So, change them."

Dinner last night flashes through my mind—the promise I made to my family, my little brother's hopeful expression lingering like an itch I can't scratch.

I promised I'd be open to change.

I guess that starts now. With pizza and Blake freaking Boden.

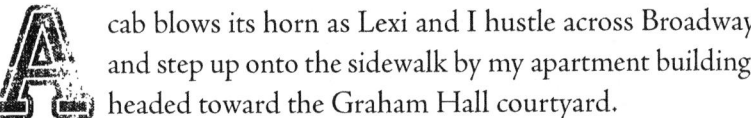

cab blows its horn as Lexi and I hustle across Broadway and step up onto the sidewalk by my apartment building, headed toward the Graham Hall courtyard.

Ace texted me fifteen minutes ago to check in and make sure I didn't need a lawyer or bail money and to tell me that he and Julia were heading to Frat Row to check out a party for a couple of hours before calling it a night. And Lexi, though grouchy, has followed me without complaint from the moment we came to a pizza agreement outside the locker room of Dragon Stadium.

I'm hopeful we'll have a breakthrough if I just keep trying, but so far, her ice has maintained an impressive resistance to thawing.

I lead the way across the courtyard, slowing slightly as two girls pass, smiling and giggling in my direction. Normally, I'd give them a quick nod or a smile back, but my mind is somewhere else—on the radiating body of my hostage, Lexi Winslow. She's oblivious to the entire interaction, her expression locked in laser-focus like she's running through every possible scenario for this pizza plan in her head.

Lexi is a puzzle. Sharp, beautiful, and stubborn as hell—a combination that has fascinated me from the moment I laid eyes on her last fall. She's different, that much is obvious, but it's what makes her so magnetic. Her mind works at a pace the rest of us can't touch, and when she starts rattling off facts like she's Google come to life, I can't help but admire it.

We're steps from the entrance to Graham when she screeches to a halt, stepping out of reach completely.

"I thought we were getting pizza."

"We are."

She narrows her eyes. "No. I know all three pizza places on Dickson's campus, and none is within a third-of-a-mile vicinity of here."

I laugh, which earns me a glare. "Okay, it's not an *official* place, so to speak, but it's a place. There's a guy from Chicago who makes deep-dish pizza in his dorm room and sells it on Saturday nights. It's the best you'll ever have."

Her face scrunches in absolute horror. "His *dorm room?*"

"Yes. Here in Graham. It's not as bad as it sounds."

"That's good. Because it sounds like an FDA violation and a call to the New York Department of Health."

I smile. "It's not a restaurant. It's just a...hobby."

"Does he have a Home Processor Exemption from Article 20-C?"

"Uh...I doubt it."

"Then he needs to be registered with the state under New York cottage food laws." Her voice is pure exasperation, and I can't help but laugh.

"How do you know that?" I ask. "Did you used to have a food business?"

She shrugs. "I just know a lot of things."

No argument there. "What else do you know?"

"About New York food law? Or life in general?" she asks, blinking at me. "Because in general is a very broad question that would take me hours to answer."

I smile, completely intrigued. "I've got hours."

She rolls her eyes so hard I'm worried they'll get stuck. "You said I owed you pizza, not hours."

"Why can't it be both?"

"Probably because of the food poisoning we're both sure to have after the first. Do you know if he even follows the 140-degree temperature regulation? And gloves. Does he wear prep gloves?"

I grin at her, a little awestruck by the sheer level of detail she applies to everything. "Why don't we go inside, and you can find out for yourself?"

She hesitates, clearly weighing the pros and cons. Her face is so expressive when she's deep in thought—brows furrowed, lips pursed slightly—and I swear, she has no idea how beautiful she is in these moments.

"Because," she says finally, "if I go inside and find out he doesn't, it'll be a complete waste of time and energy. Not to mention the dangers of going into a random building with a virtual stranger."

"I'm no one's stranger. I'm Blake Boden."

She snorts, and I'm pretty sure it's the closest thing I've seen to a smile from her all night. "Interesting take on reality."

"I'm just saying, if you need witnesses for my hypothetical crimes, you'd have no trouble rounding them up."

She sighs dramatically, but there's something softer in her expression as she relents. "Fine. But if your goal is to make me *eat* this dorm-room pizza, you might want to knock me out and tie me up now."

I burst out laughing, shaking my head. "I'll take my chances."

Lexi shrugs, resigned. "Suit yourself. But don't say I didn't warn you."

She follows me toward the entrance, and all I can think is that there's no one like her. Lexi—whip-smart, beautiful, and completely unaware of how fascinating she is to me. It's probably why I haven't been able to stop thinking about her since the day we met.

She might think she's untouchable, closed off behind her wall of logic and facts, but I see her.

And I'm not backing down. Not yet.

I pause right outside the door. "Would it make you feel any better if I told you Finn and Ace have both eaten this pizza on multiple occasions and lived to tell the tale?"

She levels me with a look so sharp it could cut glass. "Ace and Finn are hardly my guiding light for sound life choices."

She has a point. The first time she met Finn Hayes—who she recently found out is actually related to her—he fought an ex-UFC fighter at a Double C event. And she's known Ace's wild ways her whole life. Frankly, it's Ace's family's connection to Lexi's family that got me an invite into Double C in the first place.

"That's fair," I agree on a chuckle. "So, what do you want to do? I can take you somewhere else if you really want, but I'm telling you—this is one of Dickson's finest experiences. You're going to love it."

Her eyes drift to the building, scanning the scattered dots of glowing windows like she's calculating the probability of food poisoning per floor. Her posture is rigid, hands curled into fists at her sides, like she's bracing herself for war.

Ten seconds pass—ten long, quiet seconds—and then I watch her exhale, the fight deflating out of her like a popped balloon.

"Okay. You're right. Let's go visit the...*dorm-pizza guy.*" The last three words drip with disgust, but there's a shift in her demeanor. She's going along with it.

"Really? You're sure?"

She sighs dramatically, and I laugh. "Right. Of course you're not sure. But you will be afterward, I promise."

Without giving her time to reconsider, I grab her hand—not the intimate finger-linking kind, just a firm, steady grip across our palms—and head straight for the door as it swings open. A group stumbles out—a guy in a massive hoodie and two girls—laughing and jostling into the night.

The guy's head snaps up when he sees me. "Boden!" he yells, holding up his hand for a fist bump.

I oblige with my free arm, even though I'm ninety-nine percent sure I've never seen him before in my life.

"Hey, man. Having a good night?"

"Fuck yeah," he says back, spinning both girls around and making them giggle.

Lexi watches the entire interaction like it's a documentary on college-bro behavior, her expression open curiosity. I pull her through the door, and we head straight for the stairs at the end of the hall.

By the time we start climbing, she finally speaks, her tone casual but her eyes sharp. "You just…get recognized like that all the time, don't you?"

"Depends on the time of year. If it's football season and we just lost? Suddenly, no one knows me."

To my surprise, she laughs—a real, actual laugh—and it feels like I've just been handed the winning lottery ticket. Lexi Winslow is a steel fortress with a dash of razor-sharp wit, and breaking through even a little is no small feat.

"Fair-weather friends," she muses, her voice laced with amusement. "A huge part of football, I'm afraid."

"How many Mavericks games have you been to?" I ask, my curiosity slipping out before I can stop it. Growing up with a pro football team owner for a dad? Mind-blowing. "Just ballpark."

Lexi doesn't even hesitate. "One hundred and ninety-two."

I blink. "One hundred and ninety-two? You kept track?"

"I keep track of a lot of things."

"Like what?"

"Everything."

Her answer is so simple, so Lexi, it makes me grin. "That's incredible. I bet the average American's only been to, what, one game in their lifetime?"

She shakes her head like I've said something ridiculous. "Probably closer to zero. Maybe point zero, zero something. But only two percent of pro fans have been to a game, and one hundred percent of Americans aren't thinking about, watching, or fandoming over football. The real number is probably negligible."

"And yet, you've been to nearly two hundred."

She tilts her head slightly, her expression unreadable. "How many have *you* been to?"

"Ten. My dad started taking me to one game a season when I turned eleven. Different team every year. He said if I wanted to play in the pros one day, I should know what every team's atmosphere feels like."

"You're halfway there," she says thoughtfully. "There are twenty-two teams total."

I laugh, because of course she knows the exact number. "Well, I'm hoping, in a couple of years, I'll only need to be loyal to one."

"You've got the stats," she says with a small shrug. "If you maintain performance, there's no reason you won't get drafted."

"You say it like it's that easy."

She shrugs. "Relatively speaking, it is. Just like getting into college with a certain high school academic and extracurricular record. There are outliers to every rule, but they call them rules for a reason. It's statistical."

I laugh. "You know, I think I've been thinking of it like it's some magical mist or spell or something. Your take honestly makes me feel a little better. It's the numbers."

She nods. "Money being the most important number of all. Will you make them money? Your record is like a guideline for the answer to that question. And you have a good record, statistically speaking."

"Wow. Thanks."

Lexi shrugs like it's no big deal, but the corners of her lips twitch, like maybe she's enjoying this conversation.

When we finally reach the door with the Italian flag taped to it, I pause to knock, but not before flashing her a smile. "So, what do I need to do to get drafted by your dad? Any tips?"

Her soft laugh surprises me. "You'll have to figure that out yourself."

Before I can say anything else, the door swings open, and Tony Scalano's legendary dorm-room pizzeria is revealed in all its questionable glory. The air smells like warm flour and melted cheese, a fine dusting of it hovering in the air like a low-budget food television show set. "That's Amore" plays faintly from a Bluetooth speaker in the corner, and I glance down at Lexi to gauge her reaction.

Her wide eyes meet mine, a mix of horror and curiosity swirling in her expression. "Your powers of persuasion should be studied," she mutters. "Because the fact that I'm here right now is a scientific mystery."

I nod, fighting a grin. "You want to go inside?"

She sighs, resigned but intrigued. "We're here, I guess. Might as well. Though I'm absolutely certain his Blackstone pizza oven in an enclosed space is a fire code violation."

"He keeps an extinguisher under the bed."

"Oh, well. *That's* comforting."

"You're funny, you know that?"

"Really?" she asks, her eyes lighting up with something softer than her usual sharp skepticism.

"Definitely. Which is surprising, considering how scary you are most of the time."

Her brow furrows. "I'm not scary."

"Are you kidding?" I lower my voice and look around to make sure no one else is listening to our conversation before turning my attention back to her. "You run that Double C shit like you're The Godfather. I've never seen so many shriveled balls around me as the night you double-dog dared one of us to fight Donnie Marks. Finn is just crazy enough not to care."

"Are you scared of me?"

"Yes." Her expression falters for just a fraction of a second, caught between shock and confusion, but I don't give it time to settle. I can't. After tonight, more than ever, I'm determined to make Lexi Winslow mine. "But unlike most people, I like to face my fears head on."

Lexi

Blake Boden is an interesting case of data. Women follow him around in droves, offering fornication in exchange for very little, and it makes me wonder if there's more to him than a single glance could discern.

He's muscular and over six feet tall in the way a lot of women prefer in their potential mate, conventionally attractive, talented, athletic, and packs an easy smile I know puts everyone in his vicinity at ease, but what if there's more to it?

What if there's a science to the amount of attention he gets—an evidence-based reasoning for why he's so popular with women and men alike, and why his confidence isn't deterred by repeated rejection.

Dopamine is chemical and reactionary. Does something about him trigger it? A scent, perhaps?

My stomach has churned at least three times tonight, two-thirds of which occurred before the pizza. There has to be a reason, and I can't help but wonder what it is.

Normally, I wouldn't even consider the possibility of dating a football player, but after the haranguing from my family last night, I clearly need to shake things up. Maybe a good old scientific experiment with Blake Boden at the center of it is the answer.

All I'd need is a hypothesis to get started.

If I date Blake Boden, I'll be chemically happier.

Not exactly testable. I try again.

Prolonged periods of time spent with Blake Boden make a marked difference in happiness.

Again, Lex, what's the unit of measurement for happiness?

I shake my head to clear it and surreptitiously glance at Blake's carved cheekbones and freakishly charming floppy ginger-blond hair. I always suspected I'd be attracted to men with dark eyes and dark hair—but something about the combination of Blake's unsuspecting, innocent look and undeniably fascinating charisma has a way of setting me straight.

As we climb the steps in front of the Beckley Theater to take a seat in the pedestrian court, ice cream procured from Brower Center for dessert after eating our slices of pizza on the walk there, Blake slows his steps and reaches out for my arm, gently forcing me to face him. "So? What's your conclusion on the pizza? Was it really as bad as you thought?"

"Honestly?" I ask, my normal blunt delivery faltering a little in deference to his feelings.

"Yes. Of course. Tell me how you really feel."

"Okay," I agree with a nod, taking a deep breath and visualizing the smell and feel of room 517 of Graham Hall. Dirty gym socks and damp laundry, I'm convinced, hold more appeal. "It was worse."

"What?" he scoffs, a growing smile settling a small dimple into his cheek. "Worse than a New York Department of Health violation?"

I nod, taking a lick of my ice cream cone before it can melt all over my hand. Blake's eyes are locked on the motion. I swallow quickly, wincing slightly at the frigid feel in my throat, and explain. "Sanitation was nonexistent, and the ingredients were sitting in bowls on his nightstand next to a pack of cigarettes and two condoms. Overall taste of the pizza was good, but I'm pretty sure we're both in for a night of violent consequences."

"Aha." His smile looks like victory. "So, you admit…it tasted good."

I roll my eyes. "Yes…it tasted fine."

"You didn't say *fine* before. You said *good*. And you don't strike me as the type of girl who isn't precise with her words."

"Here's something precise—smug isn't a good look on you."

"Not possible." He chuckles. "Everything is a good look on me."

"Oh, wow. Okay. Smug *and* cocky."

Blake sits down on the top step in front of the theater and rubs the air atop the spot next to him to entice me to join him, unaffected, at least outwardly, by my analysis of his personality.

I have to suspect his confidence is part of his mysterious, scientific appeal.

"Come on," he insists at my lack of compliance. "Sit down. Just for a little while. At least long enough to eat the rest of your ice cream."

I do as he says with a roll of my eyes and a deep, beleaguered sigh that makes him laugh. Surprisingly, though, the real reason I sit down is because I want to.

Under normal circumstances, spending time with a football player—*the* football player, arguably—from Dickson would be out of the question. But now that I've given in, Blake's mystique raises too many questions to short-cut the evening.

"What made you choose Dickson? Given that you grew up in Southern California, I can't imagine this was a school on your initial short list."

I take a lick of ice cream, and he smiles. "Ah, see, I guess you don't know *all* my stats. My grandfather went here. Played quarterback on one of the first Dickson teams to make it to the play-offs. In fact, he was a part of the graduating class you mentioned just tonight, at Double C."

"You're kidding."

He laughs. "I'm not."

"You knew the switched seats?"

Blake winks, and I groan. "Oh my God. Why in the hell didn't you just find them, then? Win the money?"

He shrugs. "I didn't want the night to be over too soon. It's the end of the semester. Who knows when I would have gotten to see you again?"

"And your entry money…what about that?"

"Trust me, this ending is worth the sixty bucks."

My gaze jerks to his, and my stomach turns over yet again. It's a foreign feeling—one I didn't even think I was capable of having, truth be told. My mind races to figure out if this is all just a part of a smooth-talking game or if he really thinks my company is worth a sixty-dollar loss and a very close call with losing his entire scholarship.

Instead of saying anything, I bite into my cone and work at the last vestiges of mocha mint chip ice cream from the student dining hall. I expect him to fill the quiet with mindless chatter, but he sits comfortably in the silence, finishing his vanilla peanut butter mixture from his bowl.

It takes a minute, but I finally work up the courage to consider the conversation, ignoring the fact that I've pointedly excused a whole section of undeniable compliments directed toward me. "What about your parents?" I ask him. "Where did they go to school?"

"My mom didn't go to four-year college. She's a paralegal. And my dad went to USC for both undergrad and law school. They met when my dad started at his first firm."

I smile, the comfort of having something in common putting me a little more at ease. "My parents met at work too. My mom is the head on-staff physician for the Mavericks."

"This might be an overly personal question, but we are getting to know each other, so I'm just going to ask it, and if you don't want to answer, you don't have to."

I tense but nod anyway. "Sure."

"Why is your last name Winslow and not Lancaster?"

"Wes isn't my biological father," I answer simply. I know people like to tiptoe around familial intricacies, but after nearly twenty years with Wes in my life, I see our situation as fact. He didn't create me, but that doesn't make him any less of a dad. "My mom gave me her last name."

Blake nods. "And your bio dad…is he in the picture?"

"Oh. Yeah. Nick's a good dad too, really, save some stupid decisions upon my conception and birth, but he's in Germany now, heading up a world-renowned neurological research clinic. I see him a couple times a year, but we speak often."

"Siblings?"

"One. My brother, Wes Jr., is thirteen. I hardly understand anything he says, and yet, I know with an almost certainty that he's roasting me."

Blake chuckles. "I hear that's why younger siblings exist…to humble you."

"I take it you don't have any, then?"

He shakes his head. "Nope. Only child."

"Mm-hmm," I hum. "It's all making sense now. The confidence, the ego, the garish refusal to hear the word no…you're a walking billboard for too much attention and unconditional love."

"No such thing," he refutes easily.

"Oh, please. You can absolutely be spoiled."

"Can't spoil people like you can milk." He smiles. "That's what my mom always says."

I guffaw. "Well, there you have it. A complete picture."

"Now, you know that's not true," he contests. "Any given theory has many sets of data. I can't imagine you don't know that."

My eyes widen. He's right. I *do* know that. "Okay. What are some of your other data points?"

"I was born with a congenital heart defect. Had five surgeries before I turned one. I shouldn't be able to play sports the way I do…my parents never thought I would. But when they checked me at age five, all my function was normal. A miracle is what they said, actually." He laughs. "My mom took that pretty literally. My dad was tough, though. I mean, not in the horrible way you see some dads being, but he pushed me to be what I am in both life and football. He always expected excellence."

"And how did that make you feel?"

He shrugs. "Pretty good, honestly. Because he expected a lot, but he had loads of patience and a never-ending willingness to provide the tools. He spent all his time on the weekends coaching my youth team and practicing with me. He sacrificed just as much as he demanded. I can't think of a better person."

Something about Blake's fierce defense of his parents is comforting and humanizing. He seems like an enigma most of the time—like a freak star born of luck. The truth is that he and his parents scraped for every opportunity he has. It's admirable.

I, in contrast, have never had to work that hard at anything. My intelligence and academic pursuits all came naturally. My family, while unconventional, is loving, wealthy, and privileged, my dreams and possibilities endless.

It's ironic, almost, that relating to other humans—something that should be basic instinct—is where I struggle the most.

"He sounds a lot like my uncle Remy. He's given so much for our entire family, especially my mom and me, and yet, somehow, managed to make it seem like he actually enjoyed it."

"Is he your mom's brother?"

"Yes. Well, one of her four brothers. Though, I guess, technically, Finn and his brothers Reece, Travis, and Jack are my uncles too. Strictly genetically speaking, now that we know my mom's bio dad is their bio dad too."

Blake laughs so hard he almost snorts. "Pretty funny picturing 'Fighting Finn Hayes' as your uncle."

I shake my head, but I also find myself laughing a little too. "I don't think anyone has any plans to treat it that way. Finn and his siblings are my cousins' and my generation. Not to mention, there's no way I'm going to call him Uncle Finn when I'm six years older than him."

The truth of my relation to Finn—and his siblings—came out shortly before his girlfriend Scottie Bardeaux was in a terrible accident during a cheerleading competition. To say it's been a whirlwind of information over the past four weeks would be an understatement.

And while it might already seem pretty crazy, the reality of it all when it comes to Finn and my mother's bio dad is even wilder. The man, Jeff Hayes, is now sitting behind bars for a murder he committed in the eighties.

Honestly, it sounds more like the plot of Ace's dad Thatch's favorite soap opera, *General Hospital*, than real life. Ever since they started streaming *GH* on Hulu, Thatcher Kelly—billionaire and financial whiz extraordinaire—has been driving my stepdad Wes nuts with phone calls and text messages about every storyline and plot twist.

Funny thing is, if you know Ace's dad personally, his obsession with a soap opera isn't a shock. The man is a proud lover of all things romance and drama. I honestly think that's one of the reasons Ace's mom Cassie ended up finding her way to writing romance books in her free time when she's not busy on location for photography shoots.

"So, calling Fighting Finn Hayes your uncle is a no-go, then?" Blake asks, a teasing tone in his voice.

"Definitely a no-go…" I pause, scrunching up my nose. "And do people really call him that? Fighting Finn Hayes?"

"Not yet, really. So far, it's just me. Hasn't really caught on yet."

"I bet he hopes it doesn't."

"You have no idea." Blake grins. "Threatened me with lots of pain."

My phone buzzes in my pocket, startling me briefly before I realize what it is. Sitting in the cloak of darkness with Blake, eating ice cream, I almost forgot the outside world existed.

I pull it out and swipe up on the screen to read the text message.

Ace Kelly: I know you can normally fend for yourself, but Jules and I have been worrying for two hours. Did you make it out of the stadium unscathed, or do I need to be contacting Wes's lawyer?

I glance up at Blake, who's sitting quietly and patiently. He's not demanding I tell him about the sender, which somehow makes me feel even more like I should.

"It's Ace. Just checking to make sure I'm not locked up."

Blake laughs, nodding. "He texted me an hour ago. While you were picking out your ice cream. Wanted to make sure I'd still be eligible to play next year so I didn't wreck his entire sports betting scheme."

"You didn't…tell him we're together, did you?"

He cocks his head, and my throat feels thick. The last thing I need is Ace Kelly running all over campus telling people I'm dating a twenty-one-year-old quarterback or something.

"I didn't," Blake says slowly and softly, pausing briefly before continuing. "Can't say I'm loving how big of a deal-breaker it seems it would be if I had."

I shake my head. "It's just…complicated. I'm four years older than you. And it's not like there's something to actually tell. We're just celebrating our narrow escape from authority, right?"

"Right."

I suck my lips into my mouth, and Blake stands abruptly, holding out a hand to help me up. "Come on, Lex. I'll walk you home."

I'm surprised he's the one ending things, given how hard he's been pursuing me, but I have to admit I'm tired. My adrenaline crashed over an hour ago, and I've been relying on the sugar from the ice cream ever since.

"Okay."

As I stand up, Blake jogs over to the trash can at the side of the entrance to the theater and throws out his ice cream bowl, and then he comes back to me to walk down the stairs together.

I use the solo time to text Ace back with just enough to keep him from sending the police to find me and then tuck my phone away again.

Me: I'm fine.

Blake and I are mostly silent on the way down the steps, but despite my normal introverted tendencies, I find it somewhere inside myself to break the monotony.

"Thanks. For…stepping in tonight. I *would* have come up with something, but I do appreciate that I didn't have to."

Blake's laugh is soft and comforting, wielding a weird power over my stomach once again. "You're welcome. I know how painful it had to be for you to accept help, especially from me, the perpetual thorn in your side."

"Double C nights are busy. You always linger a little too much."

He guffaws. "Oh man, so I'm right? I am a thorn in your side?"

I shrug, wincing slightly as he continues. "I half expected you'd coddle me a little, you know? Tell me I'm just imagining things. Instead, I've just got really poor timing."

"One thing about me you should know right off the bat is that I don't tend to coddle. I… Well, to be honest, I'm not sure I'm capable of it."

Blake's face is a mask of nothingness in the dark of night, and I wish more than anything I could see it a little better so I could attempt to read it. Normally, I wouldn't care, but for some reason, I find myself curious what he thinks of me.

Quite frankly, I hate it. It's much easier to function when you aren't worried about what other people are doing, thinking, or feeling. *Much, much easier.*

I lead the way toward my apartment, and Blake stays in step beside me. We don't speak for nearly two blocks, through the entire journey past Beckley Theater, across Amsterdam Avenue, and all the way to the back of Dickson's parking garage.

"How'd you end up running Double C?" Blake asks, seemingly out of nowhere. It's a question I'm duty-bound not to answer, and for that, I'm thankful.

"I can't tell you that."

"Because you'd have to kill me? Or just because you don't want to?"

"Closer to the first."

"Wow. Okay. So, this really is some mob-style, family-secret type shit."

I roll my eyes. "This isn't *The Sopranos*."

"It feels like it."

I laugh and shrug. "It's not that complicated. But it *is* secretive. That's kind of the point, you know?"

"All right, then." Blake's mouth tilts into that easy, cocky smile of his. "I guess I'll just have to be okay with never knowing. But at least I'll know where you live."

I stop dead in my tracks, narrowing my eyes at him.

Blake chuckles, holding up his hands like I might call the cops. "Come on, I'm kidding. I swear I'll never show up uninvited."

"Maybe we should just say goodbye here."

"Lex," he says softly, stopping just ahead of me. "Let me walk you home. Make sure you get there safe. After that, you'll never see me in the vicinity again. *Unless…*"

I arch a brow. "Unless what?"

His gaze locks with mine, steady and warm. "Unless you invite me."

I swallow against the sudden tightness in my throat. *Why is he so good at this?* "Okay," I say, my voice quieter than I intend, as we start walking again. Every rational brain cell I have is screaming to let him go, but something deeper—something *curious*—is pulling me toward him.

I can't explain it, but I *have* to know why women react to Blake Boden like this. Why *I'm* reacting like this.

Hypotheses swirl in my head like a storm, and my brain spins through the kind of evidence-based research I could conduct to figure it out. I'd need a baseline spreadsheet—physical traits, football stats, maybe some genetic history—paired with his upbringing and social conditioning. From there, I'd track reactions, mine and others', and utilize an AI-assisted app to create a data flowchart to help correlate trends. I'd need updates…which would require future observations—otherwise known as seeing Blake more.

This is all hypothetically speaking, of course.

By the time I resurface from my internal monologue, we're standing in front of my apartment. I blink, disoriented, and realize Blake is staring at me. Not impatiently, not smugly—just staring, like he's trying to figure me out.

"Sorry," I mumble. "I was…thinking."

"Don't be sorry." He gives me that lopsided grin that shouldn't affect me but *does*. "I feel privileged to see your mind at work."

I start to roll my eyes, but Blake stops me with a light touch on my elbow. His hand is warm, and my skin heats, completely betraying me.

"Don't do that," he says softly. "I'm serious. You've got *big* things going on up here."

My cheeks flush, and all I can think is, *If you only knew the calculations I've been running about you.*

"Thanks," I say, clearing my throat. "For…you know. The save, the horrifying pizza experience, the ice cream, walking me home. And your patience."

His smile widens, and it's both charming and infuriating. "You make me sound pretty good, Lex. Are you *sure* you don't want to date me?"

I laugh, though my response lacks conviction. "Pretty sure."

Eighty percent sure. Maybe seventy. *Fine. Sixty, at least.*

"Okay, then." Blake's voice is light, but his eyes gleam with something teasing and unrelenting. "But if you change your mind… you know where to find me."

"Statistically speaking," I retort, forcing my brain to recover, "Dragon Stadium or your apartment."

He grins. "Sounds about right."

"Goodnight, Blake."

"Goodnight, Lex."

Warm air crackles between us as Blake leans in. I expect a quick, harmless kiss on the cheek, but at the last moment—probably because of some glitch in my brain-to-neck function—my head jerks.

And his lips land *directly* on mine.

Tingles erupt across my skin like a live wire, and before I can process what's happening, Blake wraps his arm around my back, pulling me closer. My hands press against his chest reflexively, and though my brain is spinning in panic, my body betrays me completely because—well, *damn*.

I push back abruptly, breaking the kiss and sucking in a sharp breath. Blake's eyes are wide and intense, like I've just hit him with a lightning bolt.

"What was that, Lex?" he asks, his voice low and slightly rough.

"It wasn't anything," I lie, shaking my head too quickly.

"Bullshit." He grabs my hand, holding it firmly but gently. "That was *something*."

"Fine," I admit. "It was something. It was research."

The first step in convincing someone of something is convincing yourself. I'm not sure I've achieved that here, but he's so caught off guard by my assertion, he goes with it anyway.

It was research. It was research. It was research.

Right? Right.

"Research?" He lifts his brow in disbelief.

"Yes. A data input, if you will."

He stares at me for a beat, then grins. "Let's input some more data, then."

"No," I say firmly, yanking my hand free. "This ends here."

He shrugs, turning on his heel and laughing as he jogs down the stairs. But before he disappears into the night, he glances back, winks, and says, "We'll see about that."

It's both a threat and a promise. Blake Boden isn't going away without a fight.

His charisma is undeniable, and once again, hypotheses swirl in my mind. *If subjected to this level of swoon for a prolonged period of time, how long does it take to fall in love?*

Hordes of excited graduates hoot and holler in their navy-blue-and-gold gowns, posing for pictures with their friends and family in front of the stadium as I leave drill practice on Monday afternoon.

It's graduation day and the official end of the spring semester, and by and large, all the students will be moving their stuff out of their dorms and apartments and heading home for the summer. I'll be here, though, practicing, conditioning, and training for next football season until our first game at the end of August and school starts at the beginning of September.

I'm thankful Ace, Julia, Finn, and Scottie are all local to New York so I'll still be able to get together with friends other than my teammates, but for the most part, I'm excited for the crowds on campus to thin out a little bit. Brower Center student dining won't be as much of a crush, and I won't have to juggle classes and training.

I read a waiting text from my mom before shooting her a quick one back.

> **Mom: A little sad that you won't be home this summer but looking forward to using your time in New York as an excuse to come shopping. LOL! Don't tell your father.**
>
> **Me: Haha. Noted. Your secret is safe with me.**
>
> **Mom: Have a good day, hun. Talk to you soon!**

I tuck my phone back into the pocket of my sweat shorts and sling my practice bag up on my shoulder. After I head back to my apartment and shower, I'm supposed to meet Ace, Julia, Finn, and Scottie for an end-of-the-year celebratory lunch at Zip's Diner, and Ace is bound to give me shit if I'm the last one there.

The sun is crisp today, but a gentle breeze means it still feels like spring. The hair on my arms stands on end, so I stop briefly, pulling my bag back off my shoulder and opening it, and I throw on a Dickson University Football sweatshirt.

As the hood clears my eyes, I notice a familiar face across the pedestrian court, headed for the southwest entrance of Ferris Research Lab.

Well, hello, Lexi Winslow. I haven't stopped thinking about her ever since we kissed on Saturday night outside her apartment building.

A small trill of excitement runs the line of my spine, my mind quickly recalling that amazing kiss, and I hustle up to get my arms in my sweatshirt sleeves and pick up my bag to jog in that direction, but it isn't without at least three people shouting my name at full volume.

"Yo, Blake!"

"Boden!"

"What's up, BB?"

Lexi, of course, hears the shouts and turns around to steal a glance, and I'm thankful and even a little hopeful when she doesn't immediately bolt inside. Instead, she slows to a stop to wait for my approach, so I settle for a few quick chin-jerks at the strangers and keep jogging.

Lexi looks at the ground and back up, her feet in constant motion as she spins herself in a circle. It's pretty fucking adorable, and I get the feeling she doesn't deviate from her route to wait for people very often.

But she's waiting for *me*. It's all the confidence boost I need.

"Hey, Lex," I greet, a smile making my mouth climb near my

eyes. "Headed to the lab, even on the last day of the semester, huh? Isn't the work supposed to be over?"

She rolls her eyes. "Not for me. There's always work to do. Research. Improvements. Plus, I don't graduate until I turn in my final dissertation at the end of summer semester."

This might be the best news I've heard all week.

"So, you're going to be around on campus all summer?" I smile. "Me too. I have training, practice, and camp with the new guys in June. Maybe we'll see each other."

"Well, if you keep stalking me, I'd say there's no maybe about it."

I laugh. "I just happened to see you. That's not the same as stalking."

"I think you're relying too heavily on semantics."

"So, give me your phone number. That way, I won't have to rely on anything else, and we can eliminate the whole element-of-surprise thing."

"No," she says quickly, her response immediate and resolute. "I don't give my number to anyone." But then, surprisingly, her expression softens a little. "It's a safety thing."

"But we kissed," I counter, grinning slightly. "Surely that makes me a safe person."

She shakes her head, unimpressed.

"No?"

"No. Statistically speaking, it makes you more dangerous. Most women who are homicide victims are killed by men they know."

"Wow. Okay. I don't love that fact at all. So, what does it take to make me safe?"

She shrugs, her lips pressing into a thin line. "I… Well, I don't know."

"That's fair," I reply with a small nod. "All trust has to be earned in some capacity, right? So, the more trustworthy I am, the safer I'll be." I pause, letting the words settle, then grin. "Guess I'll just have to keep showing up until I hit the magic quota."

"Blake—"

"Don't say it, Lex," I cut her off. After the time we spent together the other night, and the kiss she gave in to for just a moment at the end of it, I refuse to let her push me completely away again. I haven't been this obsessed with getting to know a person ever. That's got to mean *something*. "Don't tell me not to bother or that I should avoid you at all costs or that Saturday night isn't worth repeating. Let me have the possibility. Let *yourself* have the possibility."

She searches my eyes. "The possibility of what exactly?"

I shrug, the movement a dramatic flare of hope. The fact that she's asking instead of walking away is a sliver of praise for the start of my little speech. "Maybe we'll be friends. Maybe you'll get sick of me. Maybe we'll be something more. I don't know, and you don't either. But it doesn't have to be a bad thing. It can be fun."

"I don't like not knowing, Blake. My whole personality is to *know*. I know that's hard to understand, but just *winging it* isn't exactly a part of my vocabulary."

My chest tightens. Lexi is different. From me, from my family, from most of my friends—frankly, from most people. That's part of what I like about her. I can't expect her to conform to my idea of easy any more than she can expect me to give up just because she said so.

"Okay. Then…take the day. The week, even. To figure out everything, you need to have a plan. The only thing I ask is that you don't discount the idea of giving us a try completely without thoroughly analyzing the facts."

"And what if it doesn't come out in your favor?"

I shake my head, a smile growing so wide it connects my ears. There's nothing more powerful than having someone's own words to use against them. "It's about the numbers, Lex. Not some magical, mystical reasoning. As long as I keep up my performance—continue being a good human—why wouldn't you consider having me in your life?"

My words make the tiniest hint of a smile form on her lips. "Your smug use of short-term recall is painfully annoying. I just want you to know that."

"Annoying, maybe. But it's also true."

"Fine," she finally says, her tone laced with mock seriousness. "I'll consider the possibility of keeping you around this summer—for companionship *and* entertainment."

"Oh my God. Entertainment?" I ask, clutching my chest like I've been mortally wounded.

She smirks. "What will he do or say to get my attention this time, I ask myself…"

Her jab makes it impossible not to smile, but I quickly force a pout. "You're mean, Lexi Winslow."

She shrugs, completely unbothered. "Yeah. I've heard that before."

"What does it say about me that I keep coming back for more?"

"You're a glutton for punishment?"

"Or maybe I'm just an optimist," I counter, raising an eyebrow.

"Whatever helps you sleep at night," she replies dryly, her sharp wit as quick as ever.

I grin, and she shakes her head, sensing the dirty turn of my mind immediately. I had no doubts she would. She's the smartest person I've ever met.

"I better get inside," she announces, her tone brisk as she pivots to officially dismiss me. "I have a million data points to enter and a myriad of tests to run. If I don't start now, I'll be here all night."

"Yeah," I say, pretending to sound nonchalant. "Of course. I've got…stuff…to do too."

I half expect her to ask about my plans, but my anticipations for Lexi Winslow are too jaded by my experience to be realistic. She's not a pick-me girl—she's a *don't-pick-me* girl, to be honest.

"Well," I say with a grin. "I may not have your number yet, but you've got mine. Don't be afraid to use it."

I laugh. I have to. It's the only way to save myself from a hit to my self-esteem. "See you soon, Lexi."

I make a point to turn to leave first, before she heads into the lab—before she can serve me another kick to the balls. Instead, maybe, just maybe, she'll be left with a feeling of longing for more.

Water splashes onto the dock, sprinkling my legs and the edges of my towel, yanking me out of the deep recesses of my always-busy mind. The sun blazes overhead, the thick heat wrapping around us like a blanket, ushering in summer alongside our annual Memorial Day tradition—a weekend at Uncle Brad and Aunt Paula's lake house.

My family is big. So big, in fact, that if I ever had to bring an outsider to one of our gatherings, I'd probably create a detailed family tree—color-coded and annotated—just to give them a fighting chance at keeping everyone straight.

I wish I were kidding. But with Finn's family merged into our already chaotic mix, our connections are more tangled than ever.

The whole family rundown?

Well, there's my immediate family—my mom Winnie, step-dad Wes, and my technically *half* brother Wes Jr. My mom has four brothers—Remy, Flynn, Ty, and Jude—and all four are married with kids. I'm the eldest cousin within the Winslow family; everyone else is closer to my brother's age.

Remy and Maria have Izzy and Carmen.

Flynn and Daisy have the twins, Roman and Ryder.

Ty and Rachel have Emily.

Jude and Sophie have Hawk and Meadow.

Aunt Paula is married to Uncle Brad—my grandma Wendy's brother. And Howard is my grandma's husband.

Finally, there's Finn's side—my *half family* because they all share the same bio dad as my mom and uncles. Finn's crew includes his mom Helen, sister Willow, and brothers Reece, Travis, and Jack.

See what I mean? *Complicated.*

Out on the lake, my brother and several of our cousins—Hawk, Meadow, Ryder, Roman, Izzy, Carmen and Emily—are floating on every inflatable device imaginable, from tubes to noodles. My uncles Flynn and Remy are in the water with them, while Ty and Jude execute cannonballs with reckless abandon, sending tidal waves crashing through the crowd, which, of course, cues Meadow's and Emily's inevitable, high-pitched shrieks.

Meanwhile, most of the adults have escaped to the house for a brief reprieve, preparing lunch in the relative quiet while we wreak havoc down here.

Finn and Scottie are on the dock with me, canoodling on a towel with Scottie's body propped up against the front of Finn's.

I can imagine every experience she has with her newly paralyzed body is both traumatizing and enlightening, but her attitude is commendably positive. She's been all smiles since we arrived last night and hasn't even offered an emotional moment over the complete and total upheaval of her life for the last couple of months. Maybe she's different behind closed doors with Finn, but if I didn't like her already, I'd be rethinking my stance this weekend.

I flick my large black sunglasses down my nose to get a better look at the water, counting heads in the shimmering churn. I know my uncles are paying some attention, but they're also playing around, and I don't want anyone trying to drown on my watch.

Satisfied with the body count, I sigh and push my sunglasses back up over my eyes, evidently earning Finn's attention. "What's wrong, Lex? Allergic to the sun?"

"No. Overwhelmed by the chaos, maybe," I snort. "The sun, though, in measured amounts, has substantial benefits. Most of us don't get enough vitamin D."

Scottie giggles. "There are…*a lot*…of people here."

"Yeah, I can't believe how enormous my family is now," Finn says with a grin. "Every time I glance back up at the house, I wonder how the hell we've managed to stuff that many people inside."

Finn's transformation over the past few months has been incredible. From crude, guarded, gruff fighter to someone at peace, his shift has a lot to do with Uncle Ty's patience and the rest of our family rallying around him and his siblings and his mom. For years, their lives were anything but easy. Their dad—the same man who walked out on my mom and uncles and left my grandma to raise five young kids by herself—put simply, is a piece of shit.

But now, the Hayes family is safe and happy, and it's clear in the way Finn carries himself.

Ironically, his story is not far off from the rest of us, taken under the wing of a loving sector of our family to guide us through a hard time at one point or another. I, myself, wouldn't be flourishing the way I am now without my mom, grandmother, all four of my uncles—especially Remy—and Wes Lancaster, who stepped up to be a better stepdad than any girl could dream of.

I was never like the other kids. But with my family, that didn't matter.

"It's a phenomenon of theoretical physics how Uncle Brad and Aunt Paula managed to cram so many bedrooms into that lake house," I tease, shaking my head. "Are the walls portals to other dimensions? I've been trying to figure it out for years."

Both Scottie and Finn laugh, Finn leaning down right after to whisper something in Scottie's ear that makes her both blush and smile. If this weren't a regular occurrence for them, I might be tempted to spill into the thoughts of a third wheel. Given the circumstances of Scottie's injury, and the trials of their whole relationship, though, I'm just glad to see them both so happy.

It makes me wonder if I'll ever have it—the thing my parents and my aunts and uncles and Finn and Scottie and even Ace and Julia, no matter how much they don't realize it yet, have with each other. It's a level of closeness with another person I've often mused if I'm actually capable of having, or if the attempt would be like fitting a square peg in a smaller, rounder hole.

I know I'm not a freak of nature or anything, but my brain *does* work differently. Relationship-wise, it's a challenge.

"Incoming!" Jude yells, razor-knifing into the water with one knee tucked to his chest and splashing all of us once again. Scottie struggles to push herself all the way back up to sitting after startling, and Finn lifts from under her armpits to help her.

"How's physical therapy going, Scottie?" I ask, steering the conversation away from my swirling thoughts and onto a different track. "Do you feel like you're making any progress?"

"It's going well…when I don't get frustrated," Scottie hedges. "Adam, the one PT at the Hodge Clinic, says he thinks I'm only a few months away from finding some really solid independence."

"That's great," I reply warmly, pushing up off my elbows and leaning my chest into my knees as a possibility hits me. "My dad, Nick, is a neurosurgeon, you know? World-renowned, actually. And he's supposed to be back from Germany this summer. I know the teams you've been working with from St. Luke's and Daytona were top-notch, but maybe you should do a consult with him, just for kicks."

"Really?" Scottie asks. Her voice is both excited and hesitant, and I instantly know why. I'm not great at reading people, but it's a no-brainer why someone in Scottie's circumstances would be reticent with their hope. Going from a cheerleader in the prime of her career to paralyzed from the waist down is something no one expects or accepts easily. It took a lot of work to get as comfortable as she is, and any kind of false anticipation of a different outcome could really cause a setback.

"Of course." I nod. "Next time I talk to my dad, I'll mention it."

"Thanks, Lex." Finn's deep voice has an extra edge of emotion I'm not sure anyone but I would pick up on, but I notice it all the same. Part of my brain's chemical makeup is analysis. Every sound.

Every face. Every facet. I can't help but study them all. "We appreciate it."

I shrug. For as weird as it may be, given how I met Fighting Finn Hayes for the first time—in the middle of a Double C event before he went toe-to-toe with ex-UFC fighter Donnie Marks—we're family. There isn't anything I wouldn't do for him.

Internal laughter plagues me as I realize Blake's stupid nickname for Finn has rooted inside my brain. I knew I'd remember it, but I never dreamed I'd find myself using it.

"What are your friends up to this weekend?" I ask, the niggling—and lately constant—curiosity I have about Blake rearing its ugly head. Ever since we kissed over a week ago, I've been mentally analyzing his charismatic superpowers at every available opportunity. And after my interaction with him on campus last Monday, I *might've* taken my research a step further.

"Julia and Ace are in the Hamptons with their parents," Scottie answers. "Kayla's home for the summer, and I think she's with her family in Florida this weekend."

"Blake is still at Dickson, I think," Finn adds, and my stupid ears home in on the sound of *his* name. "Probably football training shit he has to do."

"On Memorial Day weekend?" A pang of worry that he's lonely hits me square in the chest with annoyance. I don't spend my time thinking about men—and I certainly don't spend my time thinking about football players like Blake Boden.

Says the girl who spent way too much of her time this week focused on her new little research project that—

"I think Blake's mom and dad might have been coming into town for a couple days." Scottie's update cuts off my thoughts at the knees. "But man, maybe we should have checked." She worries her lip. "We could have invited him here, I bet. Not like anyone would even notice one more with these numbers."

"I'm sure he's fine," I say, the panic of imagining him here with my whole family pressuring me to find some status quo. "It's not like the entire campus is empty, and he's got plenty of fans."

"Shoo," Finn remarks, his face turned up in an amused grin. "You really are a steel fortress when it comes to him."

"What do you mean?"

"Oh, come on, Lex." Finn's eyes dance with amusement. "You've rejected him more times than I can count. You act like he's not even a human."

I roll my eyes. "He's a campus celebrity."

Finn laughs. "Blake's not like that. Not really. People are interested in him, but all he cares about are his friends and football."

That little nugget of information should be easy to brush off, but my mind latches on to it like a parasite. The human brain thrives on patterns, and mine *demands* them. When something doesn't add up, I can't just let it go—I have to find the *why*.

Enter the anomaly that is Blake Boden—the man who spurs a reaction from every woman in his vicinity, including me. I *don't* do well with anomalies.

Naturally, as a consequence of my shortcomings, I've turned him into data and created the AI-assisted *Blake Boden Analysis* app I've been thinking about ever since the night dorm-room pizza with Blake ended in a kiss I still don't understand.

Technically, it's a combination of a data analysis spreadsheet and an AI-assisted program, but the app is probably easier to explain. Basically, I input everything I know, and continue to learn, about him—physical traits, social interactions, football stats, even the way his smile curves slightly higher on the left. And I log my observations—the way other people react to him, things his friends say, et cetera.

The app takes those inputs and identifies patterns and gives me updated conclusions based on my current hypothesis—**Quality of life is unchanged with Blake Boden in it.** One person can't have that big of an effect on a life surrounded by thousands and thousands of other people.

It's purely scientific. Logical. *Or a way for you to reclaim control when he's threatening to steal it.*

I ignore my clearly useless subconscious and make a mental note of data to add to my Blake Boden app—*friends are defensive of who he is as a person and of his feelings.* I'm not the app, but I'm willing to bet the supposition is a benefaction of trustworthiness.

Which, of course, suggests I shouldn't be so dismissive of the idea of spending more time with him.

Annoying.

I drop back onto my elbows and point my eyes to the sky, making Finn laugh again. As far as he and Scottie are concerned, my hatred for Blake is the running joke of the century. I, for one, wish it were that simple.

"Hey, hey!" Uncle Jude shouts, jumping through the three of us on light feet, dripping water all over the dock and our bodies. "I see Wendy and Helen waving up there, and you know what that means!"

"Food's ready!" Uncle Ty yells, shoving him out of the way and jumping over my body to be first. A roaring stampede of wet teenagers follows as everyone hustles out of the water, and I shrink into a ball to get out of the way as they charge around me. I might as well be Mufasa at the bottom of the gorge for all the care they take with me.

Logically, I know they're trampling me to avoid doing the same to Scottie, but still…I'd like to live to see tomorrow.

"Hey, watch it!" I yell as my cousin Hawk steps on my pinkie finger. He looks back in apology but doesn't slow down in his surge for the house. "My God, this is like *Roadhouse* without Patrick Swayze, and clearly, he was the best part."

"Solid fucking movie," Finn says in camaraderie as I climb to my feet and shrink into a pencil to avoid the last of the wildebeests running for sustenance. Scottie smacks his chest with a small laugh and a big smile, and he clears his throat, adding, "May he rest in peace."

Finn gets to his knees and then his feet, making sure to take care with keeping Scottie propped up and sitting, and then leans down to scoop up her body with ease. She's a petite girl, but he makes it look like she doesn't weight anything at all.

Gallantly offering them the right of way with a swing of my arm, I follow behind them, bringing up the rear of the entire dripping group. Roman and Ryder are the first in line, ravaging at the aluminum pan lineup of food the adults have managed to pull together, and Hawk, Meadow, Emily, Izzy, Carmen, Wes Jr., Willow, Travis, and Jack aren't far behind. Reece waits at the back door, leaning into the jamb and stepping to the side as Finn approaches with Scottie, while Jude, Ty, Remy, and Flynn all make plates, only to hand them over to their wives.

"Take note, fellas," Remy says wisely, a smile on his face reminding me of the carefree uncle who put me first time and time again when I was just a special needs girl with a single mom. "A happy wife means a happy life, and the root of happiness is food."

I find a place at the back of the line, my stepdad and my uncles keen on getting their own food in front of me. Balancing a plate and napkin between my fingers, I wait my turn, half listening as their conversation inevitably drifts to football.

"Mavs Kids Camp starts next week, doesn't it, Wes?" Uncle Ty asks, grabbing a burger from the grill.

"Yep," my stepdad replies, his tone casual as he loads his plate.

"What big stars are joining the fun?" Uncle Jude grins, already angling for something that benefits himself. "Anyone I might need you to snag an autograph from?"

"I'm not getting you any fucking autographs," my stepdad shoots back, rolling his eyes with a chuckle. "Though, I just got word from our media department on Friday that your favorite Dickson quarterback is going to be there."

"Boden's going to Mavs Kids Camp this year?" Uncle Jude's eyes widen in surprise, and at the mention of his name, my head snaps up like a rubber band.

"Yep," my stepdad confirms, tossing a hot dog onto his plate.

"Blake Boden was a late sign-up, but it worked out since Cam Mitchell backed out last minute. We needed an extra volunteer."

"Blake Boden is going to MKC this year?" I ask, but my question goes completely ignored.

Apparently, Blake forgot to mention this little detail during our Mavericks discussion last Saturday night. And despite the fact that Mavs Kids Camp is planned almost a year in advance, he somehow managed to get a green light from the media team.

"That kid sure is talented," Uncle Jude remarks, scooping mac and cheese onto his plate. "Tell me he's on your draft short list."

"I know his stats," my stepdad replies, a dry laugh rumbling through his chest.

"Oh yeah, baby. The next Quinn Bailey incoming," Uncle Ty crows, high-fiving Jude as I edge closer, pretending I'm just trying to grab a hot dog.

"He's good," Uncle Flynn cuts in, his tone unusually skeptical. "But calling him the next QB is a stretch, don't you think?"

"His college stats are technically better than Quinn's," I chime in, feeling strangely defensive. Blake's record *is* better than Quinn's, but I have *no* idea what drove my need to say something about it.

Thankfully, no one thinks anything of it. Spouting facts and figures is nothing outside of the norm for me.

"See." Uncle Ty grins. "Next Quinn Bailey, I'm telling you."

My stepdad just laughs. "We'll start with this week's camp and go from there." He turns to me with a smile he reserves for the people he loves most. "You're still helping, right, Lexi Lou?"

"Yeah. I'll be there."

"Good. Let me know if I can do anything to help you with the highlight reels. You should have most of the footage—"

"I'm good, Dad. I had them ready months ago."

Uncle Ty guffaws, and Uncle Jude laughs as my stepdad's face turns into a combination of amused and contrite. "Right. Of course you did."

The group of them splits off, coming to the end of the buffet line and joining their wives in every available nook and cranny on the deck. The cousins and pseudo-aunts and uncles have all gathered back down on the dock, plates in their laps as they scream and tease and taunt one another with full mouths. I glance inside the house, to where Finn's propped Scottie on the couch in the living room to wait for her plate. I consider whether I want to join them but ultimately settle on a moment of solitude.

Big crowds are still overstimulating for me, even when they're all people I know and love, so a moment with nothing but my phone and my food won't go unappreciated.

Hopping up onto the brick retaining wall in the side yard, I set my plate down beside my thigh and scroll through my running apps. The first is related to my dissertation, and the second to my weird—and probably a little creepy—experimental research and findings on Blake Boden. I input the new information from Finn and Scottie about Blake's tendencies as a friend, along with his volunteer position for MKC, and then let the app run its conclusions. AI kicks out a ninety-five percent that life with Blake Boden in it is better than life with Blake Boden out of it, and I let out a heavy sigh.

Sometimes, I frighten even myself with the lengths I'm willing to take science.

I grab my hot dog and take a bite, moving to YouTube briefly to break up the monotony. I push play on a video from the PBS Space Time channel called "The Secrets of Quantum Thermodynamics." But before it can dive all the way into the fundamental principles of thermodynamics and their connection to quantum mechanics, I'm interrupted by the buzz of a message banner as it pops up at the top of my screen.

> **Unknown: Hey, Lexi. How's your weekend at the lake with family going?**

> **Me: Who is this?**

Unknown: Oh, you know…just the perpetual thorn in your side.

No longer confused, I frown and type out another message. It seems, today, Blake Boden is *everywhere* I turn.

Me: How did you get my number? And how do you know where I am? Don't tell me you're in the bushes.

Unknown: I have my ways. You're not the only resourceful one, you know. PS: I'm not in the bushes.

Me: I thought you were focusing on building trust…?

Unknown: Can't build anything without making contact, and you've been avoiding me.

Me: I haven't been avoiding you. We just haven't crossed paths.

Unknown: That's because I haven't seen you going into the lab at all this week.

Me: Stalk much?

Unknown: Admit it…you've been using a different entrance, haven't you?

Me: No.

Truth be told, I've not needed an entrance all that much. I woke up Wednesday morning with a keyboard on my face, having spent the entire night locked away in my apartment at my computer, putting in data points for my Blake Boden research project. I'm obsessive—sometimes to the point of recklessness.

But, evidently, so is he. Otherwise, he wouldn't be texting me on a number I told him he couldn't have.

I sigh, choosing not to argue with someone as clearly stubborn as him, and save his number under his full name—just like all the other contacts in my phone. Somehow, adding him makes the whole idea of spending time with him this summer feel plausible within the constructs of reality. And according to my stepdad, avoidance—if I'd even been attempting it—ends Monday at MKC anyway.

> **Blake Boden: Come on, Lex. Give me a chance. Please?**

> **Me: I'll see you at Mavericks Kids Camp this week, and maybe, if you're convincing enough, I'll consider it.**

> **Blake: You have no idea what you've just agreed to. Let the games begin.**

I roll my eyes, but the tug of my smile betrays me. For better or worse, I guess the Blake Boden Experiment—and the fact that I'll need to spend more time with him to conduct it—has officially begun.

Monday, May 26th
Blake

With a netted bag of footballs slung over my shoulder—courtesy of one of the Mavericks' staff—I step through the tunnel and out onto the field. The stadium looms around me, empty but electric, the kind of place that doesn't need fans in the seats to feel larger-than-life. My feet hit the turf, and I almost have to stop to remind myself to breathe.

This is it. The field where legends played. Where legends *still* play.

The very field that I hope to someday call home.

I scan the expansive venue, my eyes wide like a kid who just walked into Disney World for the first fucking time.

Hot damn. I'm happy to be here.

Today is the first day of Mavericks Kids Camp. For two hours today and two hours Wednesday, this is where I'll be, and I can't remember the last time I was this hyped for something. Sure, I'm here because I've been a Mavs fan since I could throw a football, but let's be honest, I'm also here because Lexi Winslow's name came up when we were talking about this camp during my lunch with Ace and his dad last Tuesday.

Thatch mentioned the camp shortly after walking into Zip's Diner, casually sharing that he'd just gotten off the phone with his brother-in-law—retired Mavs running back Sean Phillips. Apparently, Cam Mitchell had torn his hamstring playing indoor soccer with his sons and had to back out of camp at the last minute.

Of course, I latched on to the opportunity like a wide receiver on a Hail Mary pass. By the time I got back to my apartment, I'd already roped Coach Gordan into calling the Mavs on my behalf, and by Friday, I was officially on the volunteer list.

Sure, meeting retired legends like Quinn Bailey is a dream come true. But I'm not going to kid myself—knowing Lexi is here sealed the deal.

Some people think the Mavericks should change their long-standing tradition of starting the annual kids camp on Memorial Day. *It's a disservice to those the day honors. It's a day normally spent with family. Blah, blah, blah.*

But to kids like me, who've looked up to some of these guys since they were three or four years old, football like this *is* family. I watched them on TV, rooted for them in Super Bowls, and followed their careers as they retired. I bonded with my dad over conversations about plays and going to witness them play in person, and I watched as service members were honored at their games.

Being here with them today is a dream come true, and I know, with every fiber of my being, the Mavericks will do the Memorial aspect of today right.

Add in the fact that I've kissed Lexi Winslow—stepdaughter of the Mavs' owner—and today feels like I'm living in some kind of fever dream.

"Blake Boden?" a strong male voice asks from behind me as I dump the bag of footballs in the north end zone of Mavericks Stadium to get ready for our first drills after warming up. I stand and spin from my squat, my eyes widening on the vivacious, charismatic face of retired Mavericks quarterback Quinn Bailey. Affectionately, friends and family know him as QB.

I hold out a firm hand, belying the very shaking of my confidence upon meeting my idol. "Quinn Bailey. Excuse me for being so uncool, but holy fucking shit, is it a big deal to meet you."

Quinn laughs, thank God, easing the tension in my shoulders

and solidifying all the things I've heard about what a great guy he is over the years.

"I could say the same thing about you, Boden. I've watched what you've done with the Dragons since you got there, and I've got a tingly feeling this year is going to be your year."

I smile so big my cheeks burn. "I sure hope so, sir."

Quinn laughs again, waving a hand between us. "Please, for the love of God, don't call me sir. I feel old enough as it is when it hurts to get out of bed in the morning. Stick with Quinn or QB."

After years in New York playing for one of the best football teams in the country, Quinn's southern twang has faded just a bit—I guess fifteen years surrounded by *fuggettaboutits* will do that to you. But I can still hear the hint of it in his every word, and the thought of possibly finding a home away from home with the Mavericks like he did makes me smile.

"Right. Quinn, then." I shake my head, a rumble of laughter in my throat that makes Quinn freaking Bailey match my smile. I know there are other Mavericks alumni coming today, but for as exciting as that is, it could end right here, and I'd be a happy guy. "Thanks for coming today. I know meeting you has got to be a ton of these kids' dreams come true."

"I was that kid," Quinn says simply. "We all were."

"Yo! QB!" a big man with an even bigger smile calls from the tunnel behind Quinn. He's got a beard and has changed his haircut, but Teeny Martinez is quite arguably one of the most recognizable faces in American football. He commentates some on *Football Tonight* now that he's retired from the game, and just last weekend, he was at some concert dancing in a tracksuit in the middle of the band. He's a personality and a half, and I've never met a single person who doesn't love or idolize him.

"Teeny!" Quinn greets, doing the slap, handshake, hug thing you often see us men doing. They do a complicated handshake that ends in a spin, and Teeny finishes it off by holding out a hand for me to take. "Hey, Boden."

"Teeny," I say back, my face a layer of melting disbelief that all these guys know who I am. "Thanks for coming."

"You bet, kid. Speaking of...where are the attendees? This isn't some elaborate prank you're pulling just to get some face time with me and QB, is it?"

I chuckle. "While I'm not entirely above that particular move, staging an entire kids camp through the Mavs organization is a little above my abilities. From what I understand, they were doing a meet-the-owner thing with Wes Lancaster and their parents first, touring the stadium, and then ending here, where Lexi is going to show them a highlight reel on the jumbotron before we get started."

"Lex is coming?" Quinn asks excitedly. "That's my girl!"

It's an innocent statement from one of the people Lexi grew up around, and yet, I don't *like* it.

Ridiculous, I know, but there's a small, irrational sense of possessiveness I've already developed for Lexi Winslow. If she boxes me out like she could—like she has been up until now—that's going to make for one hell of a crash and burn.

"She's great," I say, stopping myself there instead of going into a three-page essay on all the things I'd like to get to know about her.

"You friends with Lexi Lou?" Teeny asks.

"We know each other from Dickson, so sort of..." I laugh. "I'm kind of still convincing her it's worth her time to be my friend."

"Ha!" Teeny shouts. "God, I love her."

"Where's Sean?" Quinn asks then, looking back into the dark tunnel and cupping his hand over his eyes to shield the morning sun. "I thought he was supposed to be here too."

"He is, but he and Six are doing their podcast for this week about Camp. They probably went with the kids so they could catch Bossman on audio giving his little speech."

Six is Sean's wife and an incredibly famous YouTube personality turned popular podcaster turned reality television star. Truthfully, it's mind-blowing how much I know about these guys and their lives.

Quinn laughs. "Oh shiiit. Lancaster hates the limelight, that's for sure." He picks up a football, working it in his hands and spinning it constantly to get a grip with his fingers on the laces. It's a classic quarterback fidget, one I was mere seconds away from starting myself. Quinn pumps a couple of times with some fake throws, and Teeny starts cackling.

"Look at this guy. Retired and still can't stop himself. He misses the game so much, he calls me crying on the phone at night so I can put him to sleep."

Quinn holds up a middle finger before throwing the ball to one of the catch nets at the other end of the end zone. Teeny laughs and winks at me before continuing. "You'd think a married fella like himself would be content once he got in bed, but nope. He needs a phone call with Teeny to make sure he has sweet dreams."

Quinn turns around with a roll of his eyes and a shake of his head, a smile curving his mouth all the way to his ears. "Don't listen to this guy, Boden. I have plenty to do with my wife, in bed, at night. He, on the other hand…"

Teeny snorts. "My wife is an angel on earth who takes care of her man's every need and want, okay?"

"Does she also have a listening device on you?" Quinn asks with a snort. "Because holy hell, you're laying it on thick."

Teeny shrugs and pretends to whisper. "You never know."

There's a sudden jolt of noise as the jumbotron kicks on in the center of the field, the Mavericks' intro playing at full volume. It's a tiny taste of what it might be like to be a player in this stadium, and fuck, does it give me chills.

"Welcome!" the announcer's voice yells over us. "To Maverriiiiiiiickkkkks Kids Cammmp!" On cue, a surge of young boys and girls dressed in matching camp T-shirts comes running on a charge out of the other end zone tunnel, their tiny faces scrunched into warrior expressions and their screams permeating the space between us.

A golf cart zooms toward the middle of the field, and Quinn,

Teeny, and I pick up a jog to meet it there as Wes Lancaster, Winnie Winslow Lancaster, and Lexi all climb from the back and take their spots to wait for the arrival of the running kids.

Lexi's eyes are on the three of us, but at this distance, it's impossible to tell who she's focusing on. I want it to be me, but these are guys she's known her entire life, so it's probably not.

Fuck, I sound real damn annoying, don't I?

As the stampede of kids comes to a stop in the middle of the field, Sean Phillips and his wife Six running behind them with a camera and microphone, Winnie and Lexi clap, and Quinn, Teeny, and I stop just to the side, our arms crossed over our chests. The kids' parents begin to fill up the lower levels of the stadium seats, and the other Mavs' staffers who help run the camp start to set things up on the sidelines.

Wes steps up in front of the excited group in his jeans and expensive button-down shirt, offering high fives to those who can jump high enough to hit his hand. "Welcome, everyone!" Wes says on a shout, quieting the boisterous and adorable little crowd effectively. "Thanks for coming out to the Mavericks' tenth annual kids camp! I'm Wes Lancaster, the owner of the team, and behind me are my wife Winnie and daughter Lexi. Winnie is also the team physician for the Mavs. Though, I do have some disappointing news that she'll be retiring after this year."

"Booo!" the lot of us yell, the loudest of which come from Quinn, Teeny, and Sean.

"I know, I know. It's the end of an amazing era. But I'm confident we'll find someone to fill her shoes who will be with us, hopefully, all the way to your generation of players," Wes tells the kids. Sean comes to stand next to Quinn and Teeny, while Six stays on the other side to get a good camera angle, and Wes continues with the introductions. "Now, these guys, I'm sure you recognize…" He pauses, and within seconds, the kids start to scream and hoot and holler toward us.

"*Quinn!*"

"*Teeny!*"

"*Oh my God, Sean Phillips is standing right in front of me!*"

"*QBpie!*"

It's a smattering of yells and a jumble of different affections, but without any doubt, it proves the kids do, indeed, know just who the retired Mavericks players are.

It's not a surprise, given their interest in a Mavericks football camp, but what does shock me is the number of kids who start to yell my name, unprompted.

"*Boden!*"

"*Blake!*"

"*Oh my God, I didn't know Blake Boden was going to be here!*"

Quinn turns to me with a waggle of his eyebrows, mouthing, "See? Your year."

I wave to the kids with a smile, jerking my chin up when one little boy calls my name again.

"And yes, it seems you know him too," Wes says and flashes a smile in my direction. "Blake Boden is the quarterback at Dickson University and has generously volunteered his time to help you guys learn this year."

My eyes can't decide where to look, bouncing around the crowd at all the kids and occasionally looking to where Lexi stands beside her stepdad. When I see she's looking in my direction, her eyes focused in that analytical way I've seen so many times before, I can't help but wonder what she's thinking right now.

Is she mad I'm here? Is she happy *I'm here?*

Has she finally decided that she should give in and marry me?

Surely the latter is over the top, but the fact that she's not tossing glare-daggers my way is all the response I need.

Add in the excitement as the kids scream about getting to work with me, and a warm wave of pride crashes over my chest. Becoming the guy people look up to in a sport I love is an accomplishment in and of itself. Whether I end up making the pros or not, I'm certain this is an experience I'll remember for the rest of my life.

Pulling a ball from the ground at my side, I pass a quick ten-yard lateral to the sideline, where a waiting boy in a Mavericks camp shirt and black jersey shorts waits with his hands up. He completes the catch with the ball tucked to his chest and then does a quick shuffle with his feet to turn upfield. His moves are impressive, reminding me of what I was like when I was just becoming obsessed with the game at eight years old.

Lexi holds court with a group of other kids, talking shop and statistics for pretty much the entire past roster of Mavericks' football.

I haven't gotten a chance to talk to her yet today, but as things wind down, I'm hoping I can catch her before she leaves. Her highlight reel video at the beginning of the day was so fucking well done, including a huge tribute to memorialized soldiers at the end and everything.

Graphics and videography may not be her main skill set, but I'm starting to think there isn't anything her brilliant mind can't do.

I pick up another ball and repeat the process for the last two kids in line, shouting encouragement as they each make their catch, the second of which wasn't even that suitable of a pass.

"Good hands!"

They beam under the praise and run to join the group in front of Lexi, tossing their balls back to me on the way. I net them all back into the bag, pull the drawstring, and then follow them over.

Quinn, Sean, Six, Teeny, Wes, and Winnie have already left for the day, so it's just me, Lexi, and the kids.

The last time we found ourselves alone in a football stadium together, the night ended in a kiss. I can only hope this time goes as well.

"Great job today, everyone," I say encouragingly as I join Lexi at the front of the group. As in any camp like this, it's plain to see that some of the kids have more natural talent than others, but the heart of every single one of them was huge. They all put in one hundred percent effort for the whole two hours, which is a lot for kids ten and under, attention-span-wise. "I'm so impressed with everyone's effort today and can't wait to see where we can get Wednesday. My goal is to leave you with as many exercises and drills as possible that you can use at home and in your own team's training to improve your timing, hand-eye coordination, and general knowledge of the game. Speaking of which, Lexi here is a wealth of football knowledge, so be thinking between now and Wednesday of some new questions you can ask in an effort to stump her."

Lexi eyes me with a narrowed gaze I can see out of the corner of my vision, but I smile and continue on.

"In fact, if anyone can ask her for a Maverick statistic on Wednesday that she doesn't know, I'll give them a signed Dickson Football poster to take home for their room."

The kids roar in excitement, and Lexi shakes her head with a coy smile.

"Don't get too excited," I warn them. "She knows almost *everything*. It won't be easy."

"My dad knows all kinds of Mavs' facts!" one little boy shouts. "I'll definitely get her."

I laugh. "I hope you do. But until then, be practicing and get some rest. We'll be busy on Wednesday!"

I pull the kids in for a final huddle, hands-in cheer, and then off they run toward the south end zone to meet back up with their parents.

Lexi and I are standing alone on the football field again, but thankfully, this time, we're not locked in a standoff with Dickson's athletic director.

"So, what do you say, Lex? Want to grab some pizza again?" I ask, trying to keep my tone light.

She makes an exaggerated gagging noise, her eyes bulging for extra effect. "Not unless you blindfold me first and bring a stun gun for backup."

I chuckle, shaking my head. "Good thing I packed both."

"Ha-ha." She rolls her eyes but smiles just enough to give me hope. "Very funny."

"Okay, but really. Let's go do something."

She shakes her head, her ponytail swishing behind her. "I'm busy."

"Busy doing what? Avoiding me?" I tease, even though I'm silently wondering if that's true.

"Wow," she deadpans. "We're really back to square one, huh?"

"Not exactly," I argue, folding my arms. "At square one, I didn't have your number, and you probably wouldn't even be talking to me right now. So, we're at square three. Maybe two and a half."

She tilts her head, considering me.

"Just for clarification," I continue shamelessly, "at what square do I get to kiss you again?"

"That square is off the board," she replies flatly, but I don't miss the way the corners of her mouth twitch. She wants to smile right now, but she's doing everything in her power to keep her poker face intact.

"Oh, come on," I say, eyeing her closely with a grin. "You can't tell me you hated it that much. It was a good kiss, right? Technically speaking."

"It was above average," she admits, her tone neutral but her cheeks pink.

I grin, leaning in just a fraction. "By a lot of points, right?"

Her eyes narrow, but I see a flicker of amusement in them. "What is it with you and your ego? Do you need it stroked every five minutes, or can it occasionally pet itself?"

"It's like a cat," I say with a shrug. "It needs attention. Regular rubs."

"Uh-huh," she says, arching a skeptical brow.

"What? That's normal. Everyone's ego likes attention. Don't you like it when people tell you how smart you are?"

She shrugs again. "I guess I don't hate it."

"See?"

"See what?" she asks, crossing her arms.

"We have a lot more in common than you'd like to believe. You just need to spend more time with me to figure it out."

"I can't tonight," she says, turning away, her voice dismissive but not unkind.

"Then when?" I ask, a level of desperation setting in I'm not used to — not in school, not in sports, and definitely not in women.

She glances back over her shoulder, and the tiniest hint of a smirk plays on her lips. "You have my number. Guess you'll have to figure out how to use it."

I watch her walk away, but my resolve grows with every step she takes.

Fine, Lexi Winslow. You want me to figure it out? *Challenge accepted.*

Ginger Lewis startles awake as I shove her in the shoulder, and she slams her feet down on the floor, causing an echo in the deserted lab. Her eyes are wide and frightened until they lock on me, and then realization sets in.

"Oh God. I slept here all night again, didn't I?"

I laugh, taking my seat at the computer desk next to her and waking up my screen with a tap of my fingers on the mouse. "Technically, I don't know when you got here, but I do know it's morning. Eight a.m., specifically. So, I'll leave the analysis up to you."

"The last thing I remember is being here at midnight." She jolts again, panicking over her computer. "Oh my God! I better have backed up my dissertation, or I'm going to have to kill myself!"

I take a drink of my coffee I picked up on the way here and stay silent. I've never been good at comforting someone in the middle of their breakdown. After, I can rationalize and strategize, but when it's happening, I either undercut their emotions entirely or take them on as my own, neither of which is particularly helpful or friendly.

"Oh, sweet, merciful Jesus. Thank everything. I saved it. I saved it, Lexi!"

I pump a small fist in the air in celebration. "Yay."

Ginger laughs and sinks back into the chair, her head falling back in a dramatic thud. "One day, I'm going to have it as together as you do."

I sigh. "It's not always as glamorous as it seems. Trust me."

She giggles and shakes her head. "Well, given your history of being right about stuff, I'm going to believe you. But from my perspective, I can't see how it could be any worse than being as Type B as I am."

I smile and click through my email to avoid opening the not-related-to-my-dissertation app I've been spending way too much time on. I already know what emails are in there, but I refuse to let anyone see that I'm spending an inordinate amount of time on Blake Boden research.

After having to be surrounded by his magnetism and handsome smiles for two hours straight yesterday at MKC, I obtained *a lot* of new data.

Ginger yawns, stretching to standing and pushing her chair into the desk. "What are you doing here anyway? If I were finished with my dissertation already, I'd be lounging on the beaches of Mexico right now. Or, at the very least, Long Island."

The truth is way too embarrassing—that I've taken my obsession with a guy so far that I'm using my research to back it up—so I settle for a white lie instead. "Just buttoning things up. I found a couple of bugs over the weekend, and I want to make sure it's perfect before I turn it in."

Ginger isn't what I'd call a best friend, but the truth is, I don't know that I'd use that terminology for anyone. I'm more of a loner planet, who occasionally allows other people to enter her orbit. In some cases, I could see how people might think that's sad, but I'm most content in the confines of my head.

The only company I've ever craved, ironically, is the company I spend most of my time turning down—Blake Boden.

"I'm sure it's brilliant," Ginger says kindly, gathering her headphones, drink cups, and various snack bags, and packing them into her light-pink tote. "I guess I'm going to go try to get some sleep in a real bed before returning later to drudge through some more data. Will I see you then?"

I shrug. "I guess it depends how sucked in I get. Who knows, maybe you'll find my face in a keyboard."

Ginger laughs. "Sounds like a plan. Later, Lex."

"Bye." I offer a small wave before turning back to my computer screen, clicking into my self-made romance analysis app after, and only after, I hear the door to the lab close behind her with a resounding click.

I open my spreadsheet first, entering all the carefully collected data from camp yesterday.

Good with kids

Patient

Confident around celebrity figures

Likes to tease

Self-deprecating at times

Flirtatious but funny advances that make it hard not to smile

An image of Blake stretching at the front of the group comes to mind.

Muscular thighs

I hit enter to populate another run of my AI-assisted analysis and, once again, get a result in the high nineties that Blake Boden in my life would be a good thing. So far, no inputs are moving the needle downward, and I'm starting to wonder if I'm going about this all wrong.

Maybe it's not all about Blake. Maybe, just maybe, I need the app to run the analysis as a comparison instead. With both of our information, I could set up an algorithm for compatibility.

My phone pings in my bag, so I take a drink of my coffee with one hand and reach blindly to dig it out with the other. I'm expecting a message from my mom—she makes a habit of getting in a few messages first thing in the morning—but instead, it's a message from Blake.

Blake Boden: Good morning, Lab Girl. Discover anything Nobel Prize-worthy yet this morning?

I scoff. Holy hell, if he only knew.

> *Me: Just having my morning coffee. The Nobel Prize will probably take another hour or two.*

> *Blake Boden: Wow. Slacking today, huh? I've already conditioned, run drills, and jogged three miles.*

> *Me: Am I supposed to be impressed or depressed? Because that sounds miserable.*

> *Blake Boden: What? Not a fan of exercise?*

> *Me: I don't particularly like being uncomfortable. Or sweaty. So, no.*

> *Blake Boden: Ah, well. I imagine when your brain burns as many calories as yours does, it'd be way too tiring to do anything more.*

It's an obvious attempt at coddling me, and surprisingly, I find it flattering.

> *Me: You're being nice.*

> *Blake Boden: I'm always nice.*

> *Me: I don't know about that.*

> *Blake Boden: Then you don't know me well enough yet. That means we need more time together. Let's go get breakfast. Or lunch. Or dinner. Whatever meal you want. Hell, I'll even settle for an after-lab snack.*

> *Me: You're going to see me at camp tomorrow. Isn't that enough?*

> *Blake Boden: Not even close. Yesterday, I barely even got to talk to you.*

Me: What if I promise to talk to you more? Will that be enough, then?

Blake Boden: Doubtful.

Me: But isn't it better than nothing?

Blake Boden: Absolutely. When it comes to you, I'll take anything I can get.

Anything he can get? I should probably be annoyed by the confidence and his clichéd words, but my mouth *really* wants to smile. I suck my lips into my mouth and type out a dismissal instead.

Me: Bye, Blake.

Blake Boden: Have a good day, Lexi Lou.

Lexi Lou. My first and middle name—a combination only the people closest to me ever use. The list has shrunk over the years, making it all the more disarming to hear it from someone like him. I can't decide if I hate it or if I kind of...don't.

Sighing hard, I push at the rampant flapping of butterfly wings in my stomach and tuck my phone back into my purse, hoping to trap the feelings right along with it.

My mind is a mess, but at least one thing is crystal clear.

I most definitely need to update my app to test the compatibility of opposites, and Blake Boden and I are subject zero.

Wednesday, May 28th
Blake

From the moment camp started today, things have been different. Instead of avoiding me, Lexi's been involved and engaged, going so far as to participate in some of the drills while I coach her and the kids.

Eye contact hasn't been impossible like it usually is, and for the first twenty minutes, I wondered if she'd fallen and bumped her head at some point after we talked yesterday.

It's almost as if…she likes me.

And it's kind of freaking me out.

"Okay, guys. This time, we're going to break left, juke one, two, and then cut back right," I instruct my group of attentive and excited kids. "Your marks are the five yard line and the ten yard line. Spread out so you have room between you and the person beside you, okay? We don't need any injuries."

The kids shuffle their feet from side to side with their arms up and out, looking at their neighbor to make sure they're not touching, and dropping into position as they've been taught. Lexi is at the end of the line but does the same. I blow the whistle to signify the start of the drill, and they all take off on the designated route at whatever their full speed is.

Quinn Bailey stands in the end zone and picks a kid to toss the ball to in the center of the group, sailing it right into his hands with ease. All the kids cheer in excitement, and Quinn does a little victory dance.

In the other end zone, Sean does drills with the kids who think they'd like to try their hand at quarterbacking, catching while they make passes to him and employing the techniques Quinn and I taught them earlier.

Teeny wasn't able to come back to camp today due to some of his professional obligations with his contracted sports network SportsCast, but everyone has certainly missed his humor.

I blow the whistle and clap my hands, calling all the kids into a mob in front of me. Lexi and Quinn hang back to talk to each other—a regular occurrence I'm starting to get used to with how close they are.

"Okay, guys! You did awesome!" I encourage them with a big smile. "Go get water and take a five-minute break. Don't forget to stretch and keep your muscles loose and warm. When we come back, we're going to run some strip-the-ball drills."

The kids take off for their water bottles on the sideline, cheering and jabbering on the way, and I stroll to the center of the end zone to meet up with QB and Lex.

"Going well so far, Boden," Quinn comments. "What's up next?"

"Strip-the-ball drills," I comment and waggle my eyebrows. "With you and me playing running back."

"Oh boy." Quinn's chuckle is devious and amused. "You know I'm a dual-threat quarterback, don't you? I'm gonna burn you so bad on this one, Boden."

I laugh, but to my surprise, so does Lexi, coming to my defense with facts. "Blake's a dual threat too, Quinn, and he's not retired. I wouldn't get too cocky if there's going to be a competition."

I smile, hedging, "I wasn't planning on a competition, but maybe that would make it interesting. What'd you have in mind, QB?"

"How about whoever maintains possession the most times wins?" He winks. "I may be old, but my hands are sticky like glue, baby boy."

I chuckle. "I don't know if that'll be the best for the kids' self-esteem. Pretty sure we're supposed to teach technique but motivate."

"Yeah, Quinn, we're not here for you to get some glory. We're here for the kids," Lexi teases, and Quinn's so easygoing, he just laughs and shrugs.

"Right. The kids. The whole reason we're here." He winks again. "How about a good old-fashioned weight-room competition when camp is over, Boden? It's how we used to settle shit back in the day."

"Yeah, okay." I nod, tapping my chin thoughtfully. "That, I can agree to."

"Good grief." Lexi scoffs. "Would you like a side of grunts with your cavemen egos? Now I'm remembering why I don't hang around football players that often. *Macho, macho, muscle, muscle, grunt, grunt, blah, blah, blah.*"

Quinn guffaws. "Give us a break, Lexi Lou. Our brains aren't as big as yours."

"Maybe you should join in on our weight-room competition," I suggest with a knowing smile in her direction. "Even it out just a little."

She rolls her eyes. "Yeah, no thanks. Not only are my muscles more for looks than show, there's also too high of a risk of wrist injury. I'll attend, but I'll keep the score."

"Quinn and I would spot you," I offer, but she just rolls her eyes again.

"Ha. No thanks. I'll stick to the sidelines."

"All right, that's fair." I nod. "I'm just impressed you've been running all the drills today. You learn them pretty quickly. A hell of a lot quicker than I used to when my dad was teaching them to me on Coronado Beach."

She shakes her head. "It's not skill. I'm just hyperattentive to instruction."

I study her face, her bright-blue eyes steady on mine, the wind catching her blond ponytail and sending it swaying behind her.

For a moment, I let myself hope—just a little—that I'm breaking through that fortress she keeps so tightly locked.

She doesn't interrupt the silence. Instead, she holds my gaze, and time seems to slow, everything else blurring into the background. Everything tunnels into me and Lexi Lou Winslow.

And then the alarm on my stopwatch goes off in blaring rebellion.

I flinch, fumbling to turn it off, and blow the whistle to call the kids back over from their water break. The moment dissolves, but it's burned into my memory, refusing to fade.

It happened.

And judging by the knowing smirk on Quinn Bailey's face, I wasn't the only one who noticed.

So maybe—just maybe—I'm not imagining it. Lexi Winslow might genuinely be starting to like me.

God, I hope so.

10

As Mavericks Kids Camp comes to an official close, the attendees reunite with their parents, Blake breaks down some of the drill setups, and Quinn and I gather balls in the end zone to net them back in their bag, while several members of the Mavericks' staff start to clean everything up.

"So…you and Boden have a cute little friendship going," Quinn remarks as I put the last ball in the bag, and he cinches the drawstring.

I've known Quinn for as long as I've known my stepdad since when my mom and Wes got together, Quinn Bailey was the starting quarterback for the Mavericks. Even though I was just a young kid, my expansive knowledge of football stats and extensive vocabulary evidently convinced him in some way that I wasn't.

Our friendship has well surpassed any other in my life. I'm godmother to his and Cat's son, Waylon, and we've spent more time together over the years than seems realistic for a young girl and a professional football player in any universe. But Quinn's seen me grow up through all my awkward phases in life and knows me better than most people could ever dream to.

But right now, his need to insert himself into whatever he thinks is going on between Blake and me is completely unnecessary and, frankly, unwanted and unwelcome while I'm still trying to sort through the mess of it myself.

"We just know each other from school."

"Yeah, of course," Quinn comments, though, his eyes are still assessing me closely. A little too closely, if you ask me. "I just mean it's good to see you getting along with someone your own age. You always had a soft spot for kids and grown-ass crybabies like us Mavs, but I know people your age are usually a bit of another story."

"Blake's younger than me."

Quinn laughs. "Okay, Ms. Exact Science. Yes, he's a few years younger. But he's in the same age group."

I shrug. "I guess."

"I think he might even like you."

Oh, trust me, I know he does. What I'm trying to understand is why do I keep finding myself thinking about him? Obsessing about him? Creating AI-enhanced apps to analyze him and what he does to me?

But I don't even think about telling Quinn all that. Instead, I feign annoyance and roll my eyes.

"You just want me to end up with a football player so you can rub it in my face."

Quinn's smile is huge. "I admit, that would be a fun bonus, but you know all I ever want is to see you happy."

I appreciate his words, but the fact that he's tying the premise of happy into a conversation he initiated about Blake Boden pushes me a little too far out of my comfort zone.

"Do we really have to talk about this?"

He chuckles. "No, I guess we don't."

"Good."

"I'm going to, though, just a little bit more."

"Quinn—"

"All I'm going to say is to give it a chance." He holds up both hands in the air. "Don't shut shit down just because you think you should. Let the wind blow you."

"Right," I say with a groan. "Because that's exactly who I am as a person. Just letting things *happen* instead of planning them."

"Maybe it's time to adapt." He shrugs one suggestive shoulder in my direction. "Didn't you learn anything here at camp? You've got to think on your feet."

"Please." I sigh. "Don't even think about using football analogies on me."

Quinn's booming laughter sounds like it comes from his toes. "All right, I'll let it go. I'm just saying…"

"Yeah, yeah, I hear you," I say, hurrying to hush him as Blake approaches us from the center of the field, a smile on his undeniably handsome face. "Now, drop it."

Quinn slings the bags of balls over his shoulder with a gloating smile, and I consider the ramifications of stabbing him. I don't even know how *I* feel about Blake yet. The last thing I need right now is Quinn freaking Bailey complicating things by inviting outside interest in the situation.

"You still up for that weight-room competition?" Blake asks as he arrives, a bag of his own balls slung over his shoulder. The two big, muscular men look like a couple of fit football Santa Clauses.

"You bet," Quinn agrees. "Cat's busy until five anyway."

The mere mention of his wife's name makes me smile at the fond memories I have of her over the years. "How is Cat these days?"

"Excellent," Quinn says, beaming. "Better than every other person combined, in my humble opinion."

I smile. "Good you found someone who can put up with you." I was a fairly young girl when they got together, but I was aware enough to know their romance was full of struggle and obstacles. Now that I'm researching compatibility, everything about how their story unfolded seems way more interesting than it did back then.

"Please. She doesn't just put up with me. She worships me." Quinn winks. "Just like Boden's going to after I kick his ass at the racks."

"Great," Blake says through a soft chuckle. "We'll drop these balls off in the training closet on the way there, then."

"You both act like you have privileges in the weight room." I point at Quinn. "You're retired." And then at Blake. "And you don't play professional ball yet."

"Yet, huh?" Blake waggles his brows.

I shake my head, but Quinn just smiles at me.

"We're with the owner's daughter, Lexi Lou. Somehow, I think it'll all shake out okay."

I sigh.

"Don't worry, Lex," Blake chimes in. "We'll try to make it entertaining, at least. And I can still spot you if you want to participate."

"Yes. You've mentioned that."

Blake laughs, holding up both hands innocently. "Okay, I surrender. You just tell me if you change your mind."

"*Blake.*"

"Right, right."

Quinn is like a fucking drugged hyena trying to keep his smug laughter at bay, and I narrow my eyes at him in warning. He's on my short list if he doesn't cool it. I swear, people are always looking for romance in everything.

Even if it—most likely—doesn't exist.

"Just a little bit more. You got it, Lex. Come on," Blake coaches as I get close to reracking the bar on the bench press. It's only ten pounds on each side of a fifteen-pound bar for a whopping thirty-five pounds, but my wrists are shaking, and my arms feel like Jell-O.

It's official. I'm a weakling.

And a fool.

Because for as much as I fought it, here I am, letting Blake Boden coach me through weight-training exercises and trusting that he's capable of making sure I don't get hurt.

Quinn left about thirty minutes ago to meet up with his wife, and despite the act of nonchalance I've been putting on, I didn't go running into the night with my hair on fire to get away from Blake.

Instead, I hung around until he convinced me to try doing a few reps with some light weights.

The bar clanks into the holder finally, and I drop my arms to my chest, totally and completely exhausted. Blake pulls me up by my hands, and I duck my head under the bar until I'm upright again.

"See! I knew you could do it! A little bit of light training a few times a week and you'll be close to my bench weight before you realize."

"Ha!" I say loudly, shaking my head. "You're joking, right? You bench double my *body* weight. *Double.* I'm a fragile skeleton. I don't think I'll be turning into a leafcutter ant anytime soon."

"A leafcutter ant?"

"Yes." I smile for what has to be the one-hundredth time since I stepped into the weight room with him. "They lift fifty times their body weight. They are literally one of the strongest things to ever exist."

"And yet…they look so delicate. Maybe there's a lesson in there somewhere, Ms. Fragile Skeleton."

I snort. "I don't think so, unless the lesson is that weight training isn't for me. I don't mind hanging out while you do it, though."

Or watching. I especially don't mind the watching, I find. The way his muscles ripple and flex is truly fun to observe.

"That's good. I'll have to keep that in mind when I'm having a late-night sweat session."

My brain short-circuits. Something about the way he's paired *late-night* and *sweat session* makes me feel like the oxygen in the room has been sucked out. But it doesn't make me scared of him— it makes me scared of myself.

Suddenly, I'm not entirely sure if I'm capable of keeping Blake Boden at the carefully crafted distance I'd planned on.

He takes a step closer, eliminating some of the space between us, and I swear the room tilts. His eyes search mine, soft but intent, and before I realize it, I'm mirroring the movement. My heart pounds as the distance between us vanishes, and my gaze flicks to

his mouth without permission. It's so close, it would take nothing—
nothing—to lean in just a fraction more and—

No, Lexi. Absolutely not.

I jerk back, the air between us thick with tension I don't understand. "I better get going." It's abrupt and blunt, and for once, I realize it. But my mind is spiraling in confusion of what is happening with this guy, and I'm at the end of my masking rope. I need right now, more than anything, to be alone so I can drop the act entirely.

Blake's brows knit together. "Oh. Okay. When can I see you again, then?"

I shake my head, back toward the door. "I'm not sure."

He frowns. "Is everything okay?"

Not at all. "Of course."

"Okay," he says, though his tone doesn't match the word. "I'll text or call you."

"Sounds good."

"Lex—"

"Bye, Blake," I say, cutting him off before he can say anything else—anything that might make me stay. Because if I stay even a second longer, I fear I'll do something stupid like let him kiss me.

Or worse, kiss him back.

I turn and bolt out of the weight room, power walking through Mavericks Stadium, out to my car, and all the way back to my apartment just outside Dickson's campus. My heart pounds harder than it should over the simple exertion, my mind spinning like a hard drive at the end of its memory life.

I want to go back. Back to when everything was about the lab, my research, and the predictable comfort of knowing exactly who I was and where I fit.

I don't want to be *this* girl—trying to earn a third PhD in Blake Boden. A girl who has developed an AI-assisted app to decode why he has this infuriating effect on me and why my reaction to him feels so uncharacteristically…uncontrollable.

Because for someone who thrives on control, losing it is terrifying, even if it's to something that feels good.

And Blake? Well, he makes me feel good.

Too good.

And that's a problem I have no idea how to solve—a genius's uncharted territory.

I don't like it one freaking bit.

11

luorescent lights flicker above my head as I walk down the hall of Ferris Research Lab, a bag of Chinese takeout hanging from my right hand.

I've never been inside this building before, and with how deserted it is tonight, I'm starting to think no one ever has.

My footsteps echo on the tile floor as I walk the halls aimlessly, searching for the infamous computer lab in which I know I'll find Lexi. After the shift between us at MKC earlier this week, I was naïvely hopeful that she would reach out to me if I didn't reach out to her.

Instead, we've gone a full day and a half with no contact, and I've been properly humbled into being the pursuer again. I texted earlier to no response, but when my plans for dinner with Ace and Finn fell through, thanks to a prank-war emergency with Ace's dad Thatch, I decided to take matters into my own hands. They asked me to come, but I excused myself, saying I had something with my football teammates I should do instead.

And while I *was* invited to party with the team, I figured trying my hand at making Lexi Winslow notice me was a much better plan.

Not to mention, an in-person meet-and-greet is much harder to ignore.

Turning the corner at the end of a long, dark hall, I see a light finally beckon in the distance. It's the subtle glow of the lights of a room, shining through the glass window in the door.

An irrational pang of insecurity rears its head as I approach the door to find a keypad and a locked handle.

What if she doesn't let me inside?

My inner psyche both laughs and cries. Because damn, that would be one hell of a sign that I need to give it the fuck up, wouldn't it?

Carefully, I peer through the narrow window to look inside, finding Lexi sitting at one of the computer desks on the back wall, clicking away at the keyboard in front of her. I lift a hand and knock, hoping I don't scare the shit out of her.

She jolts and turns to look, cupping her hand over her eyes and squinting to see through the window. I wave, and she jerks her head back as if struck.

She doesn't look angry—just surprised. *Thank God.*

I don't know how well she can hear me through the door, but I chance talking anyway, feeling only slightly like a goober. "Hey, Lex. Let me in. I brought dinner."

She spins in her chair and types furiously again, clicking something that makes the screen go black before getting up and jogging over to the door.

I breathe a small sigh of relief as she turns the handle and pushes the wood obstruction toward me, letting me in.

"Did you say dinner?" she asks, and I smile, holding up the bag.

"I did."

"It's not dorm pizza, is it?"

"Nope," I reply. "It's Chinese takeout. From a restaurant with approval from the New York Department of Health and everything. I checked their certificate."

She rolls her eyes but laughs too. "Come on. Come inside."

I step in quickly, not about to squelch the invitation, and survey the space discreetly. There are probably fifteen computers and chairs in this room, and yet Lexi's is the only one occupied.

"You're here all alone?"

She shrugs. "It's not exactly regular hours."

"It doesn't freak you out? Being in this dark building by your-self at night?"

She frowns. "Maybe now it does."

I laugh. "Well, don't worry. I'm here now. I'll protect you."

"My God, your masculinity is smothering," she teases, cracking an actual grin for a change. It feels like a huge win.

It's not that she's not emotional—she's just hugely reserved with showing it. The more time I spend with her, the more I'm starting to understand that.

"As long as it's not toxic," I say in reply, pulling up the seat next to the one she was sitting in, placing the bag on the table, and un-packing the food.

She watches closely.

"I got a little bit of everything." I set the lo mein to the side to pull out both fried and white rice, and then I take out the chicken, beef, and shrimp. I didn't know what she'd like the most, and I'm not picky, so whatever she doesn't want, I'll take. "Pick what you want."

She considers the food carefully before reaching out and snag-ging the lo mein. I wait patiently, smiling when she grabs the chicken too.

"Hungry?"

"More than I realized. I've been here since eight a.m. and only brought coffee and a banana with me."

"Ah, well…happy to be your knight-in-food-bearing-armor."

"How'd you know where to find me?" she asks, grabbing one of the plastic forks from the table next to the food, sitting down in her chair, turning to face me, and cracking open her carton of lo mein.

"I made an educated guess. Though, I almost gave up halfway through the building. This place is almost as hard to find as Abrams was at the end of the tunnel challenge."

She smiles slyly. "Good thing you got the practice that night, then."

"How do you come up with the events?" I ask, curiosity about the mysterious Double C getting the best of me. I doubt she'll answer, but it's worth a shot.

She shrugs. "Different ways. If you know the history of Dickson, it makes it easier."

"That's the most nonanswer answer I've ever heard."

"Best you're gonna get."

"Yeah, I figured," I admit through a chuckle. "And what about your sidekick? What's his name?"

"Connor?"

"Yeah, that's him. What's his deal?"

She tilts her head to the side. "What do you mean?"

"I mean…how do you know him? Why do you trust him? Why's he involved?"

She shakes her head, digging her teeth into her bottom lip. "I've…known him what feels like forever. When we both came to Dickson, we maintained a friendship, and I don't know…the rest of it just seemed natural. He understands me better than a lot of people do."

"I'm jealous."

"Of what?" she asks, her brows drawing together.

"Of his knowledge," I reply simply. "I want to know you too."

Blushing, she turns back toward her computer and sets the lo mein on the table next to the keyboard, swapping it for chicken and popping open the top. I toss a shrimp into my mouth and then switch to the fried rice, scooping a forkful into my mouth and chewing before moving my line of conversation to something a little less scary.

"So, what have you been here working on all day? Something with your dissertation?"

She pauses briefly, her fork hovering in front of her mouth with a juicy piece of sesame chicken. I can't explain it, but it almost seems like she's more afraid of this question than any of the others.

"Uh…yeah. Sort of. I'm mostly finished with the official paper, but I'm still doing some related research."

"And what's your topic again?"

"Advancing technology with artificial-intelligence-based code."

I snort, feigning brain cells I don't have. "Oh. Yeah. Of course. I've always been really curious about that too."

"It's a fancy way of saying we should let the computer do the hard work for us. We input data, and the computer writes the algorithm to give us whatever answer we're looking for."

"But isn't all AI essentially human-taught to start with?"

"Technically, yes." She nods. "It gets all of its data from us, but it has way more analytical capability than we do. It can take in an abundance of information and build conclusions at a substantially quicker rate."

"Right. Cool."

She laughs, and I shrug. "I'm just a dumb jock."

"Jock, yes, but dumb, no," she disagrees. "In fact, I'd say you're a lot more intelligent where it counts than I am."

"What's that mean?"

She shifts in her seat a little, sighing. "I'm not good with…social things. Interacting. Understanding emotional needs. Relationships. And trust me, those things come up in everyday life a lot more than AI coding."

"I think you're better at it than you think you are."

"You do?" she asks. And before I can respond, she quietly adds in a voice that barely rises above the hum of the computers, "Because I know being neurodivergent can make me come off as quirky or even cold to other people."

There's a vulnerability in her admission. But it doesn't exactly come as a surprise to me. To me, Lexi Winslow is different in the best kind of way. I mean, clearly, you don't pursue a woman like I've been pursuing her without being completely enamored.

"Lex. Everyone who knows you loves you. They speak highly of you, and they want to be around you." I lean forward, putting just one hand on her knee and watching as her eyes jerk down to look at it and then back up to meet mine, albeit a little wider. "That doesn't just happen. If you have a weakness, you obviously have other strengths that make people want to pick up the slack." I smile. "Take your relationship with me, for example. Your weakness is pursuing and accepting my company. I make up for that by being willing to chase you all over campus like a stalker."

She laughs, just like I was hoping she would, and I run my hand a little higher up her thigh. She doesn't stop me. In fact, her body sways toward me in a promising display of yearning for more.

Leaning forward slowly, I touch my lips to hers, a soft, slow kiss of promised intention. She melts into it, sighing softly when I slip my tongue past her lips and just barely touch it to the tip of hers.

But despite the fact that every cell in my body wants to continue this, wants to keep kissing her, I break it off before it can turn heated, and she chases me forward, back toward my chair, with a sway of her body.

It's exactly what I'm hoping for, even if it's simultaneously the worst form of torture.

"Well, I guess I'll leave you to it," I tell her with a soft smile.

"W-what?" she asks, a small stutter in her normally sure speech.

"I know you're busy, Lex. I just wanted to make sure you were fed, and now that I have, I'm going to leave you to it."

"You're going?"

I nod. I am. As much as I don't fucking want to.

"But remember…I'm just a phone call or text away."

It's one of the hardest things I've done—and I've done a lot of difficult shit—but I stand from my chair and leave the lab, walking down the hall as the door clicks shut behind me, and I don't look back.

If this has any chance of going anywhere at all, I have to create the opportunity for Lexi to want me.

The time is now or never, and I sure as shit hope she's ready to play the game.

12

Twenty-four hours, ten minutes, fifteen seconds…sixteen seconds.

That's how long I've been thinking about Blake Boden and his stupid Chinese-food-tainted kiss without being able to stop, and now I'm outside the entrance to his apartment building on the west side of campus, standing under an umbrella as the rain pelts down on me and wondering where I'm going to go from here.

I look up at the illuminated windows of several floors and then back down at my feet, which are starting to tingle from being so soaked.

Finally decided, I turn around and jog across Broadway, checking first in both directions for cars, and then dip straight in the front door of Brower Center to escape both the weather and my intentions.

A few students are milling around inside the dining room straight ahead, but thankfully, nothing too overwhelming. My nerves are far too stimulated right now to handle a crowd.

I quickly shake out my umbrella and tuck it into the pile of others by the door, and then I pull off my rain jacket and give it a shake as well. Folding it over my arm, I walk toward the double doors and sneak inside, surveying the buffet of food still out from dinner.

None of it sounds good, as my stomach is currently turning itself inside out with worry that I don't even know who I am anymore, so I settle for a table in the corner and tuck myself away.

Scrolling on my phone, I pull up Netflix and pick out a rom-com to study. One of the first to pop up is called *Anyone but You* and starts with an awkward encounter in a coffee shop between Glen Powell and Sydney Sweeney. It's a cute scene full of bumbles and fumbles, and in some weird way, it makes me feel better about my propensity to overthink things.

They end up putting themselves out there and ultimately having the best night together, and I know it's make-believe. But in some way, it renews my confidence to show up at Blake's apartment uninvited and see where the night goes.

I grab my phone from the table and do something completely unprecedented—I initiate contact with Blake myself.

Me: *What are you up to?*

Blake Boden: *Just hanging out at home. What about you?*

Good. He's home.

Resolved, I stop the movie and pick up my belongings, slinging my jacket back on and pulling my hair out of the collar. I tuck my phone into my pocket and push my chair into the table, rounding it and stepping out from behind the concealing shrubbery in front. There are a few more people out, but given the lower attendance of summer semester and the late hour, it still isn't bad.

Back through the door, picking up my umbrella on the way out, I cross Broadway again. Only this time, I go straight to the door of Blake's building as someone exits, holding the door for me as they do.

"Thanks."

I head directly for the stairwell and the fourth floor, having memorized his apartment number and location long before giving in to the temptation to come in the first place, and make the slow climb up and through the door at the top. The hallway is long and stark white, the doors painted in an alternating pattern of blue and gold with their number placards at the sides in brushed bronze metal.

Apartment 417 is midway down the hall, on the left-hand side, and the door is navy blue. I pause briefly, setting my umbrella down beside the door and straightening my moisture-frizzed hair self-consciously before lifting a hand and knocking.

I hear a small shift in the sound inside, including Blake's muffled voice and some shuffling, and then the door swings open to reveal his bare chest and black netted basketball shorts, his phone to his ear. He freezes at the sight of me, his eyes widening just before his whole face melts into a giant smile.

My stomach flips, and I steady my breathing against an onslaught of nerves. "Hey, Ace, I'm gonna have to call you back," he says, which immediately seals my mouth shut with glue.

I appreciate the heads-up, and when he winks, I know he's done it on purpose.

"Yeah, yeah. Shh, it's okay. I'll hug you later and you'll feel better." He laughs so loudly it startles me, and then he rolls his eyes. "Aw, poor baby. I'm sure you'll find someone to hang with tonight."

He shakes his head, stepping aside and waving me into the apartment. When I clear the threshold, he shuts the door behind me and locks it.

"Go over to Julia's, then. She always lets you cry on her shoulder." He snorts. "Then you should have gone to the Hamptons with her. Don't even try to tell me she didn't invite you." He laughs. "Yep. That's what I thought." He shakes his head back and forth and mimes constant blabbing with his hand. "Okay, buddy. Just take a nice warm bath, then. We'll talk later."

He pulls the phone away from his ear and hangs up, even though I can still hear the shrouded sound of Ace's complaints on the other end. When I'm sure the call is over, I allow myself to laugh. "He's a character."

"I was going to say *you have no idea*, but I guess that's stupid since you grew up around him, huh?"

I nod. "Some ridiculousnesses are hereditary. For Ace, that's one hundred percent true. Both his parents are nutcases. If we could get them to a certified psychiatrist, I'm positive there'd be a diagnosis and commitment to a padded room."

"So I've heard," Blake agrees, clearing off his duffel bag from his cornflower-blue couch and ushering me to come sit down. I'm surprised he hasn't asked me why I'm here yet, and it's throwing me off a little. When I rehearsed this in my head, he started with that question.

When I struggle to get started talking, I end up using my scripted answer even though he hasn't asked the question. "I thought I'd try my hand at popping in on you like you have a habit of doing to me."

He smiles. "Great. I love the spontaneity."

I lick my lips. I wish I could say I'm as convinced.

"So…what are you up to?"

Ugh. Why do I have to make everything sound so cringeworthy?

"Just relaxing. Practice was a double today, so I iced my calves and took a shower and was just trying to decide what to order for dinner. Did you eat yet?"

"Eat?"

"Yes," he confirms. "Food. Dinner, as it were."

"Oh, no. I didn't eat dinner."

"Cool. Then I can get us both something. Any idea what you're in the mood for?"

This feels like the perfect opportunity to add in some kind of innuendo-laden suggestion about his penis, but I'm completely out of my depth. *How do other women manage to make it sound so natural when they do it?*

I cough and clear my throat, clenching my fists and steadying my anxiety the best I can. I came here to do something specific, and now that I'm here, I'm *going* to do it. "Actually, yes. I was…well, I was thinking I'd like more of what we had last night."

"Chinese? Okay. Did you want more lo mein and chicken or something else?"

"N-no. I meant…more of something else."

"The shrimp? Because they were pretty good too." He searches the coffee table, through a pile of takeout menus, sifting to find the one for the Chinese place, his phone already in hand.

It takes everything inside me, but somehow, I manage to reach out and grab his wrist, stopping him. "No… I… Well, I meant the kiss."

"Oh." His face transforms, lifting into a giant smile I just know is full of every egotistical thought on the planet. And still, I find it attractive. Go figure.

"I…well. I thought maybe we could do it a little more." I shrug. "Just to…see."

"To research?" he asks, repeating my word from the night of our first kiss.

I nod.

"Okay. And what exactly did you have in mind?"

Even though my hands are sweating and my lips feel dry, I force myself to go through with the plan. This is my chance to put myself out there, like I told my family I would, and if I don't have the courage to do it now, I'm never going to find it.

"Well…I kind of thought, maybe, we should…have sex."

Blake chokes a little on his own saliva—at least, as far as I can tell—and comes toward me, effectively tossing his phone back to the surface of the coffee table like it's a worthless brick.

I swallow thickly as he adjusts himself to sit directly in front of me, his ass on the coffee table, and I struggle to keep eye contact as he presses me. "You think that you, Lexi Winslow, and I, Blake Boden, should have sex?"

I roll my eyes. "You don't have to say it like that."

"Say it like what? I'm just trying to make sure I'm hearing you correctly and not having a stroke."

"You don't have to make fun of me."

He reaches out for my hand, snagging it fiercely and clutching it to his chest with both of his own. "I'm not. Swear, Lex. I would never make fun of you for putting yourself out there like that. I'm just…surprised. You have to understand why. It's not like you've given me more than a passing glance and a flick of your fingers for many, many weeks leading up to this moment, so this is a turn-around. I'm just trying to understand and make sure you're not asking for something you'll regret and be angry at me for later on."

"I'm not totally socially naïve, Blake. I know you don't just tell men you want to have sex and then take it back."

"Yeah, yes. I'd say, generally speaking, that's true. But what I'm trying to say is that you can take it back, with me, if you want to."

"I…I don't want to." I shake my head. "I don't want to take it back."

In fact, to my own shock and horror, when it comes to having sex with Blake, there's nothing I want more.

13

exi's eyes are wide and challenging as she stares at me from her spot on my couch, the remnants of her words lying between us.

I think we should have sex.

My heart beats fast as she intertwines the fingers on one of her hands with the other and squeezes so hard the skin turns stark white. The idea of this brilliant, beautiful woman wanting to sleep with me is exciting enough that I could pounce on it right this second and never look back.

But something tells me that would send her running for the lab, never to be seen again, and that's…not what I want at all.

"Listen, I think this is one of the best things to come out of your brain, and let's be honest, we both know it produces a hell of a lot of good. But I don't want to jump headfirst into this without exploring it first."

She blinks. "What do you mean?"

"I mean…" Cautiously, I wade into much more dangerous waters. "Are you…a virgin? Have you slept with someone before?"

She rolls her eyes, her patience with me just slightly tried. "I know what a virgin is, Blake. And yes, I've slept with someone before."

A pang of jealousy hits my chest like a baseball bat, but seeing as I'm the one who started the trajectory of this conversation and it's already tenuous at best, I make the decision to ignore it. I can tackle her horizontal scoreboard at a later date and time, when we're so in love she finds my raging envy cute.

"Okay. And what about orgasming? Have you done that before?"

"I don't see how that's relevant right now," she sidesteps, her beautiful skin mottling with an embarrassed red. "Why does that matter?"

"Oh, Lex," I counter gently, reaching a hand to her thigh and scooting it upward *oh-so slowly*. She jerks her gaze to my hand and watches with avid interest, her chest rising and falling faster with each inch it travels. "It's important because if we're going to have sex, you and I...I want there to be a connection. I want lust and hearts pounding and soul-touching intimacy. I want blinding, bonding pleasure for both of us, but more than anything in this world, I want it for *you*. And if I rush this or make assumptions or pretend it'll all come together, no matter what I do, that won't happen."

"What are you talking about, Blake?" she asks, seemingly frustrated that I'm making this more complicated. But I'll be damned if I'm going to be a dog of Pavlov's that doesn't learn lessons. Just last night, I left her longing for more...and tonight, she's here asking for sex. There's no way in hell, heaven, or on this big ball of earth I'm going to rush this process. I'm going to move one step at a time until she's so hooked to me, it'll take surgery to separate us.

"I mean that there's more to sex than *sex*."

"Are you drunk?" she questions, narrowing her pretty blue eyes at me. "Because you're making no sense."

"*No*. I'm not drunk. And I'm only not making sense because you're not paying attention. The act of sex itself is a culmination of other things. Of touch and taste and exploration and foreplay and closeness. It's a *finale*, not an opener."

"What does that *mean*, though? Are you saying no?"

I shake my head, squeezing the very top of her thigh, my fingers splayed on the denim fabric of her tight jeans at the line where leg meets torso. "I'm saying yes to the process, no to the act tonight. Tonight, I think I should touch."

"Touch?"

"Touch," I repeat. "*Everywhere.*"

Lexi swallows hard before nodding. "Okay."

My hands are slow, but my heart is the opposite. This moment is the pinnacle of thousands of hours of thinking about what it might be like to touch her, feel her, and experience her. This giving in, this relinquishment of control by one of the smartest women I've ever met, this level of trust in me to handle things with consciousness and care—it'll go down in my own personal history as a landmark point in time.

A core fucking memory.

Moving slowly, I sit down beside Lexi on the couch and drop my hands to her hips, pulling her toward me. I lift and settle her in my lap, sliding my hands to the top of her rain jacket and unzipping it slowly. Her beautiful blue eyes practically glow as she concentrates on my every move.

"You feel warm," I tell her, the heat of her lap in mine a welcome and arousing sensation.

She nods, whispering, "So do you."

Her jacket slides from her shoulders easily, and a plain white T-shirt cups her breasts underneath. Her nipples stand out, thanks to the change in temperature, and I have to restrain myself from leaning forward and taking them both in my hot mouth and sucking.

I lift her quickly off my lap and lay her back on the light-blue couch, and she gasps, her whole body shaking with anticipation. I lean forward and cover her body with my own, my lips skimming hers.

"I thought we were just touching," she says, her whisper desperate.

I smile against her mouth. "We are just touching. My body is touching your body, and your body is touching the couch. Right?"

She nods, her head so close, her forehead brushes mine, and

I slip out just the tip of my tongue to run the seam of her perfect, plump lips.

Her breathing escalates again, and I sink my weight into hers, my hand finding the tangles of hair at the back of her head. Her mouth searches for mine, and I give in to the request, melding our lips and taunting. Slow, steady, and soft, I kiss her like we have all the time in the world, like our mouths aren't strangers at all, but long-lost friends.

She moans, and I sink my tongue through the opening that creates, touching the tip of hers and swirling. She tilts her head in my hand, desperate to get deeper so she can taste more, and I follow her lead.

She tastes like sweet fruit and intrigue—like nothing I've ever experienced before.

Carefully, I pull back enough to disengage, running my lips along the corner of her mouth, to her jaw, and down her neck until stopping at her collarbone. Her body responds, arching into mine, while her hands grip at the skin of my back.

"Feel good?"

She nods. "Yes."

"Good. I want to make it feel even better."

Her head jerks. "Please. Yes. *Please.*"

Hearing Lexi Winslow beg me for more wasn't on my summer bingo card—hell, I didn't even think it was on a list of remote possibilities. But I swear, at the sound of it, I'd do anything to keep it.

I'd be morally gray, desperately corrupt, unfair, and unjust. I would walk a lava-covered volcano, fight a dragon, sell my soul to an underground world—as long as it ended in hearing her say please again.

Climbing off her, I undo the button on her jeans and lower the zipper, grabbing them at the waistband and pulling them down as gently as I can manage. She lifts her ass for me to make it easier, and a smile paints itself across my face. Her plain black cotton bikini underwear are undeniably sexy but appropriately practical. They're so perfectly Lexi.

I wouldn't expect her to wear thongs or synthetics or bother with unnecessary laces. I'm unbelievably interested to see if any of that changes the more we're together, but my guess is that it won't. And for some reason, that makes me smile.

I've seen the lingerie of many a desperate woman—none of it changed what lay underneath.

Shifting her slightly, I lie down on the couch next to her, my back to the upright cushions and her spread-out body near the edge. She watches carefully as I run my hand down her stomach, over the white of her T-shirt, around the bikini line of her panties, and then underneath, to the hot, wet apex of her center.

As I make contact, her head rolls back, and a moan falls from her lips involuntarily. It might be the first thing on scientific record that Lexi Winslow has done without meaning to.

"Yeah," I say softly, encouragement rolling off me into the soft shell of her ear. "Just relax and feel me."

Swirling moisture from her center to her clit, I stroke softly at the sensitive bud until her back arches again. I put my lips to her neck and suck gently, using my knuckle to tease at her entrance. She gasps, and I straighten my finger, sinking it to the base in one smooth motion, turning my hand so I can swipe softly at her G-spot.

Her hips jerk up and down restlessly, so I add another finger, beckoning her orgasm with a curl of my fingers over and over again at a steady pace.

"Are you going to come for me, Lexi?"

She tries to speak, but her words are stilted and awkward. The usual connection to her brain is temporarily unavailable due to a redirection of blood flow.

"Come on. I want to feel you all over my fingers. I want it to drip down my hand."

"Oh my G-od," she manages through a whisper, her breathing heavy. Her eyes flutter open and closed as she fights the lull of my fingers on her G-spot. I don't want to be fought, so I pull my fingers out quickly and swirl at her clit before diving back inside.

Her back bows and her breathing stops and her eyes fall closed with the weight of her head on my arm.

She sounds like sweet victory and no turning back.

I may be a thorn in her side, but I also come bearing orgasms. I'd like to see her avoid me now.

14

he menu for Fortress, my stepdad's newest food endeavor, is a clunky, huge thing I can barely hold in front of my face. Normally, it'd be something I might complain about, but today, I'm thankful for the shield.

My mom sits across from me in a pair of tan linen pants and a white button-down shirt, her hair pulled up in a half-up, half-down do made fancier by a twist and braid of the hair by her face. I've always thought she's one of the most naturally beautiful women I've ever seen, but today, she looks particularly content.

And I know, deep down, it's because I reached out and asked her to meet me for lunch. She already had plans with Georgia and her girls, but not wanting to miss the opportunity for some face time with her daughter, she invited me to join. She never pushes to see me or makes me feel bad for not getting together more, which I appreciate more than I can say. But seeing her heart in her eyes today, I know I need to make a bigger effort.

As for the menu, it makes everything I did with Blake last night feel just the tiniest bit less exposed. Georgia, Julia, and Evie are supposed to meet us here soon, but their driver hit traffic coming back from the Hamptons. So, right now, it's only my mom and me, and for some reason, that makes me feel anxious to take advantage.

"I think I'm going to try the harvest salad," my mom remarks, studying the menu herself as though she didn't help my dad create it. "I'm in the mood for strawberries. What are you thinking, Lex?"

I'm thinking about the thing I always think about these days, much to my chagrin—*Blake Boden*. Like it or not, memories of him fester on my brain's every available surface, waiting to be addressed. Tackling that elephant seems a little traumatic, of course, so instead, I settle for a broad question that feels like it at least scratches in the vicinity of the itch.

"When you and Dad first started dating, were you sure you wanted to be with him, or were you confused?"

"You know, Lex, I don't think that's on the menu." I roll my eyes, and she laughs. "Sorry. You just caught me off guard with that one." She hums. "Well, let's see. I'd like to say I was confident, but if I'm honest, I was definitely scared. I had you, of course, and you were the light of my life. The last relationship I'd tried to make work ended in disaster, and your uncles were operating on a pretty hair trigger when it came to new men. I knew Wes was special, but I didn't know if it was going to work." She shrugs. "Is that the kind of answer you were looking for?"

"I don't know." I shrug. "To be honest, I'm not sure what I'm looking for. I was just…curious."

My mom nods but is careful not to study me too closely. She's one of the only people who truly understands and respects how uncomfortable it makes me. "That's fair. From my own experience, relationships are always complicated. There are ups and downs and obstacles and unknowns. But when they're right, they always seem to sort themselves out. Look at me and Georgia and Cassie and all your uncles. Everyone has their moment if you wait long enough."

"I don't know if I'm…*moment material*," I admit. "I want to be, but I just… Some things are better off locked in my head."

"There's no timeline on figuring it out, you know?" she comforts. "One day, you'll know for sure what's right for you, and when you do, your father and your brother and I—we'll all be there to support you."

I swallow hard, warring with myself over sharing something about Blake or not. Deep down, I know I should, but I just can't bear the thought of exposing myself like that. I don't like topics I haven't mastered. I don't like wondering how I can learn everything I need to quickly, and I don't like feeling out of control.

What if I'm getting it all wrong?

I can't imagine what that would mean for the part of my personality that hinges on getting everything right.

"Thanks," I say, settling for a simple show of gratitude. My mom's smile is warm and understanding, and if possible, it makes me feel even worse.

Maybe I can start off by sharing Blake's pursuit? Maybe I can tell her how long he's been—

"Hello, hello!" Georgia greets hurriedly, hustling both Julia and Evie around the table to my side to take the seats next to me. "Soooo sorry we're late."

"Hey, Lex," Julia says excitedly, leaning in for a side hug before sitting down. "Never expected to see you here!"

"Yeah. I'm trying to expand my horizons a little. My brother seems to think I'm going to spend all my time in the lab until rigor mortis sets in. I told him I do other things, but he didn't seem to believe me."

Julia laughs, and I can read the unspoken words about Double C as they cross her face as though they're a flashing neon sign. *If he only knew.* "Hey, I'll take it. I always love a chance to hang out with you, expected or not."

Evie doesn't say anything, focused instead on the menu in front of her, her eyes glazed with distant thoughts. It's weird, given how effervescent she normally is, so while my mom and Georgia gab and catch up with each other, I lean toward Julia and raise an eyebrow. "What's with your sister? Is she in mourning or something? She's never this quiet."

Julia laughs. "She has her earbuds in, listening to a romantasy audiobook Cassie gave her at dinner last week. I think it's a retelling of Hades and Persephone or something with a parallel universe and monsters. She's transfixed."

Evie Brooks isn't the first daughter in our group to be folded into the romance genre by Cassie Kelly herself without their mother's knowledge. In fact, as the eldest of the group, I was first.

When I was ten and a half, Cassie gave me my first young adult romance to get me addicted. For the past few years, I've been preoccupied with other things, but once upon a time, Cassie and I had quite the interesting dealer/junkie relationship with romance novels.

Truth be told, she's a woman *full* of interesting secrets.

My phone buzzes in my pocket, startling me slightly, so I lean back into my seat and pull it out as surreptitiously as possible. I already had one text exchange with Ginger when I first got here with my mom, asking if I could help her work out some kinks on her project in the lab tonight, and put simply, I'm not normally this popular of a person.

> *Blake Boden: I've been thinking about last night all morning. What about you?*

An uncharacteristic blush steals across my cheeks as I remember how it felt to finish with his fingers inside me. It was jarring. Imprinting. Impactful. It was unlike anything I've ever had with another person before, and yet somehow, the two of us went back to conversing and having dinner together without prejudice or discomfort. Somehow, even knowing what we'd just done, I was at ease.

"Who is it?" Julia asks, obviously noticing how weird I'm acting.

"Just Connor," I lie, knowing the familiar name will at least buy me one or two casual dismissals before I'll have to explain further.

She nods. "Oh, okay."

I type out a quick message I'm hoping will keep him occupied long enough to delay needing to answer again until after this lunch is done.

> *Me: Yes, of course. It's hard not to. I'm curious what you've got in mind to happen next, but don't tell me now. I want you to really think about it.*

I tuck my phone away, only for it to buzz again immediately.

> *Blake Boden: Oh, I've thought about it already. In great detail. Where do you think the thoughts about last night led this morning?*

Obviously, I'm far too unpracticed with social games to be playing them. Desperate now that my mom, Georgia, Evie, and Julia are all engaged and paying attention to one another, I resort back to blunt truth.

> *Me: That all sounds nice, but I need to not talk to you right now. I'm at lunch with people, and I don't have the experience I'd need to hear about your plans and keep a poker face.*

> *Blake Boden: Okay, no worries. Keeping it a surprise is better anyway.*

His message urges a smile to my lips that I can't control. It takes me a good five seconds to swipe the damn thing off my face.

> *Me: I'll be in the lab later if you want to come find me.*

> *Blake Boden: I wouldn't miss the chance. Later, Lex.*

> *Me: Bye, Blake.*

Satisfied that I've curbed the explosion for now, I set my phone on the table facedown and work myself back into engaging in the lunchtime conversation.

I'm an outsider, as usual, but for the first time in a long time, I lean into the feeling of being present anyway.

Something inside me is shifting—but the jury's still out on whether it's for the good.

15

Blake

Freshly showered, with damp curls clinging to my ears in the warm summer evening air, I stroll through the pedestrian court, a bag of food swinging from my finger and a ridiculous spring in my step.

After being officially invited to join Lexi tonight in the lab, I can't help but relish the difference just a week of a little push and pull has made. When Lexi tugs, I come running, but when it starts to feel like she's pulling away, I extend my rope a little and give her space.

It's a delicate game, and I know it seems childish to make it this complicated, but Lexi Winslow isn't the kind of woman you chase without a plan. Just like in football, the right plays at the right times can make all the difference, and trick plays and strategizing are there for a reason.

"Yo, Boden!" a voice yells from the other side of the court, and I squint to see who it is as they jog across the space. Dark hair, fresh sweats, and a big-ass gold chain around his neck give him away, so I smile as my incoming freshman teammate Ron Zimmerman, who'll be playing wide receiver, makes his quick approach.

"Hey, Ron. What's up, man?"

We exchange a quick slap of our hands with a twist and snap, and he adjusts his flat-billed hat off and back onto his head. "Not much. Just heading over to that Thai place by Frat Row to get some chow. You wanna come? Some of the other guys are meeting me there."

"No, thanks." I hold up the bag of food as evidence of my

conflict of interest and explain, "I'm already running late to meet a friend for dinner at their place."

It's a bundle of small white lies, but I don't feel bad since none of them holds any malice. My goal is to ensure Ron doesn't feel rejected, while at the same time knowing I'm headed somewhere—so he doesn't feel like we can chitchat forever.

"A friend, huh?" he asks with a wag of his eyebrows. "I've heard legend about you with the female friends, dude. I can only dream of being as successful in my college career," he teases, his eyes reminiscent of an eager puppy. Which, for all intents and purposes, is exactly what he is.

All the single guys who come into the atmosphere of college sports are like toddlers in a candy store for at least the first two months. They're not used to getting so much easy attention, and they gobble it up until they're bloated.

"Nah, man. Not like that this time. Just meeting a friend." I laugh, rejecting the idea that I'm going to get some pussy, just in case he happens to see me headed into the lab. I know Lexi isn't in the place to go spreading that shit everywhere, and even if she were, I'm not eager to have people cheapening whatever is happening between us.

I really like her, new sexual escapades completely aside. I'm not just spinning wheels here. I'm invested.

"Oh, gotcha." Ron chuckles, a sizzle of misplaced understanding in his cockiness. "Next time, then."

I nod. "Catch you later."

Ron takes off again, looking back to wave a little before crossing between the theater and the stadium and, eventually, crossing Amsterdam Avenue. With the coast clear, I pull open the door to Ferris and step inside, letting the darkness overwhelm me.

The trek through the halls feels like a victory lap, compared to last time. I stride confidently, turning corners with the precision of someone who's been here before. Because I have. No more wandering the labyrinth like an amateur; I'm a seasoned pro now.

What I *don't* expect is to come face-to-door with someone exiting the lab at the exact moment I'm leaning in to peer through the small sidelight window of said door. It bumps me squarely in the forehead, and I stumble back, rubbing the spot as my vision momentarily blurs.

"Oh my God!" the girl exclaims, stepping out and practically tripping over herself to apologize. "I'm so sorry! I wasn't expecting anyone on the other side because, well…there's *never* anyone on the other side." Her expression quickly morphs into suspicion. "Wait. Who are you? And what are you doing here?"

Before I can muster a reply—possibly something dumb like, *Would you believe I'm the new janitor?*—Lexi's voice cuts through like a lifeline.

"He's here for me, Ginger. Delivering food for my overnight session."

Ginger's suspicion evaporates instantly. "Oh, cool. All right, Lex. Catch you later!" She turns to me, flashing a quick wave and smile. "Sorry again for the bump."

A small part of my ego is wounded by the fact that she clearly doesn't recognize me, despite my star quarterback status, but the vast majority is thankful. I guess most of the people who spend their lives in the lab—aside from those whose dads own professional teams—don't know or care much about football. "No problem."

As soon as Ginger disappears down the hall, I step inside, adopting Lexi's lie with full commitment. "Lexi Winslow, is it? Your food delivery has arrived."

"Shut up," she scoffs, standing to greet me with a quick hug. It's casual, sure, but it's enough to short-circuit my brain for a solid three seconds. She smells faintly of flowers, fruit, and something sweet like honey—probably from yogurt and granola, her usual morning choice. I know this because I notice things about Lexi. *Too many things.*

When she pulls back, she smooths her shirt and tucks a loose strand of hair behind her ear. I watch the motion, captivated, but choose not to comment.

"Are you right in the middle of something? Or do you want to eat now? Either way is probably fine since I brought tacos, and they wrap them in forty-seven layers of foil. Time isn't an issue. These babies could probably survive a nuclear fallout under all that aluminum."

Her face lights up. "The ones from B Street Grill?"

"Yep." I grin. "Good call?"

"Well, yes, but only if you got chicken," she says, raising a brow.

"I got chicken, beef, steak, and shrimp. You can pick your favorite."

She rubs her hands together and licks her lips, and it takes everything in me not to freak her out by leaning down for a casual kiss on the mouth. Sure, physically, we're past a single, quick kiss, but mentally, I know Lexi still sees our arrangement as much more formal than that.

"Choices," she says. "Always choices. I swear, you're better than DoorDash."

I laugh, loud and unrestrained, and her smirk tells me she's satisfied with her joke's success.

Poking at her stomach, I move her back toward her chair and set the bag of tacos on the desk beside her computer. "I don't think DoorDash has orgasms on the menu."

"No," she agrees, settling into her seat. "Not the one I use. But really, thanks for bringing me dinner. Ninety percent of the time I'm in here, I completely forget to eat."

I shrug. "No problem. I like taking care of you."

Lexi stills for a moment before turning to her computer and busying herself, and I make light work of finding all the chicken tacos first. If she wants to ignore my last remark, I will too.

For now.

"What has you here all hours today?" I ask instead, finding a topic I'm confident won't make her uncomfortable. "What are you working on?"

She glances from the computer to me, clicking through a few things before closing it out. "I was helping Ginger with something on her dissertation earlier, and that led to a thought on my own. I was running a few tests on some of my data inputs to see if it would change the algorithm in my test app for my dissertation."

I snort. "Oh, is that all?"

"Hey, you asked," she says warmly, pulling her shirt down again to meet her jeans in the front and taking a taco from my outstretched hand.

"I know. And I'm interested. It just feels like you're speaking Chinese half the time when you explain it. Normally, I could really wow a woman with some unknown football jargon, but I don't think I have a leg up on that one either."

"Listen, if you're going to spend time with the smartest person in the room, you're going to feel a little dumb sometimes."

"Ha! Wow!" I hoot. "Really putting it all out there tonight, huh?"

She winks, and unable to resist anymore, I snag her hand full of taco on the way to her mouth, pull it out of the way, and touch my lips to hers. She startles, but she chases me when I pull away, so all in all, I'd say the move is a success.

"I like dating the smart girl," I assure her while our lips still touch.

She pulls back and searches my eyes with her own. "Are we dating?"

I shrug. "We aren't *not* dating, that's for sure. Call it whatever you need to, I guess, but I plan to get a little one-on-one time with your pussy after we eat."

"Blake!"

"What, Lex? You don't like that word? Is there something else you'd rather I call it?"

"No," she says quietly. "Pussy is fine."

I laugh, sitting back in my seat and pulling a taco off the table for my own consumption. "Well, okay, then. There you have it. First, I'll eat this taco, and then I'll eat yours. Sound like a good plan?"

A soft laugh escapes Lexi as she shakes her head, but then she nods. Not just any nod either. It's subtle, but it's there, and it feels like the kind of victory that would make a touchdown celebration look subdued.

I lean back, taking a bite of my taco and letting the moment stretch, the grin tugging at my lips impossible to suppress. *Cheers to motherfucking progress.* For the first time, it feels like I'm not just running plays—I'm actually moving the chains.

———

In a quiet room filled with beakers, pipettes, and shiny silver hoods, I lean Lexi back on the solid black top of one of the bar-height table desks, skimming my fingers along the soft skin of her exposed side as I do.

I offered to relocate from Ferris to my apartment or hers, but Lexi was adamant we use one of the chemistry labs in the Caulder building. According to her, chemistry majors don't share the relentless dedication of computer science majors, and their lab would be a ghost town all night.

Plus, she said. *Isn't sneaking around supposed to make things even more exciting?*

The muffled sound of her soft panting whispers through my ears and migrates straight to my dick, hardening the length of it in my shorts and making a bid to rip right through the material like a fucking action hero.

But tonight isn't about me, and it sure as hell isn't about my dick. Tonight is about exploring Lexi's sexuality in all the safest ways possible for both her and me as we navigate the budding possibility of an us.

"Blake," she whispers into the darkness as I rub at the skin of her thighs with my hands, grazing the bikini line of her black cotton panties each time I do.

"Easy, Lex," I comfort as her back arches off the cold surface beneath her. "I'm getting there, I swear."

She sighs and I smile, the wickedness of the curve of my mouth extending straight into my tongue as I lick one long line over the material of her panties.

Her back spasms again, and I reach up to calm it, pressing a warm hand into her bare stomach. Gently, I tug her underwear off her hips, Lexi helping as I drag them over her ass and then down her legs to let them drop to the tile floor below. Kneeling in front of her, I pull her legs over my shoulders and let them rest there, closing my mouth over the heat of her sweet center and sucking.

"Oh my God," she cries, her voice stilted only by the failing effort to be quiet.

Fuck yes, to the sound of pleasure. I feel on top of the world.

She tastes better than I even imagined, and since the moment I met her, I've fucking *imagined*. Fruity and fresh and so fucking warm, it's like her mouth on steroids, and I know with absolute certainty, if she'd let me, I'd stay here all night.

I moan right against her, swirling at her clit before circling and sucking at her center until the bow of her back rivals the curve of my mouth. "Lex," I say, removing my mouth only briefly to get her attention and pull her eyes to mine.

We hold eye contact while I consume her entirely. Her eyes flutter and threaten to fold, but I reach up and grab her hand, entwining our fingers and willing her to stay with me through the peak—to stay with me until she can't anymore.

I lick and tease and suck, latching on to the bud and flicking it with my tongue in the most intense of vibrations. Her body tenses, twists, and turns, until finally, the dam breaks, flooding my mouth with the greatest surge of Lexi Winslow's pleasure.

And just like that, I'll never, ever be the same.

Thankfully, from the look in her perfect, sultry blue eyes, neither will she.

16

Blake's wicked smile, flashing up at me from between my legs on Sunday night, dances in my mind as I jot down the directions Dr. Blevin is rattling off for our dissertation presentations at the end of the semester.

Normally, I'd be obsessing over every detail, overthinking the presentation order my professor's chosen to the nth degree. Today, though? My brain is stubbornly stuck on the way Blake's hands felt on my skin. The way he murmured my name like it was the only one he ever needed to say while his face was between my thighs.

The memory flares up again, my cheeks warming as I press my pen harder into the page.

At this point in my PhD program, meetings like this are rare, and yet here I am, trapped in the conference room for an update session that feels about as necessary as a parachute in outer space. Add in the fact that my mind is cycling through an NSFW highlight reel of Sunday night, and this academia gathering is starting to feel like I'm being waterboarded. I'd rather be hauled before a high fae court, burned by dragon fire, or stabbed by a venin—anything, really, disastrous or otherwise, from my mom's friend Cassie's collection of romantasy novels—than sit here, wasting another thirty minutes of my life.

"You'll each have fifteen minutes to do your presentation, followed by thirty minutes of questioning and support," Dr. Blevin drones on, blissfully unaware of my mental spiraling. "Then another fifteen minutes for closing statements and final defense. Papers are due two weeks before the semester's end so Dr. Visson, Dr. Thomford, Dr. Leemer, and I have time to prepare your questioning."

I nod absently, but my mind stays fixed on one undeniable fact—Blake has officially taken up residence in my head, and no amount of dissertation prep seems capable of evicting him.

"Is it just me, or is this starting to sound more like a juryless trial for an impending execution than anything else?" Ginger whispers from my side, startling me slightly but also making me smile.

She's surprisingly pretty funny. Honestly, I should probably make an effort to hang out with her more outside the lab.

"Then, we'll convene as a committee to deliberate and assess your success," Dr. Blevin continues. "At which point, we will make a decision to pass you with no revisions, minor revisions, major revisions, or reject your defense altogether."

There's a small titter of gossip and overall unrest, so Dr. Blevin rushes to smooth it over.

"Now, I don't see the last option as something we'll be dealing with here, with this group, because each and every one of you has done your due diligence to go over your topics with your mentor professors and seek insight about their validity and workability." He eyes us closely. "However, that doesn't mean that if you aren't properly prepared, you won't be facing revisions and another defense at the end of the fall semester. Graduation with a doctorate at the end of this summer, my friends, is not guaranteed."

"I guess there's a reason they don't just hand them out," Ginger sidebars to me again.

I nod, penciling down a few notes—except, they have absolutely nothing to do with this meeting or my dissertation at all.

The subject instead? Blake Boden's cunnilingus skills.

Slow is better than fast, but at the end, fast is better.

The element of surprise was scary at first, but the more it went on, the better it got.

Blake's tongue muscle control is far superior to anything I could even remotely imagine mine being.

Just for kicks, I test a couple movements in my mouth, only to find my tongue clunky and unskilled as suspected.

Closing my eyes briefly, I try to picture his movements. Up and down, around in a circle, tiny little vibrating flicks, and a hungry amount of suction that all led to a swift acceleration over the cliff of my orgasm. He surprised me with his skill for reading my cues and intuition about what I would like, but I surprised myself too, by not only liking what he was doing but downright begging for it. I thought it would be embarrassing or feel overly intimate, but it didn't. Blake made me feel so at ease, I've spent the last four days talking circles around myself over whether I can show up at his apartment uninvited and ask him to do it again.

"Lexi Winslow," Dr. Blevin's voice says, cutting in on a scene that very much doesn't involve him. "What do you think?"

I glance to Ginger, complete uncertainty on the question or topic at this point starting as a raging burn in my spine and ending as a plum-hued blush in my cheeks. Ginger slyly moves her head up and down, and with no other option, I blindly follow her advice.

"Um, yes. I think yes."

"Good," Dr. Blevin says resolutely, glancing to his notebook and moving on.

I sigh a small breath of relief and mouth, "Thank you," to Ginger.

She nods, giving me a smile and a thumbs-up, and I make a mental note to ask her what the hell I just agreed to when we get out of here.

"As you all know, tonight is our monthly committee meeting for the advancement of technological sciences here at Dickson, and I expect you'll all be in attendance," Dr. Blevin announces, moving on to his next topic of the meeting. "We need to show a strong front of support to ensure the funding of this field of study continues for the next several years. Deans practically use reallocation of resources as a pastime these days."

I have to cover my mouth to hide a yawn. Just thinking about another one of those long, boring meetings is enough to put me to sleep.

And yet, I know I have to be there.

My phone buzzes from its spot in my lap, so I tuck it under the table and surreptitiously click the message notification on the screen to open it.

> **Blake Boden: *Tell me you can come over tonight. Four days is too many days.***

As discreetly as I can, I type out a response and hit send.

> **Me: *I have a meeting I have to go to that I know from past experience will last hours and have me crying for my bed. What about tomorrow night?***

> **Blake Boden: *I have plans with Finn, Ace, Scottie, and Julia. You could come along.***

> **Me: *HA. No. I'd never hear the end of questioning about why or how I'm there.***

> **Blake Boden: *There'd be an end if you'd just answer it directly.***

I freeze, my thumb hovering over the screen. My breath gets all tangled up in my throat, but I swallow past the discomfort and quickly type back a reply.

> **Me: *I can't do that. I'm not ready to start talking to people about…whatever this is.***

> **Blake Boden: *Right. "Whatever this is."***

A sharp sting pierces my chest, almost like his words have

the power to wound me physically. Which, of course, doesn't make any logical sense. Blake and I aren't exactly together. I don't know what we are or what we're not. Nothing has been made official.

We're…spending time together. But only in secret, where no one else knows about it.

> **Me: Come on. You can't believe this is well-defined at this point or that it even should be. We barely know each other.**

> **Blake Boden: I wouldn't say that exactly. I'm starting to know you very well.**

> **Me: You know what I mean.**

> **Blake Boden: We're going to have to agree to disagree on this one. Which is fine. For now.**

Ginger bumps my leg as Dr. Blevin approaches me, and I tuck my phone back away. He sets a packet of papers on the table in front of me, and I smile, ignoring the fact that I've once again been completely distracted today.

"Everything okay, Lexi?" he asks, making me swallow hard around reality.

I've never, and I mean never, attended something academia-related and treated it as irrelevantly as I have today.

Something about me is shifting. Something inside me is changing. I'm opening myself up to new things and treating the world like it's more than dissertations and new technological discoveries.

I promised my family I'd expand my horizons and try to live beyond the walls of the lab. But now, I have Blake unapologetically pushing into my world, stirring things up in ways that scare me as much as they intrigue me.

Sure, I could retreat into the safety of my Blake Boden Experiment app, feed it every new data point he's given me, and hope AI will spit out some quantifiable logic to make sense of it all.

But even AI isn't equipped to handle the whirlwind of emotions Blake stirs up in me. And lately, there have been so many, I've lost count.

For a girl who loves all things numbers, that's downright terrifying.

17

Friday, June 6th

Blake

Groove, a club not too far from campus, is alive and well on a Friday night. The bass thumps from the speakers and through the floor, reverberating up into my chest, while neon lights flicker and swirl in shades of electric blue and candy pink. The air smells like a mix of citrus, vodka, and just a hint of smoke from the fog machine near the DJ booth, and conversations blend with the music, loud but not obnoxious, as people laugh, drink, and dance like the night's got no expiration date.

Finn sets a drink in front of Scottie and leans in for a kiss. Instantly, Julia, who is perched on the couch across from me, grins and throws me a wide-eyed look that screams, *Are you seeing this?*

Julia's been on a vibe all night—buzzing about sneaking into an over twenty-one club with her fake ID, hyped that the whole gang is finally together again, and legit glowing because Finn and Scottie are back to being fucking adorable together. It's impossible not to feed off her energy, even if I'm not in the exact same headspace.

Finn turns and heads back to the bar to help Ace carry the rest of the drinks.

"Need any help, man?" I ask Finn before he can get away, but he just shakes his head and climbs down the step from our VIP table to return to the bar.

Ace Kelly made all the fancy arrangements for tonight, and it shouldn't be a surprise that he managed to get us a reservation behind the red velvet ropes. I'm sure it helped that he slipped the bouncer money out of his wallet on our way in or the fact that he knows the bouncer because Ace knows *everyone*.

We're only a half hour or so into our night at Groove, but I'd be lying if I said I wasn't already feeling the urge to call it a night.

I shift in my seat, forcing myself not to check my phone again to see if Lexi's sent me a text or tried to call me or, I don't know, fucking something since our text conversation yesterday. I try not to let myself get bogged down in thoughts of why she hasn't answered the two messages I sent her today and whether I should try to reach out again. And I definitely try not to think about what it'd be like to have her here, with me and in front of my friends, because fuck, I don't want to be *that* guy—you know, the desperate, mopey, obsessed-with-one-girl, single-minded guy. Those aren't qualities I envision or wish for myself in football or life.

I can miss Lexi and be the fun, chill, good-time Blake that all my friends know and love. Not miss-Lexi-so-much-I've-forgotten-how-to-live-my-life Blake. *Right?*

Right.

Finn and Ace return again, a drink in each of their hands. They hand them out to Julia and me and then keep one for themselves. I'm the only one old enough to purchase the drinks, but Ace gets a thrill out of using his fake ID just like Julia, so I'm letting him have his moment.

Truth be told, the only thing I ever do with Ace Kelly is *let him have his moment.*

"Gah, this feels so good!" Ace cheers, rubbing his hands together and squeezing in on the one couch to sit next to Julia. "The gang is back together!"

"Four friends walk into a bar…" Scottie adds, sipping her little pink drink through a tiny cocktail straw. "And then one more rolls in."

Ace, Julia, and I all freeze, but then Finn guffaws, devolving into hysterics rarely seen from his taciturn personality, and the rest of us slowly start to thaw.

"Oh, come on," Scottie says, reaching over to shove me in the shoulder. "Lighten up and take the joke. Please. For the love of God. I need everyone to be normal."

For the first time since arriving tonight, I realize she's right. We've been off our game and playing at having fun rather than just having it.

I don't blame Scottie for assuming her injury is the cause— for Ace and Julia, it might be—but for me, I'm having a hard time not letting my phone, and the woman I want to talk to who's only reachable with it, rule my life.

It's just weird being here, with people who know Lexi so well, and not telling them how I feel about her or mentioning her at all.

"You're right," I agree. "Sorry, Scottie. I'll lighten up."

"Thank God." She sighs dramatically. "I was starting to worry that pod people had invaded your bodies and turned your likable, playful personality into a typical jock."

"Ouch." I laugh and grin at her. "Low blow on the sports, babe."

She wags a finger. "You remember who I used to date. Other than you, I don't hold out a lot of hope for muscle-bound lovers of pigskin."

"That's because Dane was a douche burger," I comment, "It had nothing to do with football."

Finn nods, winking at me. "I shoulda killed that kid."

The guy Scottie was dating when she first arrived at Dickson last fall was a real fucking piece of work. And by piece of work, I mean he was a total asshole. Hell, Finn ended up beating his ass twice because of that very fact. Oh, and the fact that Finn was in love with Scottie but refused to let himself see it. Thank goodness he eventually came around. Now, I can't imagine a world where Finn and Scottie aren't together.

I laugh, and Ace reaches around Julia to pat Finn on the chest, coaching, "No, no. You got in enough trouble with that tool as it is. No need to spend life in prison, buddy."

"You would've gotten me out, Acer. Just last week, you told me your dad has a separate lawyer on retainer just for whatever trouble Gunnar gets into," Finn says confidently, drinking from his glass of ice and brown liquid.

Honestly, I'm sort of surprised to see him and Scottie drinking, given their stance on it during the year and their history with alcoholic parents, but far be it for me to judge. They've been through enough to do whatever they want.

Ace turns to me, a mocking smile on his face. "Just when you think a guy likes you for *you*…you find out he's only with you for what you put out."

I roll my eyes, but I also laugh. Ace is the biggest fucking jokester around.

"What are you drinking, Scottie?" Julia asks, a smile the size of Texas on her cheerful face.

"It's…oh… Well, it's a virgin Dirty Shirley," Scottie admits. "I'm still not big on alcohol."

"What?" Ace snaps, the high pitch of his voice making me laugh some more. "Finn told me virgin was just part of the name. You're not drinking?"

"Neither am I," Finn admits softly, putting his glass to his lips. "This is just soda."

"What!" Ace exclaims, his free hand gesturing wildly in the air and making Julia giggle.

"I'm not drinking either," she says and flutters her eyelashes as she rubs a hand over her stomach with purposeful, gentle movements. "I can't."

Wait…*what?* Instantly, we all freeze, and I swear my heart is about to beat out of my chest. Julia keeps rubbing her hand over her stomach. You know, like a woman *with child* would do. And I can't miss the fact that her normally firm belly does look a little rounded…

"You're…you're pregnant?" Scottie manages to ask for the rest of us.

But instead of looking at Julia, my eyes go straight to Ace.

His eyes are so wide, I swear his eyeballs are in danger of popping right out of his skull. His skin is mottled red, and his whole demeanor screams outright shock and anguish. "Jules…"

She purses her lips and then licks them dramatically. "Yes. I'm…"

"Who the hell's baby is it?" Ace screams so loudly I have to cover one of my ears—and we're in a NYC club without hearing protection just fine, so that's really saying something about the volume.

"Ace—" Julia starts to explain, but he's on a rampage.

"Whose is it, Julia? Because I'll fucking kill him myself."

Scottie leans toward me, clucking. "Is it just me, or has this night had a lot of talk of killing?"

"Who, Jules? Tell me who," Ace persists. "I swear to fucking everything, I will strangle whatever motherfucker—"

"Oh my God, Acer, relax!" Julia snaps, finally breaking character and sucking in her stomach. "I'm just kidding! I'm not pregnant!"

"You're not?" Ace's voice shakes as he rubs at his forehead. "You're not pregnant?" he asks again, almost like he needs the confirmation to be able to breathe again, and Julia rolls her eyes like a girl who doesn't realize she's given him the biggest mindfuck of the century.

"Of course I'm not freaking pregnant, Ace," she responds through an oblivious snort. "I'm on birth control."

Despite her efforts in putting him at ease, the words *birth control* make his jaw tick, and he runs a rough hand through his hair several times. It's almost as if even thinking about the possibility of Julia having sex with another guy has his head moments away from exploding.

"Goodness, Jules," Scottie says through a giggle. "You're crazy, girl."

Julia just laughs and shrugs, taking a drink from her fancy cocktail and turning to face the dance floor where the DJ is doing a remix of a familiar song I keep hearing on the radio whenever I'm in the weight room.

Ace, though, well, he's frozen in place, his jaw still ticking and his eyes wide as they stare far off in the distance.

I look at Finn and he looks at me, and it's all the confirmation I need. I don't know what's rolling around inside Ace's head, but I know he's in the middle of quite the crisis and he needs a minute. Like, *right now.*

I grab Finn's shoulder. "Hey, uh, why don't you hold down the fort here with the girls while I take Ace outside for a minute?"

Finn nods, understanding immediately, getting up to position himself in a seat where he can see the whole club. He's in charge of protection now, and quite frankly, I can't think of anyone more capable of the job.

"Hey, Ace, come on, bud." I put my hand on his shoulder. "Come with me for a second. I want to show you something."

When he doesn't move, I step forward and help him, guiding him out of the VIP booth area of our group, down the steps, and through a crowd of writhing bodies. A few women brush up against us on our way out, but I push onward without making eye contact.

Ace's body is pretty heavy for the first half of our walk, but as we approach the front door, his legs finally start to work again.

We walk down the long hallway to the front door and step outside, moving down the sidewalk toward a group of people who've come out to smoke their cigarettes.

My phone buzzes from my back pocket, but it only takes a quick glance at the screen for my chest to deflate when I see it's not Lexi. Yes, I'm aware it's fucking pathetic to be thinking about her when my friend is in the middle of a breakdown, but I can't help it. When I realize it's just a text inside the ongoing group chat with a few of my fellow teammates, where we mostly just send one another funny TikToks and shit, I confirm it can wait.

Once I find a spot away from the drunk chain smokers, I guide him to relax against the wall of the building.

"Take a breath, Ace," I instruct, clamping my hands on his

shoulders and squeezing. He's still staring off into the distance, but so far, he's not showing any other signs of life. "Come on, buddy."

With a shake of his head, his shoulders rise and fall dramatically as air finally fills his lungs. He starts to pace the space in front of me, eventually spinning in place and putting his hands atop his head.

He's a tall guy, so I have to work to get a read on his upturned face, but based on body language alone, I'd say we're right smack in the middle of a life-changing epiphany, and it has everything to do with his best friend Julia.

"Dude, are you okay?" I ask, waiting for his eyes to meet mine again.

He shakes his head, four times back and forth in short, manic shakes, and I nod.

Yep. It's just as I thought.

"Blake." His eyes peer into mine, as if he's waiting for me to confirm his feelings. His feelings *about Julia.*

"Yeah, buddy."

"Blake."

"Yep."

"I...Jules...me...her."

My head bounces up and down once again. He's almost there. Just a little bit more and he'll be capable of full sentences again.

"She's... I... My heart...might explode."

"Okay, buddy," I comfort, stepping forward again to push him even farther down the sidewalk past a new batch of smokers. "Just relax and breathe. I think you're having a panic attack."

He lets out a scream out of nowhere and I check around us, but no one is looking. One good thing about New York—you'll never be the weirdest person in any given area, no matter what you're doing.

"I...Julia."

"Yes," I agree. "Julia."

"Me and...Julia."

I laugh, but it's not mean-spirited. Ace can seemingly tell, rubbing at his eyes with the heels of his hands and breaking into his own chuckle of sorts. It's not exactly carefree, though. "When she said she was pregnant, I…saw red. And then black. And then blue and green and every color of the rainbow. Fuck, I might have seen my own fucking stomach at one point. I always thought… I thought we were just friends. I thought…"

I smile. "Oh, I know. We know what you all thought, but we also know you thought wrong."

"You've known?"

"Oh, Acer, we all know, buddy. You and Julia are the *only* people who don't know, and I mean that with every literal fiber of my being." I point back down the street. "You see the security bouncer guy?"

He nods.

"Even he knows."

"Well, fuck! What am I supposed to do now? Just go back in there and act like everything is the same as it's always been?"

I shrug. "That part is up to you. How do you handle being in love?"

He scoffs. "If I fucking knew that, I wouldn't be asking you. I mean, what would you do?"

I say the only truth I can and the first thing that comes to mind—*Lexi*.

"I'm still trying to figure it out, Ace. Just like you."

18

Ginger packs up her notebook and headphones and fifty-five snack wrappers, while I put away everything I've brought to the lab with me today. It's going on eight o'clock, and I'm ready to go home and enjoy some solitude.

At least, that's what I've been telling myself after a week of not seeing Blake. The last time I saw him was the Sunday night that ended with his face between my legs. And the last time I spoke to him was via text on Thursday while I was in my meeting with Dr. Blevin's PhD cohort.

I didn't try to reach out to him all weekend. But that's probably a good thing.

Though, you certainly wanted *to respond to all five texts he sent you...*

I internally shake my head at myself. Blake's effect on me is unlike anything I've ever experienced with anyone else. When he's near me, I don't think straight. I get caught up in pheromones and hormones and straight moans, and I lose my mind. I let myself get distracted from school and from myself and from the complicated part of being several years older than him and the fact that he's the star freaking quarterback of Dickson University's football team.

I forget who I am and what I want and how unconcerned I am with having a relationship or companionship or for someone else's feelings altogether.

But given a little distance and time, I'm finding my rhythm

again, settling into keeping to myself and my computer and working on graduating from Dickson with my final doctorate and moving on with my life.

It's business as usual.

And I'm happy about it. Really. I am.

I think.

"Man, Lexi." Ginger lets out a deep sigh. "I can't believe we only have a month and a half left of school before we have to go out in the real world and do real-world things. Can you?"

I shake my head. These days, I can't believe a lot of things.

"I have three weeks' worth of work left to cram in a two-week bag, but I'm not panicking. See?" she asks, widening her eyes in what she thinks is a calm expression. "This is me...not panicking."

"Oh yeah." I laugh. "You look calm."

"Yes. I'm calm. Calm, calm, *calm*."

"Ginger, it's going to be okay."

"Are you sure, Lexi? Because it doesn't feel like it sometimes."

Ironically enough, I know what she means—though, for me, it has absolutely nothing to do with school.

I know I've been avoiding Blake, but it also feels like he's been avoiding me. And, as it turns out, I don't like that very much at all.

"I am sure, Ginger." I try my hand at comforting her. "I think, from what I can tell, all of this won't feel so important anymore when we get out in the real world. Out there, there are real problems and real solutions, and none of this performance art the university puts us through."

"I don't know if that makes me feel better or worse," she muses with a snort.

"I know." I shrug. "I'm sorry."

"Hey, you want to go get something to eat?"

I shake my head. "I think I'm just going to go home." After a quick realization that this is an opportunity to grow a friendship with someone I don't hate being around, I add, "But thank you for inviting me. I'd love to go another time."

Ginger beams. "Awesome. Maybe later this week?"

"Sounds great," I agree.

Ginger hoists her stuffed bag up onto her shoulder and heads for the door, waving as she does. I wave back and look down, only to startle when she clears her throat.

"Hey, Lex?"

"Yeah?" I ask, glancing her way and then down at my bag again as I tuck my water bottle into its pocket on the side.

"DoorDash is here."

My gaze jerks to the door just as Blake scoots inside, a bag of food, again, hanging from his strong, capable fingers. Ginger smiles shyly and waves again. "Lunch soon, Lex."

I know now it's more than a promise for a meal—it's a sworn testament that I'll need to be spilling some beans as well.

I've never had a girlfriend expecting gossip before. Really, the closest friend I've had since childhood is Connor. And he's way too self-involved to be worried about the details of my secret love life. Not without me very plainly pointing them out anyway. Plus, it's never ever felt right talking to Connor about stuff like that.

As Ginger leaves, Blake steps inside, pulling the door to the lab shut behind him with a click and standing just inside. "Hey, Lex."

"Hi, Blake."

"Hope it's not a bad time."

I shake my head. "I was just packing to leave."

"How about I walk home with you? We can eat there."

"Yeah. That works."

I grab my tote and hike it up onto my shoulder, scooting my chair in under my desk and heading for the door. Blake stands next to it, waiting patiently, but when I reach for the handle, he blocks it with his hand. "Just…one thing first."

"Yeah?" I ask, my breath catching in my chest.

"You wouldn't happen to be avoiding me, would you?"

"Blake—"

"Because I've texted a few times, and you haven't responded,"

Blake says, his voice sharp, but the hurt beneath it is unmistakable. His jaw tightens as he holds my gaze. "And I don't know, maybe this is crazy talk, but as a guy who had his face between your legs the last time we saw each other, I thought reaching out would at least garner a response."

The heat rises to my cheeks, and my grip tightens around the strap of my bag. "I've been really busy," I mutter, my voice barely above a whisper. *Avoiding you because you make me feel out of control.*

"Oh, I imagine you have been," he shoots back, running a frustrated hand through his hair. "*Very* busy talking yourself out of liking me and out of whatever this special thing is between us. Very busy figuring out how to scrape me off without having to say it out loud. Very, very busy."

"That's not what I've been doing," I snap, my voice trembling slightly as my defenses kick into high gear. My chest feels tight, like there's a weight pressing down on it, and I force myself to meet his piercing gaze. I need to hold the line, but his words threaten to crawl under my skin and dig into places I don't want exposed.

"No?" he asks, stepping closer, his eyes searching mine with an intensity that makes me want to squirm.

"No."

"Then what have you been doing, Lex?" His voice softens, but the frustration remains. "Because I'm trying to understand here. Should I cut and run now, before the heartache really sets in? Before it hurts so much to be shunned by you that it turns me inside out? Or should I hang in there a little longer, hoping you'll change? Hoping you'll see the potential in the two of us like I do?"

"It's more complicated than that, Blake," I manage, my voice shaky. I fidget with the strap of my bag as if the motion can steady me. "You don't…you don't understand what it's like in my head. You don't have the thoughts or the pressures that I do. You don't… Your brain doesn't work like mine."

"Well, of course it doesn't. No two people think the same, Lex. None. So, what makes us so different? If I'm willing to learn and understand who you are as a person, why can't you do the same for me? Why can't it work? Opposites end up together all the time. Look at Finn and Scottie, for shit's sake. You want to tell me they're the same? Not a chance."

"It's just easier this way."

His face crumples at my words, and I know immediately that I've hurt his feelings—I've hurt my own too. But it's true. Trying to make it work with him is the harder road. Period.

He nods then, his eyes a little sad as he holds out the bag of food. I lick my lips to try to stop myself from freaking out. Emotionally, this all feels like *too much.*

"Here. You can have the food."

"Blake."

"Take it, Lex." I grab the bag before it drops as he shoves it off his own finger. "I, for one, am not feeling all that hungry anymore."

I flinch as he pushes open the door to the lab, effectively nudging me and the abandoned food bag out of the way. The door slams against the wall outside from his powerful shove, echoing through the empty, dark hallway as he powers down it without looking back.

My heart pounds and my stomach flips over, sick to itself.

What have I just done?

19

Blake

My calves burn as I push to run harder and harder with every suicide. We take the field in ten-yard increments, back and forth, back and forth, back and forth, until we cover the whole thing, and for as much as it hurts, I wish it would suck just a little more.

Maybe that makes me insane, but the last ten days have been more fucking pain-ridden than any football hell week training could even dream to be, and it's all my fault.

Fucking cocky, stupid, ornery—I just *had* to prove a point to Lexi by standing up for myself, and look where it's gotten me. Alone, sad, ten fucking days without her in my life at all and no choice but to hold my dick in my own hand and dream of what it was like to touch her.

Fuck.

"Boden!" Coach Gordan yells, his voice hoarse with irritation. "Take it easy, would ya? I don't need a fucking injury before the season even starts, for shit's sake!"

I power even harder for the last fifty-yard sprint, and Coach blows the whistle when I'm halfway there. I don't stop, though. I pump and I pump and I pump until my heart feels like it's going to blow a hole wide open in my chest.

"Holy shit, Blake!" Ron Zimmerman yells from somewhere behind me. "What are you on today, brother?"

I keep pushing until I cross into the end zone, collapsing

immediately to the ground and rolling over onto my back to stare at the sky. Clouds drift from east to west, falling from my head to my feet and continuing downfield until they clear the bleachers on the other side. I can hear the guys yelling and celebrating and shit-talking from all around me, but by and large, all I can do is remember to breathe. In and out, I work to bring my pulse back to normal.

"I think he broke himself," Nick Fisher, my center and one of the biggest fuckers on the team, whispers as he finally crosses the finish line himself. I hold up a single middle finger, making them all giggle to themselves like little schoolgirls.

When Coach Gordan leans over me, blocking out the sky with his face, I know I'm about to get my ass chewed for real, though.

"Hey, Sleeping fucking Beauty…what the ever-loving hell was that shit?"

"Coach," I wheeze, closing my eyes when breathing still doesn't come naturally, and a cramp attacks me dead in the side.

"I swear, you kids are going to be the death of me. What are you trying to do, kill yourself? Trying to be some hotshot for the new guys?"

I shake my head, but he keeps going anyway.

"I don't give a fuck. Whatever it is you're doing, quit it, okay? Goddammit, I hate this job sometimes. Hit the showers!"

He climbs away from my corpse, and Hank Lewis, my tight end and go-to guy, steps in to take his place, holding out a hand to help me up. "Come on, Boden. Time to rise and shine."

I sigh as he pulls me to my feet, groaning slightly at the pain in every single part of my body. "Certainly seems like you're being driven from a different place today. Everything okay?"

I nod, giving him a thumbs-up. "Oh yeah. I'm swell."

Hank smirks. "Well, whatever it is, it makes you really fucking fast. None of us could even catch your ass."

I laugh. "Oh well, glad there's an upside."

"For real, though, is everything okay?"

I nod, clapping Hank on the shoulder. "Yeah, yeah. I'm fine. Just a weird week, that's all."

"Okay, dude. You coming to the club with us later?"

I shrug. Honestly, I'm undecided. It's not a *bad* idea per se. I mean, it might lead to some questionable choices, but it'd surely improve my mood. Instead of committing, I offer about all I'm able to right now—a chance. "I might. We'll see. Cool if I let you know?"

"Of course, dude. The guys know you aren't much of a partier, so either way'll be cool."

"Later, dude."

Hank takes off, and I take my time walking through the end zone to my abandoned gear, gathering my pads and helmet from earlier and scooping them up to carry them to the locker room.

A wave of sadness crashes over me, and all of a sudden, I'm decided. I jog to catch up with Hank in the tunnel to the locker room. I spot him about fifty yards ahead, his helmet and pads hanging from the fingers of each of his hands. "Hank, wait up!"

He stops in his tracks and turns around, and I keep running until I meet up with him. "Hey, man, what's up?"

"I changed my mind. I think I'm going to come out with you guys."

"Really?" he asks, his whole face lifting with unbridled excitement.

"Really. We haven't had a chance for a ton of bonding this summer, and hell, I don't have anything else going on. So, what the fuck, you know?"

"Shit yeah, my dude. Fuck, this is gonna be good." He pounds knuckles with me as we start walking toward the locker room again, explaining the plan. "We're going to hit a restaurant first, check out that new club Tau, and then just go where the night takes us. We can meet up beforehand and go together if you want. Like seven or so?" He pushes through the door to the locker room, and I follow him, looking up at the clock on the back wall as I do.

It's only a little after four, so that gives me plenty of time to head back to my apartment, shower, change, chill for a bit, and mentally talk myself into believing this shit is a good idea. "Yeah. That works."

"Cool. It's downtown near the Financial District, so we can just meet here and then catch the subway together?"

I nod. "Cool, man."

Hank heads for his side of the locker room while I head for mine, tossing my pads and helmet into my locker with just a little more force than I intend. I sit down in front of it and start undressing, trying my best not to think about why I'm so fucking pissed off.

I sigh.

Fuck.

Tossing my clothes and shit into my locker and grabbing a towel, I head for the showers and make quick work of rinsing off the grime and sweat. I'll take another shower when I get home, one where I can soak and fucking mope, but this one, with fifteen other fucking dudes, is purely mechanical.

Sufficiently clean, I shut off my shower, wrap my towel around my waist, and head back to my locker in silence. I dress in a pair of loose shorts and a T-shirt and toss my duffel over my shoulder before heading for the door.

No one bothers me as I get rid of my towel in the hamper and exit, so I take the opportunity to put in an earbud and crank up some music. It's old-school Yellowcard, and the frantic cadence of "Way Away" matches the desperation of my mood.

I let myself jam and feel the music as it blares in my ears, all the way down the hall to the player exit, and shove through the back door into the surprisingly still high sun of summertime. The door falls closed with a thud behind me, though I can barely hear it over the volume of my music, and the street in front of me is mostly quiet.

Maybe that's why I startle so hard when I feel a tap on my shoulder from behind, and I spin around like a top.

Lexi Winslow is the very last person I expect to see.

I hurriedly take out my earbuds and tuck them into my pocket, the volume of my song still playing slightly in the background. "Lex? What are you—"

She lunges forward and slams her lips into mine, effectively cutting me off and answering me all at once. Maintaining my boundaries, it seems, has paid off in a big way.

I kiss her back, wrapping one strong arm around her back so firmly I almost lift her feet off the ground and sinking my other hand into the back of her blond hair. I get lost in the feel of her body and the smell of her hair and push her backward, all the way until her back is against the hard brick exterior of the stadium. I taste and touch and feel every bit of her mouth with my tongue, and when she finally manages to push me back, the two of us are breathless.

"I'm sorry," she whispers, her eyes looking up to meet mine. "For avoiding you."

"Shit, Lex, if it always resolves like this, you can avoid me all the time."

She laughs through a sigh, pushing me back just enough that there's a six-inch space between us. I frown, but she smiles. "I…I want to really try this. It's not been fair that I've been fighting you every step of the way, and these ten days of no contact from you… Well, they've helped to make me see that. But I'm not ready for anything to be public yet, Blake."

I look around at the space on either side of us. "We're in public right now, Lex."

"I know. Which was pretty stupid of me, I can see now, but at the time, I just…needed to talk to you as soon as possible and I knew you would be finishing up with practice now."

It's not exactly a Shakespearean love poem, but damn, coming from Lexi Winslow, everything she just said is practically a sonnet.

I can be patient on the public thing if it takes a little longer. The important thing is that she wants to give this an actual try.

"Okay."

"Okay?"

"Let's try this in private first. I can do that."

"You can?" she asks, a beautiful beacon of hope shining in her voice.

"Yeah. In fact, let's go—"

The door bangs open beside us, and Lexi jumps as I turn, distancing myself from her warm, beautiful body just a little more. Hank and Ron are laughing and chatting on their way out, when Hank spots me standing there. "See you tonight, man."

I nod. *Fuck.* "Yeah, dude. See you tonight."

He jerks up his chin, and he and Ron move on. I blow out a breath, reality having smacked the air clean out of me. "I…well, I told the guys I would go out with them tonight. I'm supposed to meet them at seven. I didn't know you were going to show up here, though, because I sure as fuck wouldn't have if I had. But I'm not supposed to meet up with them until later."

"It's fine," she says. "Just get in touch with me later tonight when you're done."

"Wait…what? But I have a few hours. I can—"

"Later, Blake." She steps forward to press a quick but discreet kiss to my lips. "I promise."

"Because we're really giving this a shot?" I ask, the need for confirmation undeniable.

"Yes."

"Well, Lex," I say and wink at her, "I think it's going to be a very short night."

She laughs and waves, walking away with only one look back. My pulse pounds and my ears ring as I think about just how down the river I've already sold myself.

How I might already be in love.

I sure hope she gets in a boat and follows because, if not, it's going to be a hell of a long row back to reality.

20

Lexi

After I left Blake at the stadium, I decided to busy myself at the lab, adding a particular algorithm into my test app for my dissertation just to see if it changes any of my conclusions. But when I ran into Ginger there, she all but forced me to follow through on the meal I promised her a week and a half ago.

And since it's already seven, it's technically a dinner meal, not a lunch meal, but Ginger clearly doesn't mind.

Now, I sit across from her in a corner booth at Zip's Diner, my burger and fries untouched as I mentally catalog what I've learned about Ginger Lewis over the course of this meal that I surprisingly didn't already know about her from all the time we've spent together in the lab.

For starters, she's older than me by a few years—twenty-nine to my twenty-five—and this is her first PhD. She's laser-focused on finishing it and has a very clear vision of her future—developing code for a tech giant like Apple or Google.

And she's also weirdly obsessed with hot chocolate, which she's now sipping with what can only be described as reverence.

"So," Ginger says after a particularly long sip. She leans in slightly, her red hair brushing her shoulders. "Tell me about the guy."

"What guy?" I already know who she means, but I reach for my cup of water like it's a shield and take a sip.

"Oh, come on, Lexi," she says through a snort. "The guy who shows up with food. You know, tall, muscular, and devastatingly handsome?" She smirks. "Don't play dumb. I've seen him twice now, and I'd bet all five hundred dollars in my checking account he's not your *DoorDash* guy."

I pause, debating how much to share. I've never really done the whole girl-talk thing, and spilling details about Blake feels equal parts terrifying and cathartic. But there's a whole reason I want to keep our relationship a secret. I'm simply not ready for anything more than that.

But man, for once in my life, it sure would be nice to talk to someone about something like this. Someone who isn't Connor or my family or someone who is friends with my family. A completely neutral party who doesn't know all the ins and outs of my life.

"His name is Blake," I eventually tell her, testing the waters to see if she knows who Blake Boden is to Dickson University. Truth be told, Ginger Lewis is a lab rat like me, and she either knows who Blake is because everyone on campus does or she has her head so far up her computer's ass that she doesn't even know our college has a football team.

"Okay, *Blake*," she repeats, her eyes lighting up with curiosity but her expression not showcasing any recognition to his name. "And? What about this Blake guy? What's the story with you two?"

This Blake guy. I almost want to laugh at how oblivious she is. I also feel the biggest sense of relief. It's one thing for me to be reckless not even two hours ago and show up at Dragon Stadium to tell Blake that I want to try to be together—in secret—and kiss him, but it's a whole other thing for me to actually talk about that reality with someone who knows who he is.

Ginger's total cluelessness is a welcome breath of fresh air. Though, that doesn't mean I feel comfortable enough to tell her all the sordid details.

"It's complicated," I say, going with vague.

"Complicated how?" She raises an eyebrow. "He seems pretty straightforward—brings you food, smiles like he invented happiness, and looks at you like you hung the stars. What am I missing?"

"You're not missing anything." I shrug, unsure of how to answer her question, but also, not answer it at the same time. "It's just very complicated."

"Well, dating someone generally is complicated."

"We're not dating per se," I clarify quickly. "I mean, we're dating, but we're keeping things on the down-low and seeing where it goes."

"So, it's a secret relationship, then?"

"Well, yeah. It is. I mean, that's how I want it for now."

"You're the one who wants it to be secret?" she asks, surprise in her voice. "Why? He seems great. And he's easy on the eyes. Why the need to keep all that goodness locked up behind closed doors?"

"Honestly, it's not about him," I admit, my voice softer. "It's more about me. My life is already full and busy, and I can't exactly lose focus, you know?"

"Lex, you sound like Dr. Blevin right now." Ginger leans back, crossing her arms as she studies me. "Dating someone shouldn't be as complicated as a PhD dissertation. It should be simple."

Yeah. Hah. I wish it were.

"Do you like him?"

I nod.

"Do you feel good when you're around him?"

"Yes." Clearly, I feel good when I'm around Blake. I have an entire, currently unused AI-assisted app I created with him in mind that's showcased that to me in graphs and charts at least a hundred times.

"Then what's the problem?" she asks, throwing her hands up. "If being with him makes you happy, why are you turning it into a mathematical equation? It's not about optimizing variables. It's about what feels right."

I stare at my food, her words hitting harder than I expected. "It's not that easy for me, Ginger," I say quietly. "I don't know how to be all in with someone. Honestly, I've never really been capable of that in the past, and I'm not sure I'll ever be capable of that. The last thing I want to do is hurt him."

She reaches across the table, her hand resting lightly on mine.

"Lex, no one knows how to be all in until they try. You're overthinking it. Just take a breath and let yourself feel."

Feel. Oh man. If only it were that easy for me.

I smile faintly, appreciating her sincerity even if it doesn't magically solve my dilemma.

Her advice isn't based on all the variables of Blake's and my reality. It doesn't take into account that he's the star quarterback here at Dickson or the fact that I'm a few years older than him and soon to be finished with academia and taking that giant leap into adulthood.

And it certainly doesn't consider my lack of emotional intelligence and clear uncertainties on whether I'm even capable of being in love with someone like my mom is with my stepdad or Finn is with Scottie.

Thankfully, Ginger senses my hesitancy to continue this line of conversation and changes the subject toward her dissertation and everything she still needs to do. I nod along, but my mind is still spinning over her advice.

Even though she doesn't know all the sordid details of Blake and me or the intricacies of my complex mind, I know there's some truth to her words.

And deep down, I do want to try. With Blake. It's why I ended up kissing him outside of Dragon Stadium just a few hours ago, without even calculating the risk that anyone could have witnessed it.

But the biggest question that gnaws at me the most is, will my pace with our relationship ever be good enough for Blake? *More like, will your fear of the unknown and inability to let go of control ultimately hold you back from something extraordinary?*

I don't know, but I'm sure as hell going to try. I'm going to follow through with what I told him I wanted. I'm going to do my best to give this whole Blake and me thing a shot.

I'm going to follow through on my promise from earlier.

And the play clock officially starts now—or, you know, whenever Blake gets home tonight.

It's just a little after ten, and I'm standing outside Blake's apartment door, constantly glancing around the hallway to make sure no one sees me.

I worry my teeth into my bottom lip, my mind racing with the abnormal behavior I am so clearly displaying right now. Frankly, I don't know who this girl is—who chases down football players outside of stadiums and kisses them out in the open and begs them to give her another chance and waits outside their apartment door for them to get home from their night out with friends because they can't wait to see and touch and kiss him again any longer—but that hasn't stopped her from robbing me of my normal eccentricities and replacing them entirely.

That hasn't stopped her from checking her phone a million times to see the time—10:04 p.m.—or the butterflies from flapping all throughout her stomach either.

I'm not someone I recognize, but for the first time since the start of this transformation, I'm starting to be okay with it.

I peek under my trench coat again at the lacy bra and underwear I went out and bought from a boutique after I left dinner with Ginger, and I roll my eyes.

I have a feeling if I entered the current data—that I'm wearing sexy undergarments for Blake and waiting outside his apartment for him to come home—into the app I created, AI would spit out some conclusion that lands on an incredibly high percentage in his favor.

I check my phone again, reading the messages Blake and I exchanged about thirty minutes ago for the nineteenth time.

> **Blake Boden: Night's coming to a close for me, Smart Girl. Should I head your way?**

> **Me: No. It's late. You should go home.**

Blake Boden: You're kidding me, right? I'm coming to you.

Me: Go home, Blake.

Blake Boden: Wait…is there a reason I should go home?

Blake Boden: Lexi????

Me: Blake. Seriously. GO HOME. TO YOUR APARTMENT. RIGHT NOW.

Blake Boden: OH SHIT. I'll head right home, then. Promise. ;) ;)

I click the power button on my phone to put it to sleep once again and tuck it away, resting my head on the wall beside Blake's door.

I haven't been this mixed-up waiting for someone to be somewhere, I think, ever. Maybe on the first night of hosting Double C when I was waiting on things to get delivered to the secret location, but even that's a stretch.

This is anticipation personified.

The stairwell door opens with a bang, and I glance out and around the edge of my hood to check. What I'm not expecting is to be scooped up before I can get a look, Blake having literally sprinted the length of the hall to get there before I could.

"Oh my God," I yelp, my whole body panicking at the rush of cool air on my very exposed parts underneath my coat as Blake picks me up, opens his door, and sets me inside, all in one smooth motion.

The door closes behind us with a thud, and Blake pushes me backward until my butt hits the couch, following me down.

"This is the best surprise of my life, Lexi. Truly."

I laugh. "You almost spoiled it by going to my place."

"I did. I was hell-bent on seeing you. Good thing I texted, or we'd both be waiting for each other all night."

"Nope. I would have lasted maybe another hour before I went home and found you eventually."

"Oh wow. Are you saying you wouldn't wait for me all night?"

"That's exactly what I'm saying." I adjust myself under him, and his eyebrows draw together. "I don't know how people wear this all the time."

"Wear what?" I shake my head, but he catches my chin in his palm, his eyes boring into mine. "Wear what, Lexi?"

I shrug. "I guess you're just going to have to wait until I take off my coat to see."

"Coat? What are you wearing a coat for?" He scoffs, pretend-scolding. "It's *summer*, for Pete's sake. I think you should take off the coat right now, just for your own comfort and convenience, of course."

"You do, do you?"

"Yes. Very much. I will, however, if it's any consolation, help you every step of the way."

"You're very supportive," I mock.

"Oh, you have no idea. On certain nights, like tonight, for example, I'm available for your *every* whim, need, or service."

"Blake."

"Take off the coat, Lex. I want to taste your pussy."

"Blake." Courage bubbles in my throat as Blake's warm blue eyes curl up at the corners.

"What, Lexi?"

"I want to taste you too."

"Oh yeah. The coat is coming off now." Blake scoots back just enough to undo the knot at my waist, pulling open the tie until it falls to the sides and then slowly, reverently, opening the coat. My skin goose bumps around the black lace underwear the salesgirl talked me into buying, and Blake's whole face heats with lust of an eleven if the scale is from one to ten.

I blow out a breath to steady my nerves, and Blake's entire

being quiets, one large, long-fingered hand splaying around the flesh of my thigh.

"You look so fucking good, Lex."

"Yeah?" I ask in a breathy whisper.

"Yeah. *Fucking incredible.* And to say I appreciate the effort is an understatement. I want to stress how impressed I am with it. But with that said…you don't have to do this for me."

I scrunch up my nose in confusion. "Don't have to do what?"

"Dress up in shit you'd never in a million years dress up in. Wear lace panties and lace bras and do it so I'll get a thrill. I like your black cotton panties just fucking fine."

Even with all the effort and the excitement and the thrill of seeing a different perspective on myself, hearing him say I never have to do it again is the biggest, swooniest, sexiest relief.

It's hard to be something that I'm not. And while I think it's a good exercise to be willing sometimes, I think it's even better to find someone who says you don't have to.

Who says *I* don't have to.

Gently, Blake puts a hand to my chest, pushing me flat on my back on the couch and pulling my arms out of the sleeves of the coat. I watch avidly as he sinks to his knees on the floor beside the couch, turning my body with two strong hands on my hips before gripping the flesh on the insides of my thighs. He licks his lips in a soft, unintentional gesture, and I have to swallow hard to send my heart back down into my chest.

Blake leans forward and closes his mouth over the top of my panties, and my back arches off the couch like a junkie taking their first hit.

How in the world can it be like this? I haven't had it that long, and yet, after the last ten days, I've *missed* it.

Missed *him.*

In a way I never thought I could. I don't know when it happened, but somehow, someway, Blake went from thorn in my side to my newest hyperfixation.

Eggs, football stats, math, weather, data, computers, and now, Blake Boden. At one point in my life, I've driven myself to obsession over all of them.

Some I've kept, and some blew away like the wind.

It's too early to tell with Blake, but I really hope my brain doesn't find a reason to get sick of him.

21

Lexi snores lightly from the other side of my bed as I climb out as gently as I can and sneak off to the bathroom.

I relieve myself, wash my hands, and brush my teeth, and then I scoot into my closet to throw on a clean T-shirt and a pair of shorts. When I pad back out into the bedroom, Lexi is still sleeping peacefully.

I skirt the bed on her side, leaning in to place a gentle kiss to her forehead, tuck my navy comforter up higher under her chin, and slide out of the room without making another sound. I pull the door closed gently behind me and run down the hall to my kitchen to grab my keys, wallet, and phone, and then slip out the door into the hall, locking it shut behind me.

God. The high of this morning feels good.

My mouth on Lexi—Lexi's mouth on me. I'll remember that shit for the rest of my life and then some. When I'm a fucking ghost, I'll be whispering about the time Lexi swirled her tongue around the tip of my cock until I came all over her hand for any stranger who'll listen. I'll be haunting the new owner of that apartment until they burn the building down to put up a new one, with illicit pictures in their cereal and distant spirit groans.

My couch—that stupid blue couch that I got at a thrift store before my freshman year—will be a staple in my homes, no matter how big they get, for years to come.

I jog down the final flight of stairs and out the front door of my apartment to the gentle light of morning sun as it beams in between the high-rise buildings on Broadway to the south. It pierces my eyes, but not even the sun itself can dim how brightly my spirit is shining today.

Checking both ways three times before crossing the street to avoid being the Brad Pitt in my own *Meet Joe Black*-style fairy tale, I make my way into Brower Center dining with my mind on donuts and coffee for the girl of my dreams who's waiting in my bed.

There's a pep in my step and a whistle on my lips as I step inside the French doors of the dining hall, and then there's an Ace Kelly right in my chest as we bump directly into each other.

He's been nearly manic since his moment of self-discovery nearly two weeks ago, but when he smiles at me as we step back from each other this morning, he almost seems like he's back to his normal self.

"Hey, Ace."

"Holy shit, everybody, it's Blake Boden!" he yells, effectively blowing my cover and making me roll my eyes. "How's it going, man? You're up and about pretty early."

"Me?" I question with a laugh, realizing quickly that Ace isn't even supposed to be on campus right now. He's not attending the summer semester at all. "What about you? What are you doing on campus this morning?"

"I have a meeting with my peer counselor in a little bit to go over my schedule for the fall. I'm planning to make some changes to my original plan, so I wanted to get ahead of the game."

"Changes? You switching majors or something?"

He laughs. "Oh. No. I'm putting myself in a position to be in every single one of Julia's classes, that's all."

Oh my God. Fucking hell, this guy. So much for everything being back to normal.

"Ah. I see we're still coming to terms with the Julia thing."

"Oh no. I've come to terms. The thing is, she doesn't even know the terms exist, and all these fuckers all over this campus sure as shit don't either. No way in hell I'm letting some preppy kid with bad breath scoop her out from under me before I have the chance to convince her to love me back."

I nod with a laugh. "Well, as long as you're handling it reasonably."

"Reasonable is my middle name, bro."

"Of course."

"What are you doing? Grabbing breakfast?"

"Yeah," I agree since it isn't exactly a lie. "Grabbing something quick so I can chill a little before practice."

Ace jerks up his chin, holding out a hand for me to shake, which I do. "All right. Well, hit me up later. I think we're all going to get together and do something. Feels like we've barely gotten to see you this summer, you've been so busy acting like you're a fucking football savant or some shit."

I chuckle. "I'll see what I get into later and let you know."

"Fine. But you have to at least come to Fourth of July with us." He points an index finger in my direction. "We're all going to Finn's uncle's lake house. It's a big Winslow family tradition that now includes the Hayeses, my crazy-ass parents, and Julia's mom and dad. Despite the parental units being there, I swear it'll be a good time."

Big Winslow family tradition means that Lexi will be there too.

"I'll see if I can make it, but it sounds as if it has potential," I reply, a wink rolling off my face right along with the lie. The truth of the matter is, if there's a chance I can spend the Fourth of July with Lexi and my friends without the world imploding, I'm going to jump right the fuck on it.

"*Potential?*" He scoffs. "It's going to be a good fucking time, Golden Boy. My dad and Gunnar apparently went out and bought a shit-ton of fireworks. Your ass needs to be there, bro… Anyway, I gotta run. I'll catch you later," Ace says with a smile, slapping me on the back and running straight out the door. I turn to watch as he goes and then scope out the area to make sure no one else is watching me too closely before approaching the buffet line.

I snag a to-go box, six donuts, and two cups of coffee, then bolt out of there like my life depends on it, determined not to get side-tracked by anyone else.

In my haste, I didn't think to leave a note—a realization that hits me like a truck now that I've been gone way longer than I intended. Big mistake. *Huge.* The last thing I want is for Lexi to wake up, find me missing, and assume I bailed. Or worse, for her to freak out and sneak out, never to be heard from again.

With my arms full and my nerves on edge, I check for traffic and dart back across Broadway, my pace quickening as I near my apartment building. The goal? Get back inside before anyone else spots me and tries to stop me.

As the lobby door closes behind me, I let out a breath I didn't realize I was holding. Now, all I can do is hope Lexi's still there.

I take the stairs two at a time, working overtime to keep the coffees from sloshing all over the place with the unexpected pace.

I have to set down the box of donuts to open the door on my floor, prop it open with my foot, and then pick them back up, and I run the rest of the way down the hall to my apartment and unlock my door by doing the same thing.

I set the treats down on the kitchen counter and then hustle back down the hall to the bedroom, opening the door so quickly in my panic that I accidentally wake up a still-sleeping Lexi.

Immediately, I start apologizing. "Sorry. I'm sorry. I just… Yeah, I'm sorry."

She rubs at her eyes and looks me up and down, pushing up to sitting in the bed and taking the sheet with her to cover her still-bare chest. "Did you go somewhere?"

I smile. "Just to get coffee and donuts. You want some?"

She nods, her cheeks lifting noticeably. "I could do coffee and donuts."

"Great. I'll go get them." I move to the door before lunging back inside, settling on the bed beside her so quickly that she laughs.

"Yes?"

"I just remembered. I ran into Ace at Brower earlier, and he had an interesting suggestion that I join everyone at Finn's uncle's lake house for the Fourth of July." I pause for effect. "You wouldn't happen to know anything about that, would you?"

Her brows knit together as she sits up a little straighter, her hair still mussed from sleep. "You saw Ace?"

That's when it hits me. I've just unloaded this at lightning speed on someone who literally just woke up. Maybe I should dial it back a notch before she thinks I've lost my mind.

"Yeah, sorry," I say, softening my tone. "I saw him at Brower. You know, where I went to grab coffee and donuts."

Her lips press into a thoughtful line. "What's he doing on campus?"

I laugh lightly. "It's a long story—one I promise to explain at some point. But yeah, he mentioned he's heading to Finn's uncle's lake house for the Fourth. Said it's some kind of big Winslow family tradition. He also suggested I should tag along. I figured…maybe you were planning to go too? Thought it'd be a way for us to spend some time together…you know, without anyone noticing anything."

Her sleepy eyes blink a few times, processing, before she finally replies, "Right."

"I didn't mention any of these details to Ace, by the way, in case you were wondering," I expand. "I heard you when you said you want to keep it secret for now. Especially last night, when we had our mouths on each other." I waggle my brows and smile at her. "I *really* heard it then."

"Oh my God." She shakes her head, giggling as she shoves my shoulder—lightly, but enough to let me know she thinks I'm ridiculous. "Blake, you're already scheming ways to secretly be with me on the Fourth of July, and that's two weeks away." Her eyebrow quirks, her lips pulling into a sly smile. "What exactly are we supposed to do until then?"

I let my smirk grow, leaning closer like I'm about to share a well-kept secret. "Oh, don't worry, Lex. We'll find plenty of ways to keep ourselves entertained."

She rolls her eyes, but I don't miss the way her smile softens, like she's secretly looking forward to whatever chaos I bring next.

We feel officially together. Maybe not in the conventional sense, but even in secret, it feels like we're building something real. And whatever this is between us, it's not a gift I'm willing to squander.

22

The Ferris Research Lab is quiet tonight, but despite the calm, my head is a thunderstorm of swirling thoughts, every single one of them centered on the one man with whom I've been spending all my free time.

Stolen moments, secret kisses, and nights spent wrapped up in each other's arms, the past six days with Blake have been a whirlwind.

The fact that I've managed to keep up with some of my normal routine at all is something I attribute entirely to his obligations to the football team since he can't be texting, chasing, or sexing me when he's there.

When he's Blue 42'ing, I'm in the lab. Though, I admit, I've spent more time dissecting the way Blake makes me feel than I have obsessing over the microscopic details within the algorithms in my dissertation test app. And given how hard I've worked for this PhD up until now, that's…terrifying.

At least, it *should* be.

I should be fighting, running, pulling away. Instead, I'm consumed.

On Monday and Tuesday, I adjusted my usual lab routine to his practice schedules just so we would have more time together. On Wednesday, I skipped the lab altogether so we could go to the Bronx Zoo and dinner afterward.

We haven't had actual sex yet—*even if I've tried valiantly to convince him we should*—and yet, I'm giving him nuclear-level energy. It's the antithesis of everything I know myself for.

It's *boy craziness*, and for the first time in my twenty-five years, I truly understand the term.

The Blake Boden Experiment app—the one I fondly named *Polarize*—of course, continues to support the mental lapse. In the last seven runs, it's yet to produce a result with anything under ninety-eight percent viability of our opposites attracting.

My phone buzzes on the desk, pulling me out of my recycled thoughts. Unfortunately for my dalliance with overconsumption, the sender only adds to the problem.

> **Blake Boden: Just finished weight training. I'm starving. Thinking I might eat you for dinner.**

A blush creeps up my cheeks as I quickly type back a response.

> **Me: I'm at the lab. A little busy.**

I'm not busy with anything but Blake-centric pet projects, clearly, but he doesn't need to know that. Pretty sure, actually, that's data I *need* to keep to myself.

> **Blake Boden: I could come to the lab and enjoy my meal there...**

My fingers hover over the screen as memories of the night we did a lot of dirty somethings in the chem lab down the hall flood my mind. The warmth of his mouth paradoxed by the cold of the lab table underneath. The sureness of his tongue and his hands and his confidence, intertwined with the danger of being discovered at any moment. It was romancelandia-level fantasy at its highest form—and yet, it was just that: fantasy. And right now, I want real.

The smell of Blake's things and the feel of his bed and the opportunity to wake up there, drugged with exhaustion from being together all night in the morning.

Not to mention, risking Dr. Blevin or someone else walking

in on us while we're right in the middle of *getting to know each other* isn't exactly a calculated risk. It's garish and unnecessary, and my practical side knows it.

> **Me: *I'll meet you at your place. Be there in 30 minutes or so.***

> **Blake Boden: *I'll see you soon, Lexi Lou.***

I catch myself smiling at his use of my nickname and shake my head over my own ridiculousness as I start gathering my things to leave. I'm eager and overtly peppy in the most disgusting of simple ways.

The lab door swings open, and Ginger strides in, her arms full of papers and her hair tied up in a messy bun. She smiles at the sight of me and charges dead ahead, freezing my hands mid-reach for my bag.

It's painfully obvious what she's here for, and it isn't the computers.

Without saying a word, she drops a newspaper onto the table beside my bag with a flick of her wrist, settling her free hand on her hip. "Oh, Lexi Winslow," she crows, her voice on sublet from Ricky Ricardo. "You have some 'splainin' to do."

I glance at the paper for context clues before offering an explanation for every transgression I've ever committed, but all I find on the front page is an article on inflation, based on what I'm sure are amateur-hour economics. I immediately scrunch up my nose. "You want me to dissect the current state of the economy and whether inflation is going to lead us into a recession or not?"

Ginger tsks her lips and bends over the table diligently, flipping the paper to the sports section, and there, staring back at me, is my Blake's handsome face. It's a full-page spread, with several flattering photos of him both in action and on the sidelines in focus, and it highlights his importance in the upcoming season if the Dragons are going to have a chance of winning a championship this year.

"Boy, he looks familiar," Ginger muses, tapping the photo with a knowing smile. "Almost as if he's the same Blake you've been hanging out with."

I feel my stomach drop as I scan the article, the warring of pride and prejudice the likes of which even Jane Austen herself hasn't seen. Blake is an incredible, accomplished, talented football player—the spitting image of everything I said I'd never date.

"He does sort of look like him," I say weakly, my joke both pervasive and cagey. Ginger bursts into laughter.

"Girl! He *is* him! You know it, and I know it!" she exclaims, her laughter filling the empty lab. "I can't believe you didn't tell me your Blake is the I Ching of Dickson University. According to this article, he could fight a cobra, score a touchdown, and explain to you in great detail how he did it all at once."

"In my defense, I think you're the only person on campus who doesn't know who he is."

Ginger waves a dismissive hand, nonplussed. "I live in the lab, Lexi, just like you. But you're dating the guy *The New York Times* is raving about, and I'd say that's worth pulling my head out of the sand for—at least, every once in a while!"

Her excitement and support are appreciated, but if I'm completely honest, all it's serving to do right now is make me nervous. Suddenly, the reality of how deep underwater I am has it feeling like the fourth wall is closing in. "It's not out in the open, Ginger, and I don't want it to be. I'm not ready for that."

She must sense my panic because her expression softens, and she places a gentle hand on my shoulder. "It's okay. I get it, Lex. And your secret is safe with me." She smiles softly. "Plus, who am I going to tell? Dr. Blevin? The only thing I do these days is sit in this freaking lab. Pretty sure there's an actual indent from my ass cheeks on that chair over there."

I search her face, and relief washes over me. I trust Ginger. Really, I do, but the idea of anyone knowing the truth about Blake and me feels like handing over a part of myself I'm not ready to share.

My phone buzzes again, and I glance at the screen before thinking better of it.

Blake Boden: *Just ordered tacos from your favorite spot. All your favs. You can dine on them while I dine on you.*

My cheeks flush, and a smile creeps on to my face before I can stop it.

Ginger doesn't miss it. "Girl, if that text is from Mr. Sports Star and he makes you smile like *that*, I'd say there's no reason to keep him a secret."

"There's just a lot more to it than that, Ginger."

"Just don't overthink it, is all I'm saying, okay?"

I nod. "Okay."

"Good." She nods, already moving to set up at her favorite computer. "Now, if you don't mind, I'm going to spend the next several hours beating my head against this keyboard."

I laugh, grabbing my bag and heading for the door. This conversation may have rattled me, but it hasn't scared me straight.

I don't pause. I don't reconsider.

I head straight for Blake's, stupid smile on my face.

———

The sound of water shutting off from the bathroom echoes softly through the apartment, and I glance up from where I'm lounging on Blake's bed, my stomach full of tacos.

A yawn escapes my throat as I hear him moving around in the bathroom.

The air conditioner kicks on and it forces the bathroom door to crack open a little, and a small curl of steam escapes the room. I peer inside the bathroom, through the crack, transfixed by the slivers I get of Blake standing there, completely naked, using a towel to dry off his hair.

He doesn't notice me watching him, but I sure as hell notice the way his muscular body shifts with his movements. I swear, the man has twelve-pack abs, and every single one of them stretches and flexes as he dries his hair.

Surprising myself, I fixate next on the way his cock hangs between his thighs. I've never craved to put my mouth on a man or understood the fascination with men in gray sweatpants. A utility of function, sure. But something to be looked at? I never got the memo. But right now, my body is rewriting its own manual.

My nipples are hard beneath my tank top, and my tongue sneaks out to lick against my lips. My center aches and pulls, willing me to fill it promptly, and my heart pounds at one and a half times its normal rate.

Cocks in general may not affect me, but Blake's certainly does. Wrapping my mouth around him for the first time the other night is a core memory, cemented by the fact that my taste buds can vividly remember every detail of his taste and texture at a simple thought's whim.

Blake hums softly to himself, completely unaware of my gawking and the dirty path my mind has taken, and for some reason, that makes the mouthwatering need for another taste of him even stronger. Before I know it, I'm getting off his bed and walking into the bathroom.

The air is warmer in here, still humid from his shower, and the mirror is fogged at the edges. Blake's back is to me, but when his eyes catch sight of my reflection in the mirror, he freezes—and then his entire presence seems to radiate pure light. His smile is bright, his mood welcoming—he doesn't make me doubt myself for even a moment.

"Need something, babe?" he asks, turning around to face me.

But I don't say anything. I can't. My eyes are focused between his thighs again, and before I can second-guess it, I step forward and get on my knees in front of him. I look up at his surprised face beneath my lashes and reach out to touch his now-hardening cock.

"Lex," he whispers my name, his voice a mix of awe and growing need. I don't squander it. I lean forward and swirl my tongue

around the tip, trialing a taste. It's fresh and manly and personal—
it makes me feel good.

When I suck him into my mouth, his gasp of surprise is deep
and raspy, just like it was the very first time I did this, and it only
emboldens me further.

I feel confident and powerful as I move my mouth up and down
his length. And I savor the way he grows completely hard against
my tongue, letting myself relish the way he feels like silk and stone
against my lips.

When I take him deeper, letting the tip of him tap against the
back of my throat, a guttural groan escapes his throat that causes
goose bumps to roll up my spine and a throbbing ache to form between my thighs.

"Fuck, Lexi. You're going to ruin me, you know that?"

He might think he's the only one who is being affected right
now, but the truth is, I feel like I'm the one falling apart. I don't
think I've ever let myself be this vulnerable with another person in
my life. I feel bare and uninhibited and safe.

So incredibly safe.

It's a far cry from the woman who wouldn't give him her
phone number, and it's all thanks to him. His open and honest
and self-sacrificing pursuit has completely robbed me of my shields,
and when I'm alone with him, I feel no need to put them back up.

And right now, all I really want to do is make *him* feel good.

So, I do.

I feel his body tense beneath my fingertips, and instead of pulling back like I did the first time, my desperation to taste *all* of him
overcomes me. I let him come inside my mouth, and astonishingly,
it feels almost as good as the orgasms he's given me so many times
with his mouth and lips and tongue and fingers.

The logical part of my brain wants to scrutinize every single
second of the intimate interaction, but when Blake lifts me off the
floor and carries me to his bed, I can't focus on anything besides the
fact that he's smiling down at me as he removes my clothes.

"Now, it's my turn," he says, waggling his brows at me as he slides my panties down my thighs.

And when he puts his mouth on me? Well, the logical part of my brain goes straight into sleep mode, leaving only this wild, wanton Lexi that I didn't even know existed at the helm.

Blake Boden has changed me.

My ship is in uncharted waters with an untested captain in charge—who the hell knows where it's going to take me now.

23

Friday, July 4th

Lexi

ust like Memorial Day weekend, Fourth of July at Uncle Brad and Aunt Paula's lake house is always an extravaganza for the Winslow clan. Though, every year, it feels like we're adding more and more people, and speaking from a purely square-footage perspective, that's a miracle.

Everyone is scattered, some inside the house, some swimming in the lake, and some sitting on the deck outside. I pour a glass of my grandma Wendy's famous lemonade into a glass, give her shoulder a friendly squeeze as I pass by her in the kitchen where she cuts up a watermelon, and head out the deck doors to take in the chaos.

All the Winslow family is here. My parents, my brother, all my aunts and uncles—both Winslow and Hayes—Helen, my grandma Wendy and her husband Howard, and all my cousins. Not to mention, my parents' best friends Kline and Georgia and Thatch and Cassie, along with their sons and daughters Ace, Gunnar, Julia, and Evie.

Finn brought Scottie along, and Blake tagged along with Ace—just like he suggested he would two weeks ago—and since Cassie and Georgia both graduated from Dickson too, many years ago, and the guys are all football freaks, everyone has been thrilled with the addition.

If I don't lie to myself, I am too.

Which is categorically insane, considering how much time we've been spending together and how strong-willed I've been about keeping us a secret. In this close of quarters, being as addicted to each other as we are, with this many eyes and ears everywhere, it'll be the eighth wonder of the world if we don't get caught.

As I look down at the lake, I take stock of everything. Looking outward is way easier than looking inward, as it were. Ace and Julia swimming side by side, and even from up here on the deck, the way he looks at her is unmistakable—like she's the only person in the world. His smile is broader, brighter, and his focus on her is unrelenting, like she's gravity itself, anchoring him in place.

Blake told me about the night out at Groove a few weeks ago, when Julia's joke about being pregnant catapulted Ace straight into the big I'm-in-love-with-my-best-friend moment that we've all been silently waiting for one of them to have.

The problem? Ace hasn't told Julia yet. Instead, he's channeled all his energy into something completely Ace-like—overhauling his entire class schedule to match hers for the fall semester. Blake described it with a mixture of amusement and exasperation, shaking his head at Ace's plan to ward off any loser who dares to talk to her.

Frankly, I can't decide if I'm excited or terrified to find out how their fall semester ends up turning out. It feels like it's all going to come up roses or go down in a fiery inferno.

I watch Blake hop out of the water, onto the dock, and I bite my lip to hide my smile when he cannonballs back into the water, purposely splashing a wave of water toward Ace.

Blake resurfaces, laughter spilling from his lips, carefree and alive as he revels in the moment with his friends. Watching him like this, so unguarded and full of joy, I feel it again—that irresistible pull he has on me, one I can't seem to fight, no matter how hard I try.

"You motherfucker!" Ace shouts as he shakes the water out of his hair and swipes a hand down his face. His mom, Cassie, sighs from her current spot on the deck, sitting at the table with my mom and Georgia.

"Is it too late to trade my kids in for new ones?" she asks, and my mom laughs.

"I think the statute of limitations is up on that, Cass."

"The party can officially fucking start!" a booming voice yells from the deck door, startling everyone's attention. Though, with who it is, I'd say that's exactly as he intended it.

Thatch walks out holding a big box of fireworks and wearing nothing but aviator sunglasses and swim trunks that have a smiling bald eagle and the words *Fuck Yeah* on the crotch. His youngest son Gunnar is right behind him, wearing a matching pair of swim trunks and sporting a new haircut—a mullet straight out of *Joe Dirt*.

"Thatch, I swear, if this ends in us having to call the fire department because you and Jude set a canoe on fire, I will cut off your dick," Cassie says.

"Have no fear, Sweet Tits." Thatch winks and pulls a fire extinguisher out of the box. "I've come prepared."

"Yeah, Mom," Gunnar adds. "Chill. We got this."

Both Thatch and Gunnar head down the deck stairs, and Cassie lets out another deep sigh.

"What about trading in my husband?" she asks, her attention back on my mom and Georgia. "Is it too late for that?"

"How's your prenup?" Georgia questions, already smiling at what she knows is a total joke on Cassie's behalf. She and Thatch, while entirely crazy, are meant to be together. Truly, no one else on the planet could put up with them.

"I don't have one."

My mom laughs. "Looks like you're stuck with him."

Cassie groans. But she also smiles as she looks back toward the lake where Thatch is twerking on the dock while Gunnar holds up the box of fireworks in the air. "He is such a fucking idiot. I love him so much."

"Is it just me, or does Gunnar's new haircut have a lot of… party…going on in the back?" Georgia asks, her voice careful as she watches Thatch and Gunnar continue to act like fools down by the lake.

"Georgia, it looks like a mullet because it *is* a mullet," Cassie answers on a laugh. "A terrible fucking mullet that I'm tempted to cut off while he's asleep."

"It's not *that* bad, Cass," Georgia says, always the eternal optimist.

My mom laughs, and she looks across the deck to meet my eyes. Her smile is loving and full of affection, and I can't help but return it. "Lex, how do we feel about Gunnar's new haircut?"

"It's bad," I answer, direct and to the point and with zero regrets about it. Gunnar Kelly's mullet is nothing to admire. It's, at most, rural kid cosplay on a billionaire budget.

Cassie cackles. "Thank you, Lex!"

"I'm sure it's just a phase," Georgia offers, and Cassie rolls her eyes.

"Georgia, sweetheart, I love you so much, but you don't need to sugarcoat my idiot teenage son's life choices," she says with a knowing smirk. "What you should do is offer up some prayers that he gets through high school in one piece and a diploma in his hands."

Georgia laughs. "Fine. Your son's mullet is the ugliest thing I've ever seen. And I'm offering my deepest condolences and prayers."

"Finally." Cassie nods and grins. "That's more like it."

I look out toward the lake again and note that Blake is now sitting on the dock beside Julia and Ace, watching toward the water as Thatch and Uncle Jude and Gunnar row around in a canoe. Their current destination is the other side of the lake, and I silently pray that whatever they have planned involves no actual fires this time.

Though, it is a little concerning that they now have Gunnar as an accomplice. The Fourth they planned a big fireworks show that ended in the fire department having to put out a flaming canoe, Gunnar was too young to join in on the fun.

But now, he's a full-fledged teenager who seems to be a combination of both of his parents' wildest, craziest genetics. No doubt, he's a certified risk for the whole damn planet.

Ace and Julia laugh at something Blake says as he points toward the canoe full of crazy and fireworks, and a part of me wishes I were down there with them, listening in on whatever Blake is saying.

To distract myself from my FOMO-style envy, I pull my phone out of my pocket and discreetly type out a text before hitting send.

> Me: *Whatever you do, don't get in that canoe.*

I suck my lips into my mouth, holding back my smile when his response comes in a moment later.

> Blake Boden: *You worried about my safety, Lexi Lou?*

> Me: *I'm worried about everyone's safety when Thatch and Gunnar have fireworks.*

> Blake Boden: *You want to come down here and go for a swim with me?*

> Me: *Pretty sure that would make it a little obvious to everyone.*

> Blake Boden: *Make what obvious to everyone? That you like me? That you can't resist me? That, faced with the opportunity, your hands have absolutely no choice but to fondle me all over?*

> Me: *Maybe you should stick to the fishing you can do with a pole. We are on a lake after all.*

> Blake Boden: *When it comes to you, Lex, I'm fishing for anything I can get. All the fucking time.*

> Me: **rolls eyes**

> Blake Boden: *Just admit it, Lex. You like me.*

> Me: *Don't be so painfully naïve, BB. It's beneath you. You KNOW I like you, as you have evidentiary support in droves.*

Blake: *clutches pearls* Lexi Lou...are you...talking about all the dirty things we've done in bed while using legal speak??? And is it turning me on?

Me: You DID admit the other night that Legally Blonde *is one of your favorite movies. So, I wouldn't be surprised. Should I continue?*

Blake: FUCK YES.

I start to type out another message, but a hand to my shoulder startles me so much I bobble my phone in my hands.

"Ha, shit. Didn't mean to scare you, Lex," Finn says, his face morphing into a curious but soft smile.

Quickly, I slide my phone into the back pocket of my jean shorts and turn to face both him and Scottie. He stands behind her wheelchair, his hands gently gripping the handles, and Scottie smiles up at me.

"We just wanted to say thanks," she says, and I tilt my head to the side.

"Thanks?"

"Yeah," Finn chimes in. "For talking to your dad about Scottie. He's already reached out and wants to do a consultation when he's back in the States."

"Oh," I answer with a little shrug. "It was no big deal."

"Actually, it *was* a big deal," Scottie says, and she reaches out to gently grip my forearm. "I know the odds of him being able to do anything are probably slim, but any opportunity is an opportunity, you know?"

I nod. "For sure."

But as the words settle in, my gaze drifts back toward the dock, almost instinctively. Blake is there, standing at the edge, his silhouette outlined by the golden shimmer of sunlight reflecting off the lake.

Any opportunity is an opportunity. Scottie's words echo in my head, but they've taken on a completely different meaning now.

The thought of finding secret moments with Blake this weekend—moments hidden away from prying eyes, when it's just the two of us, like it's been night after night in the quiet intimacy of our apartments for the past two weeks—sends a heady rush through me.

And maybe, just maybe, this weekend's secret moments will include the one thing I can't stop fixating on—*having actual* sex *with Blake.*

24

Sunday July 5th
Blake

"I can't believe you talked me into this," Lexi says as I carefully guide the canoe off the dock in the pitch darkness of an eerily still night. "If we end up in the water, I will be so mad at you, Blake Boden."

"I promise we won't." My laugh is quiet as I use the paddle to guide us toward the center of the lake, my sights set on a discreet bank I noticed this afternoon. It's about half a mile from where we are and on the opposite side of the lake, but it's a spot Ace said his dad and Lexi's uncle Jude had cleared out just for their Fourth of July fireworks antics. There are chairs and a firepit and even a fucking electrical outlet they had put in a few years ago so they can play music.

It's well after two in the morning, and after the wild day of celebrating and shooting off fireworks without any casualties, everyone is asleep inside the house.

I was almost asleep too—until I got the text. Lexi's name lit up my phone with the simple demand: *Meet me at the dock.*

Tiredness evaporated, I didn't hesitate to leave a snoring Ace and Gunnar to sneak out of the house and give in to her demands.

"Where are you taking us exactly?" she asks, and I glance over my shoulder to where she sits behind me.

"Just a little spot I know."

"A little spot you know?" She laughs. "How many times have you even been to this lake house, again?"

"Just this once, but I've really gotten the lay of the land."

She rolls her pretty eyes at me, but I just turn around and focus on paddling.

"Only a few more minutes, Lex, and I'll have your grumpy little ass safely on land."

"I'm not grumpy," she counters, her tone sharp with wit. "I'm simply being pragmatic about the probability of our capsizing and sinking to the depths of an unlit lake at two in the morning. Dive teams may find our bodies, but given how much effort I've put into living, that doesn't seem like much consolation."

I smirk but concentrate on easing the canoe toward the bank, careful not to jostle us too much as the front bumps into land. Since her whole ramble was based on the need for me to keep us safe, I think it's a fair use of my skills of prioritization.

Without delay, I hop out, willingly tolerating the water that's soaking my sneakers, and reach forward to lift Lexi into my arms before I grab the blanket I brought from the house and toss it over my shoulder.

"Oh my God!" she exclaims on a giggle. "What are you doing?"

"Keeping my promise," I tell her, smiling down at her as I carry us toward dry land. "After all that complaining from your pretty little lips, there was no way in hell I was going to let even a drop of water get on you."

She rolls her eyes at me again, but fuck, it's so adorable that I can't stop myself from leaning in and pressing my lips to hers. Our kiss lasts longer than I expect, and I have to stop my forward progress because it's so fucking distracting.

A little moan escapes her throat, and I swallow it down as I kiss her harder.

"Lex?" I whisper against her persistent mouth. "What are you trying to do to me here, babe?"

"Convince you to have sex with me."

"Convince me?" I say, leaning back to meet her eyes. I'm smiling like a fool. "I can assure you I'm already convinced."

She just stares at me, her big blue eyes searching mine. "Prove it."

When she asked me to meet her on the dock and I got the idea to come to this bank for privacy, I didn't have this in mind. But I didn't *not* have this in mind either.

Without overanalyzing the whys and hows of holding back from having sex with the fucking girl of my dreams, I know the effort hasn't been made in vain. The looks, the texts, the begging—Lexi has completely left her avoidance in the past, and I know I have taking it slow to thank for the change.

Still, for all the success they've achieved, the past two weeks have been nothing short of a master class in restraint. And even for a guy like me who prides himself on his discipline, Lexi Winslow has tested every ounce of it.

But she's not just another girl. She's not even a maybe-this-could-turn-into-something girl. To me, she's *the* girl.

And once I have her—fully, completely—there's no coming back from it. For me *or* her.

It'll be real, and with the way Lexi's track record with me has been skittish from the start, I can't risk rushing this and losing her.

She's too fucking special to me.

I guide us over toward the chairs that are placed around a small firepit and sit her down in one of them before I remove the blanket from my shoulder and unfold it over the grass. The light of the moon is the only thing that's guiding our movements, but my eyes have adjusted so well to the darkness that I don't miss the way Lexi watches me with already hooded eyes the entire time.

Once I have the blanket spread out, Lexi rises to her feet. She slips off her flip-flops and steps onto the blanket, and with her gaze purposefully locked with mine, she starts to remove her clothes.

Her tank top is first, then her bra and jean shorts. And her black cotton panties are the last thing that leaves her body before she's standing before me, beautifully bared with the glow of the moon bouncing off her naked skin.

"Fuck," I mutter, running a hand through my hair as I kneel down before her. I grip her thighs as I look up to meet her big blue eyes. "You're the most beautiful thing I've ever seen."

A shuddering breath escapes her lungs, and I lean forward to press soft kisses to each of her thighs. I move my lips to her belly and press kisses there too. But eventually, the temptation of her perfect pink pussy is too much for me, and I lift one of her thighs over my shoulder and bury my face between her legs.

She's wet and sweet on my mouth, and I can't stop myself from sliding my tongue inside her to feel how warm and tight she is.

My cock is already hard, damn near capable of cutting through steel, but I focus all my attention on Lexi and how good she tastes and how good she feels and how fucking amazing it is to hear her moans escape her throat.

It's not long before her hands are gripping my hair and she's bracing herself through the waves of her orgasm. Her arousal coats my tongue, and I savor every fucking drop she gives me.

Her body grows lax against mine, and I carefully brace her in my arms as I ease her down onto the blanket until she's lying on her back. And when she blinks her eyes open, locking them with mine, they're hazy and off focus in the best kind of way.

She reaches out to grip the elastic of my shorts, and before I know it, her hand is inside my boxer briefs, stroking my hard cock.

Fuck.

My eyes shut of their own accord, and Lexi takes it upon herself to pull my shorts and briefs down so my cock is bared to the warm, night air.

"I want you inside me," she whispers into my ear, pressing kisses to my neck and face and lips as she continues to stroke me. "I need it, Blake."

Double fuck.

She adjusts her body so she's straddling my hips, her bare pussy taking the place of her hand and just barely brushing against my dick. I look up at her, completely entranced by how fucking beautiful this girl is.

She's everything. *Fucking everything.*

"Do you have contraception?" she asks, and I nod, reaching into the pocket of my shorts to pull out a condom. She snatches it from my hand, tearing the wrapper with her fucking teeth and sliding it down my cock before I can even process what is happening.

But when she starts to lift her hips, her focus solely on getting me inside her, I take control, gripping her waist and flipping her onto her back.

"Are you sure?" I whisper, my lips brushing hers. "Because… you know…we don't have to rush this. We could—"

"Blake," she begs. "Please. We've waited long enough."

Disciplined from years of boot-camp-style football training or not, there's no fucking way I can say no right now. I want this just as much as she does. Hell, I probably want it *more*, but it's not for the pure act of sex itself.

It's because it's *her*.

It's because it's Lexi.

My dream girl. Only in real life, she's better than in dreams.

25

Lexi

The air is warm and sticky against my skin, and I feel a bead of sweat drip down my spine, but I'm too focused on Blake to be annoyed by it.

His body hovers over mine, his cock is perched at my entrance, and a moan escapes my lungs. Needy and desperate and practically coming apart at the seams, I don't even recognize the girl I am right now. I feel frantic and anxious and aroused and a million other things as I simply wait to finally feel him inside me.

But he keeps us like that, one strong hand on my hip, and his face is so close to mine that his eyes look midnight blue beneath the dark sky. He releases my hip, and he reaches up to cup my face, brushing his thumb gently over my warm cheek.

"You're so beautiful," he murmurs, his voice a sexy rasp of seduction and need. "Do you have any idea what you do to me? Do you know that you undo me every time you deign to look in my direction?"

I shake my head, his words slipping into my ears and rolling around inside my mind. The way he's looking at me, combined with what he's saying, makes me feel powerful and confident and sexy in ways I've only ever felt with him.

He moves his big hand from my face to my neck until he starts to trail a path between us with his fingers, moving them from my lips to my chin and between my breasts. I shiver under his touch.

"I don't know if I'll ever get enough of you," he whispers, his lips mere inches from mine. "Every time I get to touch you feels like the first fucking time, but better." He presses a slow and deep and delicious kiss to my mouth. Our tongues dance and another moan escapes my lungs, and my breasts brush his chest with each erratic breath I take.

All I can think is how badly I want to feel him inside me.

I've had sex before, but I've *never* felt this insane with need for the sex to start. I'm overwhelmed and yet, at the same time, completely *under*stimulated. I need to feel him everywhere, on every surface of my skin and in every facet of my senses.

"Please, Blake," I beg against his persistent lips.

Those lips of his curve up into a smile against my mouth. "Tell me what you need, Lex. Tell me, and I'll give it to you."

I grip his chin with my fingers, forcing his gaze to mine. "I need you inside me. Now."

Without breaking eye contact, he presses the tip of his cock inside my entrance. And with the most deliciously slow pace he can manage, he starts to fill me up. A little more and a little more and a little more until I'm so full of Blake, I don't know where he starts and where I end.

He's big, stretching me to limits I've never experienced, but it's right—the perfect kind of intense pressure and pleasure. I've never been with a man as big as Blake. He's well above the statistical average of 5.13 inches erect. Well, *well* above it. I kind of wish I had access to a measuring tape just to get an accurate number.

After all, I do love numbers, don't I?

Blake starts to move himself in and out of me, stroking his cock against my vaginal walls, which massages a spot deep inside me that urges goose bumps to form on my skin.

Blake Boden is the only man whose ever been able to find my Gräfenberg spot—*aka the infamous G-spot.* I've studied that specific area of the female anatomy before, the one that's located inside the vagina and can be highly sensitive and capable of enhancing sexual arousal and orgasm when stimulated. But from everything I'd researched, it's not an easy thing for most men to find or under-stand how to incite.

Clearly, Blake isn't most men.

The more he thrusts, the more he massages the very spot in-side me that only he can find, and the pleasurable tension starts to stretch tight within me like a rubber band.

"It was like I was made to fit inside you." His words melt into my skin as he whispers against my neck. "You are the best thing I've ever felt in my life."

I can't offer a counterargument to his words because I don't disagree with a single thing he says. Sex has never felt like this for me. Not once in my life.

And the more he moves himself inside me, the more intense and overwhelming it all feels. The building pleasure is so intense that I have to shut my eyes because it's the only way I feel like I can stop myself from exploding into a thousand pieces.

Which is crazy, I know. A true impossibility. But it's exactly how I feel. Like, eventually, the pleasure will be too much for my body.

But at the same time, I want more of it. So much, I can hardly remember to breathe.

"More," I pant. "Just like that. God, just like that, Blake. Don't stop."

"I won't stop until you come on my cock," he whispers, his lips brushing mine. He kisses me, locking our mouths in a way that feels synchronized with his cock.

My skin tingles, and a warmth spreads through my entire body. I reach out to grip his shoulders to steady myself, but when it doesn't feel like enough, I dig my nails into his skin and a deep moan jumps from his lungs, his persistent mouth still kissing mine.

My body feels tight, like a bow ready to release an arrow, and Blake leans back to lock his eyes with mine.

"Come for me, Lexi," he demands. "I need to know what you feel like when you come while your pussy is wrapped around my cock."

I don't know what it is about his words, but they flip the switch.

They unleash whatever it is that's been building since the moment he slid inside me.

In an instant, the most intense waves of euphoria wash over me, and sounds I don't even recognize escape my throat as Blake strokes my climax out of me. I can feel myself rhythmically pulsating around his hard length, and his eyes grow hooded and heated as he watches me completely come apart.

The entire time, he keeps thrusting himself inside me, deep and swift moves of his cock, and he doesn't stop until I feel his body tense up beneath my fingertips and hear the raspy growl of his orgasm leave his throat.

I don't know how long it takes me to come back down from my orgasm, but I know when I do, I've never felt more relaxed, more sated, in my entire life.

I've had orgasms before, but I've never had one like this. Never felt anything that was so all-consuming, both mentally and physically.

Even satisfied, I still want more.

26

Monday July 7th
Blake

The instant I step into my apartment, I drop my duffel by the door and slip off my slides. My phone and keys follow, hitting the small island inside my kitchen, and after I guzzle down an entire bottle of water, I head straight for my bedroom.

Coach Gordan ran us like dogs today. And I swear, Coach Jimmen, the Dragons' offensive coach, made me throw over one thousand passes. This year is the first year in over two decades that the Dragons are looking at the possibility of a national title. We came damn close last year, and with the addition of five freshman recruits who have upped both our running game and our offensive line, the entire coaching staff is bound and determined to take us all the way. Even if that means kicking our asses for this entire summer.

And this isn't even Hell Weeks—otherwise known as the two-week-long conditioning we'll be diving into at the beginning of August. We're talking two-a-days that feel closer to training Navy SEALs to go into war than getting a college football team ready for the season.

I yank off my sweaty T-shirt and kick off my briefs and shorts, tossing both haphazardly into the laundry basket across from my bed, and head for the shower. But I don't even get the water turned on before I hear my phone ringing from the kitchen.

Naked as the day I was born, I head out of my room, but I don't make it to my phone in time before the call is sent to voice mail. Though, not even two seconds later, a text chimes in.

Lexi: Are you home?

Instantly, I'm grinning like a fool, and images from the weekend at the lake house surge forward in my mind, unbidden but welcome. The mental reel plays vividly—Lexi's body moving with mine, the soft gasps of her breath against my neck, the look in her blue eyes when she fell apart on my cock. It's enough to steal my focus for a solid minute before I manage to snap back to the present and send her a reply.

Me: Yeah.

I hit send, but when that short response doesn't feel like enough, I send another.

Me: Want to come over?

Lexi: Already here.

A moment later, three soft knocks sound from my door.
Hell yes.

Excitement to see her is the main focus of my mind, and I head for the door, swinging it open with a quick arm. But right before I can reveal the fact that my dick is out, I hold the door precariously in front of me, just kind of peeking my head around the edge of it.

She furrows her cute brow, her blue eyes looking like the fucking ocean beneath the hallway lights. "You have a strange expression on your face."

"Well… I was just about to hop in the shower and…" I tilt my head to the side and glance down at myself pointedly. "I'm not exactly wearing any clothes right now."

"You're naked?"

I cringe, but I also smile. "I am, in fact, naked."

She doesn't bat an eye. Instead, she shrugs and steps inside, closing the door behind her as she does.

And even though I'm just standing here with my dick out, I

can't deny the fact that every time I see this girl, I swear, she gets more beautiful. Her blond hair hangs down her shoulders, and she's wearing this tight-fitting white tank top with jean shorts and sandals. It's a simple outfit, but she makes it look like it belongs on a runway. No joke, Lexi Winslow could make a fucking garbage bag go couture.

She stands in the entryway of my apartment, her gaze not at all shy in looking at me. I'm talking *all* of me. And I can't decide if I should cover my dick with my hands or head into my bedroom to grab some shorts.

But she doesn't give me any time.

Instead, she does the one thing I don't see coming at all.

Straight for me, she slides her hands up my biceps, over my shoulders, and stands on her tippy-toes to lean forward and press a kiss to my mouth. But it's not a chaste kiss or simple touch of our lips. It's deep, passionate, and she slips her tongue into my mouth to dance it seductively with mine.

I'm hard as a rock in exactly two seconds, my cock basically poking her in the belly.

"Lexi," I say, her mouth still gloriously busy with kissing me. "I just got done with football practice. I should probably take a shower."

"You can shower after."

"After?" I question, leaning back to meet her eyes.

"Yeah." She pointedly glances down at my cock, the damn thing just jutting out from my body. "After we have sex."

"That's why you came over?" I tilt my head to the side. "For sex?"

"Yes."

No hesitation. No tripping over her words. Just...*yes*.

"I enjoyed the sex on the lake," she adds and shrugs one petite shoulder. "So, I want to do it again."

I tsk playfully. "Lex, is this your way of telling me you just want me for my body?"

She smiles and shrugs again. "And the pleasure it gives me."

I laugh. I can't help it. And then I pull her into my arms and lift her up until she wraps her legs around my waist.

"I've got an idea," I say as I walk us toward my bedroom. "How about we take a shower together?"

"How are we going to have sex in the shower?" she questions, a little frown creasing her forehead. "The space is cramped, and the water makes it difficult to find a good rhythm where you can activate my G-spot."

"Oh, Lexi," I say, my lips quirking into a grin. "Haven't you learned that I'm a determined kind of guy?" I lean forward to press my lips to hers before walking us into the bathroom. "I'm going to make you come. That's a guarantee. Though, how many times is up for debate."

"I don't think multiple orgasms in one session is realistic, Blake. Statistically, it's not the norm for most women."

"Well, you're not most women, and I'm not most men."

The faintest hint of a smile lifts the corners of her lips.

With her still in my arms, I lean forward to turn on the water, ensuring with a quick hand that it's the perfect kind of warmth.

Her smile grows as I make a show of setting her to her feet and removing her tank top, revealing the white cotton bra underneath. Though, that bra is gone quickly after that, as are her perfect black cotton panties and jean shorts.

And when she's gloriously naked, every inch of her beautiful body on display for my eyes and my eyes alone, I kneel down in front of her. Steam is already billowing from the shower, and I take one of her hands, encouraging her to steady herself on my shoulder as I lift one of her thighs and put it over my shoulder.

"Blake?" she questions, confusion in her voice. But I'm too busy staring at her perfect pussy that's now directly in front of my face.

"Every good athlete knows the importance of the warm-up," I say, glancing up at her with a wink. "Just a little something to make you feel good and limber all the right muscles before I blow your beautiful fucking mind."

I press my mouth against her pussy, giving myself a long moment to inhale her delicious, sweet scent before I slip my tongue inside her. She's soft and warm, and I can feel her get wet against my tongue.

When I hear a small moan leave her throat, I suck and eat at her clit until I can feel her thigh shake against my shoulder. Both of her hands go into my hair, gripping the strands with a strong hold, and I love every single fucking second of it.

It doesn't take me long to bring her to the edge. I've been studying Lexi's body like I'm going to take a final exam on it worth a hundred percent of my grade. I know what she likes and I know what she loves and I certainly know what makes her come.

When her body tenses up like a bow and her fingers threaten to rip my hair out of my head, I keep sucking at her clit, but I let myself look up at her, watching the way her perky tits bounce and the way her eyes fall closed when her first orgasm of the night barrels through her.

It's the most beautiful fucking thing I've ever seen in my life, and if I have anything to say about it, I'm going to make her do that over and over again tonight.

I don't give a shit that every muscle in my body is sore from practice today. I don't give a shit about anything but making Lexi feel good.

Her body goes lax against mine, and I guide us both into the shower. Her eyes are heavy-lidded, her mind still soaring from the orgasm high, and I use that time to let myself touch her skin. I grab some body wash and gently rub it over her arms and her belly and her legs, and I quickly wash myself off as I do.

My cock is still hard, solely focused on the gorgeous woman standing in front of me, but I turn Lexi around and rub the body wash on her back, massaging my fingers into her muscles as I do.

She lets out a little moan of approval, her head falling back as she does, and it only makes me want to touch her, caress her, love her more.

It's not about sex anymore; it's about taking care of someone I love.

Because fuck, I *do* love her.

If I'm honest, I'm fully in love with Lexi, and I have been for a while. Heartbreak at stake or not, there's no going back.

27

I wake up wrapped in warmth, and when I blink my eyes open, I find my body curled against Blake's big, muscular frame—the little spoon to his big spoon. He's still asleep, and I carefully glance over my shoulder to take in his face.

His chest is bare, and his hair is a sleepy but sexy mess. His eyes are shut, and his lashes are thick and long. Those lashes would be a true envy for women who are fixated on their physical appearance, but for some reason, on Blake, they're just right. They're one of many pieces of his alluring puzzle—tested and retested via extensive app—that make him the kind of guy who can pretty much get any girl he wants on campus.

Sure, his persona as the Dragons' star quarterback certainly helps his appeal, but there's more to it than that. Blake Boden is one heck of a specimen for the male species. Not only does his impressive athleticism give off modern-day gladiator vibes, but the way he straddles the line of confident and cocky but down-to-earth and relatable at the same time only adds to his charisma.

The more I get to know him, the less I need an AI algorithm to explain the appeal to me.

Frankly, his sexual prowess alone would take several hours of data entry in Polarize, and I'd much rather spend that time letting him prove his worth via orgasms.

I've never had more than two orgasms in a single session—with my own hands—but last night, Blake gave me *four*. The final orgasm, even more impressively, didn't fall off in intensity at all and, instead, felt like my entire body had been turned inside out.

If only I could create technology that would help men and women alike mimic Blake Boden's appeal, our modern-day society—that's so fixated on social media and popularity and achieving aesthetic perfection—would probably applaud it more than if I'd managed to cure cancer. Who knows, I guess. Maybe, if I'm really lucky, I'll be able to do both. I haven't even officially turned in my dissertation, and I already have big corporations trying to set up meetings with me to discuss the logistics and price tag, so it's not outside the realm of possibility.

I snag my phone off Blake's nightstand to check the time, and when I realize it's quarter to seven in the morning, I carefully slip out from beneath his sleepy embrace and head into his bathroom.

I'm wearing nothing but Blake's oversized Dragons Football T-shirt, and a lazy, satisfied smile stretches across my lips when I see myself in the mirror. Apparently, four orgasms come with an endorphin high that rivals any runner's. I silently wonder if I should consider delving back into my Polarize app and adding an additional hypothesis related to the correlation between pleasure and relationships. *Is there a statistical connection between orgasms and how much a woman wants a man?*

When a woman has an orgasm, is there an internal physiological response that increases her attraction to her mate?

And if that's the case, would relationships last longer and divorce rates go down if more men understood how to give women pleasure?

I shrug and make a mental note to consider playing around with it when I get the chance.

I turn on the faucet to splash some cold water over my face, wafting an unexpected hit of the scent that's coming off Blake's T-shirt up to my nostrils. The scent is a heady combination of warm and spicy, and I'm more than a little curious if whatever cologne he wears is another piece of his captivating puzzle.

Trust me, I know only I would be half dressed in the guy I'm in a secret relationship with's bathroom, trying to analyze the power of scents and orgasms and their implications on modern relationships.

What can I say? I'll live and die by the sword of science.

I take another sniff, and another lazy smile etches across my lips. A warmth spreads beneath my skin, and the urge to bury my face in the T-shirt creates quite the temptation. Clearly, I like his cologne. Instantly, my brain goes back into research mode, already forming another hypothetical I could put in Polarize. *If Blake Boden's proximity is universally appealing, does his cologne play a measurable role in enhancing his charisma?*

And if yes, is a person's choice of scent a significant factor in enhancing their perceived charisma, social appeal, and sexual attraction?

There are an abundance of academia-backed research papers on pheromones I could include in my inputs.

I toss my long blond locks into a messy bun and lean forward to wash my face, but just as I'm drying off with the white hand towel by the sink, two strong hands grip my hips. I peer over the towel to meet Blake's eyes in the reflection in the mirror.

"Big plans for today?" he asks, an adorable grin making his lips quirk up.

"Not too much. Just my usual lab routine." I shrug and turn around to face him. "What about you?"

"Practice in about an hour," he says and steps forward to wrap his arms around my waist. "And then, I was hoping, you know, I'd get to see you again."

His close proximity forces another strong waft of his delicious scent into my nose, and I blurt out, "What cologne do you wear?"

He tilts his head to the side. "What do you mean?"

"I mean exactly what I said. What cologne do you wear?"

"I don't wear any cologne," he says, his eyes glinting with amusement. "That's all Eau De Me."

"Oh my God." I laugh. Outright. "You're so full of it, and you know it."

He grins wider, unapologetic. "I have no idea what you're talking about."

I roll my eyes at him and head back out of the bathroom and into his bedroom. I make no apologies for going straight to his dresser, where I can see a cologne bottle sitting on the top, but I only have the bottle in my possession for exactly three seconds before Blake takes it away from me with teasing hands.

"Ah, ah," he says through a chuckle. "A man needs to keep some secrets."

"Too late," I say, quirking a defiant brow. "Tom Ford Tobacco Vanille."

"Fuck, you're like a speed-reader," he responds, and I try to grab the bottle from his hands again, but he just holds it above his head, a spot that is far too high for me to reach, even if I try to jump.

Though, he is pretty close to the bed, so I hurriedly hop up onto the mattress and dive onto his back. Blake lets out a hearty laugh as I try to steal the bottle of cologne from his hands, but he just stretches his long arm out farther.

"Just let me see it," I say, giggles leaving my lips.

"Why?"

"For research."

"Oh, more research?" he asks and somehow manages to spin my body around so that my legs are wrapped around his hips and our chests are pressed against each other. "You want to kiss me again?"

"I think we're far past the point of kissing, Blake. We had sex three times last night."

He waggles his brows. "You want to do it again? For research, of course."

I roll my eyes at him. "We don't have time. I need to be at the lab. You need to be at practice. And it's been proven in many research studies that men having sex before engaging in athletics weakens their leg muscles."

"I'll just lie back and let you ride me like a cowgirl, no leg muscles involved."

Many dirty images float around inside my head, the teasing offer proving to be an actual temptation for my body. And trust me, I am tempted. But I am also Lexi Winslow, who has an important meeting with Dr. Blevin, and that is something that I refuse to be late to.

"I can't."

"But you want to," he retorts, one sexy eyebrow raised in my direction.

"Sometimes we can't always get what we want."

He leans forward to press a cute kiss to my lips. "See, Lex, that's not something I can go along with. When it comes to you, I want to give you everything you want."

His words hold power, my body and mind reacting to them in ways I don't quite understand.

"Consider it a rain check." He presses another kiss to my lips before slowly setting me back onto my feet. He also hands me his bottle of cologne. "For your research." He winks and heads back into the bathroom.

I stare down at the bottle of cologne, double-checking that I got the name of it right.

Tom Ford Tobacco Vanille

The urge to dissect this cologne's components, to compare its data against the known effects of each scent on human attraction, flares so strongly it's hard to ignore.

I set the bottle back on the dresser and quickly change into my clothes, brushing away thoughts of analysis and data points.

But just as I'm about to leave, I hesitate. I grab the T-shirt Blake let me borrow last night and spray a light mist of the cologne onto it.

Then, without a second thought, I shove it into my purse.

For research, of course.

Saturday, July 12th
Blake

Bonnie Boden looks exactly how I'd expect my mother to look after taking a last-minute trip to NYC to spend the day shopping and have lunch with me. Her hands are full of bags from various luxury stores, and her skin is tanned in the way you only get if you live in Southern California.

"Blake!" she greets with a huge smile when she spots me in the back of the fancy French restaurant she secured a reservation for yesterday when she was busy making her big New York plans. "Oh, it's so good to see you, darling," she says when she reaches the table, and I stand up like the gentleman she and my dad raised to take the numerous bags from her hands. "I swear, I don't know how you tolerate this city on a daily basis."

I nearly laugh. She's so far removed from the *daily toleration* most New Yorkers deal with it isn't even funny. She has a driver, a steady stream of money, and access to reservations at *Maison Fleur*, the kind of French restaurant where the lighting is soft, the linens are pristine, and every waiter wears a pressed black suit. It's intimate without trying too hard—exactly the kind of place my mom loves.

Her light-brown hair is perfectly styled, not a strand out of place, and her cream pantsuit is unwrinkled. She adjusts her oversized sunglasses, and her blue eyes are bright-eyed in a way that says she probably slept like first-class royalty on her red-eye flight here.

Hermès, Louis Vuitton, Cartier, the logos read like a who's who of luxury brands as I set the bags under our table's unoccupied side.

"How are you?" she says, leaning forward to press two European-style kisses to my cheeks.

"I'm good, Mom." I pull out her chair for her to sit down and don't even bother asking her how she's doing because I know it will lead to a lengthy rant about whatever inconveniences she's faced in the past eight hours.

Once she's comfortable in her seat, I sit back down in mine across the table. A menu is already in her hands, and it's not long before she's gesturing for a server to come over to our table.

I give him my order—a steak and vegetable combo—and my mom goes into her usual diatribe of asking him a hundred questions about the menu.

I love my mom. Really, I do. But I also know she's an acquired taste for most people. She's bossy and particular and direct. Not to mention, she was born and raised with a silver spoon in her mouth, paralegaling in her early days as a gateway to marrying a lawyer.

And land one, she did.

Both of my parents are great in their own right, even if they're a little too much when they're together. I've always had a good, close relationship with my mom, and when it comes to advice—whether about friends or girlfriends—she's never steered me wrong.

"What is the white sauce on the escargot made out of?" she asks the server, and he doesn't hesitate to answer her question.

"Butter, cream, garlic, parsley, and thyme," he answers. "It's a very nice accompaniment to the dish."

"Okay." My mom nods and hands him her menu. "I'll take that. And a glass of your best Chardonnay, please."

The server heads off toward the kitchen, and my mom moves all her attention back to me.

"Let me guess," she says with a secret smile as she glances down at my attire of a Dragons Football T-shirt and jeans—clearly out of place in this fancy French scene. "You had football this morning."

"That's pretty much the story of my life." I smirk. "But I did manage a shower before I headed here."

"Well, I certainly appreciate that, Blake." She grins.

"Didn't want to scare any of the clientele in this swanky place."

She rolls her eyes. "If I'm going to do lunch in New York, Blake, I'm going to eat good food."

"And I gave you a great pizza recommendation."

"Pizza?" Her laugh is of the hoity-toity variety. "You know me better than that, darling."

It's my turn to laugh. "I guess I should just be thankful you chose a restaurant close to campus."

"Exactly," she says as the server sets down her glass of wine in front of her. She takes a sip, and my phone vibrates inside the pocket of my jeans. I pull it out to find a text message from the one girl I haven't stopped thinking about since I left her apartment this morning. *The one girl you technically never stop thinking about.*

> *Lexi: I just saw you this morning, and I have two mandatory meetings with my professors today. I have to make a little time in my schedule for things other than you right now and get back to you when I can.*

Her response is in relation to the text I sent her five minutes after I walked out of her apartment door: *When can I see you again?*

> *Me: You're not going to sleep at the lab, though…we could plan on that.*

> *Lexi: I thought standard booty calls came in after 2 a.m. It's not even three in the afternoon.*

It feels like an alternate universe for a brilliant girl like Lexi to even type the word booty call. But damn, it sure does make me want to laugh.

> *Me: No booty call, babe. I just want to see you. Not sure if you know this, but I really like seeing you. Can't get enough of it, actually.*

Lexi: I should be home around nine.

Me: I'll be there.

Lexi: That text was factual, and yet, somehow, you turned it into an invitation.

I can't help the laugh that bursts out of my lungs, and when I glance up, my mom's curious eyes are locked on me. Her perfectly sculpted brow arches, but I just flash her an apologetic smile before looking back down at my phone.

Every so often, Lexi's boldness zings you with that sharp, dry wit of hers. And when it hits, it's like a curve ball out of nowhere.

Me: You didn't invite me? Because it felt like it.

Lexi: I think you're just making assumptions based on what you want.

Me: And what do I want, Lex?

Lexi: I don't know, Blake. What do you want?

Me: You.

My mom clears her throat, and I glance up from the screen of my phone with an apologetic smile. "Sorry about that."

But I also send one last message.

Me: See you at 9.

My mom watches me closely as I shove my phone back into my pocket, and her eyes never stop assessing my face until I reach forward to take a drink of the water I had the server bring me before she got here.

"What?" I eventually ask, and my mom's face splits into a knowing smile.

"Who were you just texting with?"

"Just…a friend."

"A friend makes you smile like that?" She arches that brow, her tone teasing. "Because that looked like more than a friendly smile, darling."

"Is this your way of asking me if I'm seeing someone?"

"*Are* you seeing someone?"

"I am," I admit, but when she starts to open her mouth—no doubt ready to bombard me with a hundred questions—I hold up a hand. "But we're keeping our relationship on the DL."

"The DL?"

"Down-low."

"What in the world does that mean?"

"It means we're not telling anyone about it yet."

"And why would you do that?"

Her question catches me off guard. At first, I understood the secret-keeping, but at this point, I'm just going along with it because I've been asked to.

It's not what I want. It's not even who I am.

Truth is, I've been so wrapped up in spending time with Lexi that, outside of football, I haven't even considered the other things our relationship has made me give up.

I haven't been attentive to my friends or my teammates—other than Lexi, I haven't spent much time with anyone at all. Ace alone has sent me at least fifty texts this week, begging me to hit up some random party or club with him. I've said no every time, even knowing he's neck-deep in his I-just-realized-I'm-in-love-with-my-best-friend crisis. It's a dick move, and I don't like the weight of the realization as it hits me.

"It's just all really new," I finally answer, hoping it'll be enough to stop her from digging further, but my mind doesn't quiet. I don't want to hide in the shadows of our apartments anymore. I want us to be out in the open. Official.

I deserve to be treated as though I'm real, and my friends deserve my honesty and respect.

"Do you like her?"

"Yeah," I admit. "I like her."

That's the whole problem with my newfound bravado. *I love her.*

"So…do you think this secret relationship is going somewhere?"

"It definitely has potential." In fact, it has so much potential, I'm dead certain I don't want to be with anyone else. *Ever.*

The server arrives with our food, thankfully pulling my mom's attention away from her interrogation, but it's too late for me. I'm down the rabbit hole with no escape.

I want to be with Lexi. And I want the whole fucking world to know it.

Which means I have to find a way to convince her to feel the same.

No matter what it takes.

29

Lexi

I walk out of my bathroom to a tangle of muscular, peachy-tan limbs in my bed. Blake's chest is bare, and while the comforter covers his lower half, I'd bet good money he hasn't bothered putting on anything down there since our latest round of sex ended just over an hour ago either.

I pause for a second, letting my gaze linger on him longer than I probably should. He looks so at ease, so utterly Blake, that something stirs inside me—something I can't quite name and don't know if I want to examine too closely.

I'll admit it—spending time with Blake isn't research anymore. It's something else entirely that feels too big, too abstract, and too subjective for me to wrap my brain around just yet.

All I know is that he's *different*. Not just from other guys or relationships past, but from the world at large from my place on "the spectrum."

He doesn't leave me feeling drained or overstimulated the way most people do, instead, filling me with longing and a quiet ache I'm not used to and don't know how to make sense of.

There's no logic to lean on, no data to analyze, just emotions I don't know how to control, swirling around in a way that excites and intrigues and outright terrifies me.

He's the one person who manages to sneak past all my defenses, the one who makes me laugh more, smile more, feel more. And yet, I keep telling myself I'll deal with it later, that for now, I can be content to enjoy the companionship at no cost to myself or anyone else.

It's a lie.

For every action, there's a reaction, and my actions, while self-serving right now, will have consequences I'm wholly unprepared to face. I'm too smart not to know it.

But being smart doesn't protect you from willful ignorance, a human compulsion I'm manifesting in spades these days.

"Penny for your thoughts?" Blake asks, pulling me out of my own head and crashing me straight into the present.

"I always have a lot of thoughts," I reply, and he grins, shifting to rest his back against my headboard. He folds his arms behind his head, the movement effortless yet impossible to miss. The flex of his biceps draws my eye, a not-so-subtle reminder of just how much time he's spent perfecting his throw.

Statistically, if I had to estimate, I'd say Blake Boden has thrown at least ten thousand passes in his life. Though, to be fair, that's purely speculative based on some quick math of averages. To know the exact number, I'd need every detail of his practices, training sessions, and games from the moment he first held a football. And something tells me even Blake wouldn't know that number.

"And you're still having lots of thoughts," Blake teases, his grin turning into an amused smile that's directed solely at me.

I glance down at my feet, my mind still spinning with how one person has managed to take up so much space in my brain. It's… confusing. I normally reserve that space for data.

When I realize I'm still standing here, at the threshold of my bathroom door with Blake watching me curiously, I force myself to change the subject of my thoughts entirely. "And you're looking very comfortable in my bed."

"I am." He waggles his brows. "I really like your bed. Especially when you're in it too." He pats the open spot beside him, even adjusts the comforter to give me room to climb in. "How about you join me?"

Describing a man as adorable feels like it goes against the societal pressure to see men as men, but I can't deny that Blake's boyish grin is looking all kinds of adorable right now. It's an attractive look, but at the same time, it makes me feel like I'm going into battle without any armor.

"You look like you're planning to stay the night," I remark, climbing back into my bed beside him. I adjust his T-shirt that is currently covering my body over my bare butt as I do.

"Of course, Lexi. Thanks for asking. I'd love to spend the night with you."

I snort. "That wasn't an invite."

"It wasn't?" he questions and wraps his arm around my shoulders, tucking me close to his side. "Are you sure?"

I roll my eyes, looking up to meet his gaze as I do. "You're going to have to learn some new tricks, little puppy dog. Most girls use their memory as a superpower."

"I don't care about *girls*."

I flash him a pointed look.

"Well, at least not anymore." He presses a kiss to my forehead. "Lexi Lou Winslow is the only girl I care about now."

"I think you're spouting bullshit, Blake," I challenge him. "It's a known fact of life that men enjoy looking at other women. Even married men."

"Enjoying seeing a pretty girl pass by and only wanting to be with one beautiful girl are two different things, Lex."

"You really think I'm beautiful?" I ask, searching his eyes closely as I do. I've heard him say that word in the heat of the moment, but this feels different for some reason. I know I have aesthetically pleasing features, but I've never been very busy with my looks. I let my mom choose my clothes and how I'd wear my hair, and when I was sixteen and getting ready to go to prom with Connor, I even let her do my makeup.

When I started college, I repeated her routine, step by step, just as she'd taught me. I know hair and makeup and clothes are big priorities for most women my age, but they're not even on my radar.

"It'd be easy to say yes here, Lex, but fuck if that truly conveys what I'm trying to say at all. And yet, I don't know if you're ready to hear how I really feel about you."

A strange sensation fills my chest, even vibrating like a rocket down to my belly and my toes. It's such an off-putting feeling that I have to swallow hard against it just to find my equilibrium again.

I kind of want to forget this conversation altogether, but something deep down is urging me to ask.

"Well, ready or not, it's out there now, I think. So, Blake…how *do* you feel about me?"

"Lexi…" Blake searches my eyes for a long moment. He even presses a kiss to the top of my head, his lips brushing against my hair as he does. "I think you're the most beautiful, intelligent, intriguing, amazing woman I've *ever* met in my life. I don't think there's anyone on this continent, or any other, who could rival you in any or all those things. I think you are the sum of greatness in human form, and I find myself increasingly desperate, every fucking day, to convince you to be mine."

"You want me to be your girlfriend?"

He laughs, a dry, quick rebuttal to the simplicity of my statement. "More than *anything*."

"I…don't know what to say to that," I say, but my voice is so quiet I can hardly hear it over the hard pounding of my heart.

"Say you want to be official, out in the open, where everyone knows that you're my girl and I'm your guy."

"Blake." My voice is a whisper.

"You don't need to say anything right now. I know you well enough to know you need time to process." Blake smiles down at me, reaching up to brush a rogue piece of hair behind my ear. "Just think about it."

My brain takes his edict as permission, diving right into an in-depth analysis.

Blake is four years younger than me. He's still in college. After this summer is over, I'll be done with college and starting whatever

career path I end up choosing. Our lives are entirely disproportion-
ate in almost every aspect, and yet, I feel happiest when I'm with
him.

There are so many things I want to do and accomplish—so
many goals I'm setting out to achieve—and I've already proven Blake
is more than a simple distraction I can brush off.

I have a feeling I could spend the rest of the night creating
a spreadsheet that weighs out all the pros and cons, and it still
wouldn't be enough to be conclusive.

"And while you're thinking on it," Blake says, pulling my attention back to him. "Why don't you lie back and relax, and let your
body feel."

"Feel?"

"Feel."

When he puts his mouth to my clit, the thoughts in my head
vanish in a dramatic poof of nothingness.

Just as he intended, all I can do is feel.

30

Blake

"**A**rkansas!" Coach Gordan yells from the sidelines as first string lines up against second string on our practice field. We're already two hours into this morning's training session, and my T-shirt is soaked under my pads. It's a balmy ninety degrees in New York, and the sweat dripping down my brow beneath my helmet proves it.

"Set! White 80!" I call toward Nick Fisher, my center. "White 80!" I repeat, giving Nick the final confirmation.

He snaps the ball, but it just might be one of the shittiest snaps he's ever given me.

It takes me a hot second to get a good grip on the ball in my hands, and I can hear the helmets and pads of my O-line crashing against the defense.

I drop back three steps, fake a handoff to Drake Martin, the Dragons' top running back, and it pulls enough of the defense's eyes that I have the time I need to look downfield.

One of my receivers is fighting for his life against Ryan Clark, a freshman walk-on from Texas who I have a feeling will end up gaining a starting spot by midyear. And my other receiver, Danny Ash, is dragging some serious ass. *Fuck me.*

My O-line is losing steam, and when I spot a big, burly defensive end heading my way, I know I'm in for a world of hurt. Quickly, I look at my options again, and when I see that Danny's managed to run a route that's given him some space from his defender, I send a rocket his way.

Though, what I don't account for is how close the defensive end is to me, and with one lift of his arm, he tips the ball and sends it ricocheting toward the sidelines.

Immediately, a hard whistle is blown.

"What the fuck was that, Boden?" Coach Gordan shouts at the top of his lungs. "Please fucking tell me you know Arkansas stands for a simple fucking play-action pass and not a goddamn interception!"

"Sorry, Coach," I apologize, fully prepared to take whatever ass-reaming Coach Gordan deems I deserve. Sure, there was a lot more bad shit that went down with that play than my nearly intercepted pass, but I'll never be that guy who tries to throw his teammates under the bus to save himself.

Any quarterback who lets himself be that guy isn't a fucking quarterback at all. A QB's job is to be the leader of the team, and when mistakes are made, he holds himself accountable.

Coach sighs, glaring at me from the sidelines, but when one of the defensive coaches calls for his attention, he waves an annoyed hand in the air, blows his whistles, and says, "Take fifteen!"

"Sorry about that snap, man," Nick says as we jog toward off the practice field.

"Don't sweat it, Nick." I give him a hearty pat on the shoulder.

Everyone stops at the cooler, guzzling water and bottles of Gatorade as quick as they can.

"Worst part about football is training in the dead of fucking summer," Drake comments, taking off his helmet to squirt water on his face.

"Dude," Bear Donahue says through a sigh. He's one of the big guys on our O-line, a man I'm thankful for one hundred percent of the time. Well, unless he lets my ass get sacked.

"Yo, Clark," I say, grabbing the attention of the freshman. He looks up from his spot on one of the benches, an empty Gatorade bottle in his hands. I don't hesitate to walk over to him, briefly giving him a pat on the shoulder. "I see you out there, man. Keep it up."

He smiles at me, both gratefulness and surprise making his eyes squint. "Thanks, Boden."

I give him one final pat to the shoulder and head over to my duffel that's sitting in the shade behind the benches. The rest of the team continues to bitch and moan about the heat—can't say I blame them—but as I guzzle down an entire bottle of water, I'm also pulling my cell phone out of the front pocket of my bag.

I frown. I only have a few texts from Ace and Finn, and all hope of hearing from the one person I really want to hear from goes out the window.

I swipe up to my ongoing text chat with Lexi and smile like a fool when I briefly read through some of our most recent texts.

> *Me: Lexi Lou Winslow, would you do me the honor of being my girlfriend?*
>
> *Lexi: No.*
>
> *Me: Would you possibly enjoy coming over to my place tonight so I can lick your pussy?*
>
> *Lexi: Oh my God, Blake.*
>
> *Me: So, yes?*
>
> *Lexi: I didn't say yes.*
>
> *Me: But you said, "Oh my God, Blake." Which seemed like a "Hell yes, I'm super excited to have you lick my pussy tonight" kind of oh my God.*
>
> *Lexi: Quite the postulation you made there.*
>
> *Me: And was it correct?*
>
> *Lexi: I'll be done at the lab tonight around 8:30.*

Me: See you then, babe.

That was last night. And it certainly did not disappoint. Neither did the night before that nor the night before that nor the night before that.

Any free time I have, especially at night, I spend with Lexi. Sometimes I stay at her place, sometimes she stays at my place, but every morning for the past seven days has involved me waking up with her in my arms.

She's a tough—insanely intelligent—nut to crack, but I'm bound and determined to show her why we'll be so damn good together.

Which is why, as much as I've wanted to, I haven't spammed her with any messages this morning.

She doesn't need a man riding her ass. She needs a man who is willing to stand on her sidelines, cheering her on and supporting her in the ways that she needs.

And fuck, do I want to be that man for her.

Fingers to the keys, I type out a message.

> *Me: I'm done with training at noon. I'm going to drop off lunch to you at the lab. Your food should be there around 12:30.*
>
> *Lexi: And how would you even know what I want?*
>
> *Me: Burger with ketchup only. Side of fries, but well-done. Coke, but no ice.*
>
> *Lexi: LOL. Are you keeping spreadsheets of my favorite foods?*
>
> *Me: I don't need spreadsheets, Lex. You're my favorite subject.*
>
> *Lexi: I can't decide if that line is cheesy or cute.*

Me: Pretty sure it's a healthy combo of both.

"Back on the field!" Coach Gordan shouts, blowing his whistle right after his words. I hustle to send Lex one final text before I get my ass reamed.

Me: Gotta get back to practice. See you at 12:30 p.m., babe.
PS: Will you be my girlfriend?

Her response is instant.

Lex: Sounds great. No.

Me: But will you sleep over at my place tonight?

Lex: Yes.

Another night with Lex in my arms means another chance to convince her to give in. One of these nights, she's going to realize we're made for each other.

31

Zip's Diner is alive with the warm hum of chatter, the clinking of silverware against plates, and the faint scent of burgers and milkshakes lingering in the air. The place is filled with everyone who loves and cares about Scottie Bardeaux: my mom and stepdad Wes, the rest of the Winslow family, Finn's mom Helen and all his siblings, Scottie's cheerleading teammates, Kline, Georgia, Thatch, Cassie, and even Scottie's dad, sister, and—surprisingly— her mom, despite the rocky relationship I know they've had.

The lights twinkle above us, adding to the festive atmosphere as the group waits in hushed anticipation. And the moment Finn pushes Scottie through the front doors, the room bursts to life, everyone, including me, shouting in unison, "Surprise!"

Ace and Julia and Kayla stand at the front, ready to greet her. And Blake is there too, a big, breathtaking smile etched on his handsome face. I don't miss the way a few of the girls from the Dragons' cheerleading squad flit toward the star quarterback, their eyes aflutter with overzealous flirtations.

Everyone on campus knows Blake Boden, but none of them know him quite like I do.

Maybe one day, if I can ever get over myself or if he ends up on the Mavericks like it seems as if he might…maybe one day, everyone will see all the things I do because I let them.

Scottie's eyes are as bright as a fully lit Christmas tree when her mind starts to process what is happening, and when she spots

Blake and Ace and Julia and Kayla, she exclaims, "What? I thought you were all out of town!"

A big smile covers her lips, and she also glances over her shoulder to where Finn stands behind her chair. "This is your doing?"

He nods proudly. "Yep."

From my spot in the back corner of Zip's Diner, I can't make out what else they say to each other, but whatever it is, it earns an equally big smile on Finn's normally stoic face. He even leans down to whisper something into her ear that makes her cheeks blush pink, and he presses a kiss to her lips.

If I compared this version of Finn to the version of Finn I first met nearly a year ago, I would hardly recognize him.

He's calmer. More relaxed. His smiles come easier, and he doesn't look like a guy who is walking around with a proverbial chip on his shoulder. He's *happy*.

I know his family life has changed dramatically, with his dad behind bars and his mom and siblings in a better school district and better house that's located in a safer part of town than where they were living.

But there's more to Finn's happiness. It's written all over his face, the real-life embodiment of the heart-eyes emoji as he watches Scottie move through the crowd, getting hugs and "happy birthdays" from friends and family alike.

A hypothesis instantly takes shape in my mind: **Could love be defined as finding genuine happiness in someone else's joy? Is that the true measure of connection—when their happiness feels inseparable from your own?**

The problem with my hypothesis, of course, is the same as always—the subject of love itself. It's abstract, elusive, and defies the laws of logic in ways that can't be studied, even by me.

It's the part of it I hate the most, and yet, it's the very thing that makes it so special. Love *can't* be analyzed or duplicated—it's recklessly intrinsic.

That doesn't stop me from picking my new conjectures apart.

I look across the room to where my mom and stepdad stand chatting with Uncle Remy and Aunt Maria, and I don't miss how my stepdad embraces my mom or how my mom's hand never seems to leave its gentle spot on his chest.

And when I think about all the moments growing up that I've seen my mom or stepdad at their happiest, not a single event or memory is one where their happiness was solely wrapped up in themselves.

A visual of the way Wes looked down at my mom after she had delivered my little brother Wes Jr. into the world is permanently etched inside my brain. He had tears in his eyes, and he looked like a man who was in absolute awe of his wife.

Feeling and understanding other people's emotions is always a challenge for me, but in that hospital room with my baby brother in my mother's arms and Wes looking at my mom like his whole world was her, I felt the strangest urge to cry. Wes's emotions were raw and cutting in a way even I couldn't deny.

My gaze drifts back to Blake. He's hugging Scottie, and whatever he says has her laughing, her smile wide and infectious. I catch my own lips twitching, an almost involuntary smile threatening to appear. But before I can even begin to dissect what that reaction means, a gentle hand lands on my shoulder, startling me out of my thoughts.

"Sorry," a guy with dark-brown hair and chocolaty-brown eyes apologizes with a gentle smile. "I'm Adam Houth, one of the physical therapists who is working with Scottie at the Hodge Clinic."

Confusion over why this guy is talking to me right now tugs at my expression, but I quickly compose myself and offer what I hope passes as a friendly smile. "It's nice to meet you. I'm Lexi Winslow."

"I know who you are," he says with a slightly self-conscious grin. Adam is an aesthetically attractive guy and looks to be a year or two older than me, but other than that, he's just another man.

"You do?"

He nods. "Scottie loves showing pictures of her family and friends when she's trying to procrastinate on her PT sessions."

I snort. "I can't say I blame her. I know her PT sessions are brutal."

"They are," he admits. "But she's strong."

"Yes. She is." There is no denying that Scottie Bardeaux is strong. After everything she's been through with her family life and her devastating spinal cord injury, she's more than proven her strength and tenacity.

"So, your father is Dr. Nick Raines?"

I nod again. "Yes."

"I had the pleasure of having a Zoom meeting with him last week," he updates. "He wanted to know Scottie's current PT schedule and progress and was telling me about his plans for a consult with her next week when he's back from Germany."

Everything he's telling me is stuff that I already know. And when I don't say anything, he adds, "Dr. Raines is a brilliant man."

"He is considered one of the best neurosurgeons in the country and even most Western European nations."

"Yeah," Adam replies through a soft laugh. "That definitely makes sense. I mean, he gave me a basic rundown of a few of the options he felt might be a possibility for Scottie. Though, he prefaced that he couldn't be sure until he ran more tests." He shrugs and runs a hand through his hair. "Not going to lie, I had a hard time digesting it all."

I tilt my head to the side. "What was hard to digest?"

"Well…" Another soft laugh leaves his lips. "Just about all of it, honestly. But I mean the part about some kind of molecular inhibition technology."

"You mean the NVG-291?"

"Yeah." Adam smiles. "That."

"Basically, when someone suffers a spinal cord injury, chondroitin sulfate proteoglycans collect at the site of injury and create scar tissue that prevents any type of axonal growth and natural nerve regeneration," I explain what already feels very straightforward to me. "NVG-291 is utilized to mitigate those inhibitory effects and aid in the nervous system working to repair itself. There's been a lot of success with this technology in small clinical trials too. It's proven to reactivate important regenerative processes, including axonal regeneration, remyelination, and enhanced neuroplasticity, which are vital for repairing nerve damage and restoring lost functions in patients with spinal cord injuries."

Adam's eyes go wide for a moment, his lashes fanning against his cheeks several times in the process. "Are you in residency for neurosurgery?"

"Oh no." I shake my head. "My interests are more research- and lab-focused. Particularly, focused on computer science and artificial intelligence."

"Well, it's safe to say you're definitely Dr. Raines's daughter." Adam smiles and runs a hand through his hair. "You know, if you ever want to come to one of Scottie's PT sessions or grab lunch or coffee, I'd love to pick your brain some more."

"Thanks, but no. Neuroscience isn't my specialty."

The dismissal is swift, easy, and painless—at least for me. I don't feel bad or war with my decision, and I don't have any trouble being the stalwart girl I've always known myself to be.

And isn't that an interesting tidbit of research?

As it turns out, Blake Boden is the only guy I can't turn down.

32

Blake

Zip's Diner is packed to the brim, Scottie's surprise birthday party in full swing now that the guest of honor has arrived, and the noise and activity are teeming with sensory input.

But *my* eyes have only a singular direction of focus—to the darkest corner by the back booth, where Lexi stands talking to some douchebag I've never seen before for the sixth consecutive minute.

I try to distract myself, heading over to where Finn and Ace stand to greet Finn and let them redirect my thoughts so I don't do something stupid like walk right over there and tell that guy to take a fucking hike. But my mind is so fucking one-track, instead of joining their ongoing conversation about pulling off Scottie's big surprise, I start a new one of my own—topic: motherfucker in the back corner with my girl.

"Who's that guy?" I ask, and Finn shakes his head in confusion.

"What guy?"

"Seriously? The one talking to Lexi." Frustration finds its way into my veins, but Ace, the asshole, laughs.

"You're fucking intense right now, Boden."

"I don't care." I look at Finn. "I need to know who he is."

"He works at the Hodge Clinic, dude," Finn finally explains. "He came because he's been working a lot with Scottie. Just wanted to give her his support."

I nod. *Okay, okay.* That's not as bad as I thought. Though, I still don't like the way he's smiling at Lexi and watching her with fucking awe in his eyes as she talks.

Say hello and move on, fucker.

Finn's hearty laugh fills my ears. "You know you sound a lot like a jealous boyfriend right now, right? For a girl who won't give you the time of day."

His words ricochet inside my chest, striking me first with pain, and then following up with audacity. *A girl who won't give me the time of day? Ha.* If only they knew that most nights, that beautiful, perfect, intriguing-as-fuck girl is in my arms, my mouth, and my hands.

Too bad you can't tell them that. Can't tell anyone *that, in fact.*

I brush off the thought and choose to focus on the positive— behind closed doors, Lexi Winslow *is* my girl. Every part of her.

Both Ace and Finn are looking at me curiously, and I just lift one nonchalant shoulder. "We must not allow other people's limited perceptions to define us, Finnley," I comment through a secret but knowing smile. "There are things known and there are things unknown, and in between are the doors of perception."

"The fuck did you just say?" Ace asks, and Finn cracks up.

I shake my head. "Never mind. I'm going in."

"You're going in? What does that mean?" Ace tosses back, but it's too late. I'm already on the move, striding across the restaurant and heading straight for Lexi.

I may have intimate knowledge of all the ways Lexi Winslow is already mine, and I may be secure in that—but I'll be damned if I'm going to let that fucker have ten more minutes of unfettered access to the brilliant recesses of her mind. I want to hear her theories and musings and data for myself.

"You're incredibly intelligent," the douchebag says to her, Lexi-inspired stars in his stupid eyes, as I approach. He's in deep— the admiration for her genius sinking in one nugget of information at a time—and it won't be long before he's groveling for more. I know, because that's exactly what happens to me anytime I'm around her.

"Lexi Winslow is the smartest girl you'll ever meet in your life," I correct as I join their conversation uninvited, startling both Lexi's attention and beautiful blue eyes. I purposely but calmly position myself between her and the physical therapist as I smile down at her. "Hi, Lex."

I don't wrap an arm around the small of her back, and I don't place a kiss to the soft skin behind her ear—I know she wouldn't approve. But my presence is commanding, my intention clear. Just like on the field, I'm unrattled and in control, even if I can't run the plays I want.

"Hi…" She tilts her head to the side, and her eyebrows crease in the center as a warning. I smile, knowing confidence is the best and only approach in situations like these.

"Who's your new friend?" I ask, and she blinks a few times, searching my steady gaze for insecurities I won't bare.

"Blake, this is Adam Houth," Lex introduces us. "He's one of Scottie's physical therapists at the Hodge Clinic."

I nod and glance briefly at Adam to offer a half smile, holding out a strong hand. "Nice to meet you. I'm Blake Boden." *Lexi's fucking boyfriend.* I clear my throat. "Glad to have you here to celebrate Scottie."

"Nice to meet you too, man," Adam replies, but I'm already looking back at Lexi, ignoring him completely.

"You need anything, Lex?" I ask, playing the role of boyfriend in all ways but the physical. "Something to drink?"

"No…thanks. I'm good, Blake."

"Okay," I say with a flash of a smile and a coy wink that makes a blush steal across her high cheeks. "Let me know if that changes."

She glances between me and Adam with a flutter of lashes, but in almost no time at all, she's once again staring at me. Her chest rises and falls quickly, and her tongue peeks out to wet her now-dry lips. She's craving me, just as I'm craving her, and it's all she can do to hold back the will of her body as she fights it.

It's all I need to see to feel confident in leaving her here to talk to Adam—in leaving her to talk to any stupid, awestruck fucker at this party. I spin on my heel and head back to where Finn and Ace stand, renewed and at ease.

The idea of some other schmuck flirting with her, going out with her, *touching* her, is skin-itching. But from what Lexi just showed me, I don't have anything to worry about. She wants me just as much as I want her—even if she isn't ready to publicly admit it.

"So…?" Ace urges. I shrug and slide my hands into my jeans pockets, a teasing smile lifting just one corner of my mouth.

One good thing about keeping this secret from my friends is that it makes them fucking with me over my rejection much more tolerable.

"I obviously asked her to share our love with the world, and she very graciously said no."

"What?" Finn blurts out on a snort. "Get real. You got rejected."

Ace is nearly wheezing from laughter. "Why do you look so happy about that and, please, even more than that, why are you talking like a fucking poet tonight?"

I briefly glance over at Lexi again, who is no longer talking to Adam, but instead, chatting with Ace's parents, and I can't stop the smile that spreads across my face. "Because it's only a matter of time."

Ace and Finn both look at each other in confusion.

"Mark my words," I add confidently. "That girl will be mine."

"Finn. Help me out here," Ace says. "Bring this man back down to earth."

"Dude, I can't judge," Finn responds. "I spent four weeks in hospital waiting rooms for Scottie."

"That's what I'm saying." I wrap my arm around Finn's shoulder. "When you know, you fucking know. Right, Finn?"

"When you know, you know," Finn agrees.

And trust me, I *know*. Lexi is the only girl for me.

I pull a naked Lexi closer to my chest, and everything feels right with the world.

It's only a little after nine, our usual nighttime habits moved up a few hours because Scottie's party at Zip's made Lex take a day off from her evening lab routine, and while I was a little worried she'd be gun-shy about getting together after I cut into her conversation with Adam at the party, she's been nothing but proactive since her first text around six when I was getting back to my place.

Are you at home? she asked.

To which I responded, **Yep. Just waiting for you to get here.**

She showed up thirty minutes later.

Confidently setting the hook and letting her take the line out, it seems, has worked just as I'd hoped—I pull her tighter in my arms, reeling her in and smelling the top of her hair.

Sex is always incredible with Lexi, and this time was no exception. She's this perfect combination of innocent and uninhibited. She's direct in the best ways, telling me the things she likes and doesn't like, and she dives headfirst into her pleasure.

I fucking love it.

But that shouldn't be a surprise either because I fucking love *her.*

If only you could tell her.

I lean my head back slightly and slip my fingers under her chin, pulling her gaze to lock with mine. Her eyes are still a little hazy, but I don't let that deter me from dancing around my truth a little.

"I like you, Lexi."

"I like you too, Blake."

"Actually, I *really* like you, Lexi." I up the ante a little. "I'm talking *a lot* of liking you. Like, a lot."

"Okay…" She scrunches up her nose. "Is this some kind of riddle I'm supposed to solve?"

"No riddles." A soft laugh leaves my lips. "But I do have a question."

She quirks her brow.

"Will you be my girlfriend?"

"Blake." She flashes a knowing look. "We've already been through this."

"Have we?" I question. "Because it feels like there are a lot of unspoken things happening between us related to our secret relationship but not a hell of a lot of spoken ones. Maybe we *need* to talk through it in scientific terms, if you will. You eggheads usually love the details, don't you?"

She searches my eyes for a long moment, and I'm on pins and needles, wondering what her response to that is going be.

"You want to know a secret?" she eventually asks, and it's my turn to search her eyes.

"I'd love to." *Because I love you.*

But she doesn't respond with words. Instead, she leans forward to press her mouth to mine. Her kiss starts out soft and slow until a little moan escapes her throat, and she adjusts her body so she's on top of me. Her thighs straddle my hips, and my bare cock is already growing hard again when she grinds herself against me.

"I'm on birth control now. Have been for a full cycle," she whispers toward me before kissing me again. "And right now, I want to know what it feels like to have you inside me…bare."

Fuck. Little Blake with the rapidly swelling head is happy—undeniably, physically so—but Big Blake is devastated that she's completely avoided the entire subject of our relationship.

When she starts to grind herself against me some more and then begins to slide the tip of my cock inside her, my brain fucking buffers over how good she feels, and Little Blake officially wins.

"Lex."

"Please," she begs, and I'm too far gone on this girl to deny something she wants.

So, I slide myself inside her a little deeper. And a little deeper. And a little deeper until I'm pressed to the hilt. She's warm and tight and fucking perfect, and I have to hold my breath for a good ten seconds just to keep myself from coming on the fucking spot.

"It feels so good." She lets her head fall back, and her breasts bounce up and down with each panting breath.

"*You* feel so good," I tell her and reach out to grip her hips, guiding us into a slow rhythm.

Her eyes meet mine again, and I swear, for the briefest of moments, I see her rare vulnerability. I see the way a sheen of emotion coats her beautiful eyes. In that moment, I know again, just like I did when I interrupted her with Adam this afternoon, I'm not the only one who has feelings.

She has feelings too. *For me.*

I'm going to do everything I can to make her mine, starting right now, with fucking her raw.

St. Luke's Medical Facility smells like antiseptic and memories as I head straight for the elevator, ride up five floors, and follow my dad's quick text instructions on where to find him.

After our reconnection, I spent nearly Meredith-Grey-level amounts of time in these halls, meeting my bio dad for lunch or hanging out in his office when he had to work weekends. He wanted me around, in any way I could be, even when he was called to duty fixing people. I resisted at first, but the more he reached out, asking to see me for any amount of time I'd be willing, the more I started to cave. By the time a couple years passed, the hospital became my second home. He got job offers constantly, but he never moved from St. Luke's—because I was here.

I practically had to bash him over the head to get him to accept the job in Germany. I appreciate the dedication to being an active parent, considering how we started, but I'm a grown woman now. Chaining himself to New York until he's six feet under seems like overkill.

I smile when I spot a shiny gold-plated name on the door—**Dr. Nick Raines, Head of Neurosurgery**—a niggle of actual excitement at seeing my dad in the flesh reminding me that I really am human after all.

Crossing the threshold of his office, I find my father sitting behind an impressive desk, his face entranced with whatever he's looking at on his laptop.

"Even after a yearlong stint in Germany, St. Luke's has welcomed you back with open arms," I announce as I shut the door behind me.

My dad looks up, a grin spreading across his face and crinkling the crow's-feet around his eyes. It's been a whole year since I've seen him in person, aside from a few FaceTime calls, and except for a little more gray threaded through his hair, he hasn't changed a bit.

"I never resigned from my position here, Lex," he corrects, and I just roll my eyes as I round his desk to check out whatever has him so invested in his computer screen. A comprehensive list of clinical data for a drug called NVG-291 sits at the forefront, and I already know this is related to Scottie.

"You think she's a candidate for it?" I question, and he shrugs as he closes the screen of his laptop before my eyes can read through all the statistical data on the cutting-edge treatment.

"I think I'll know more when I conduct a few more studies myself."

"You're not happy with all of the labs and tests you had her team run over the past month?"

"I'm definitely satisfied with the information I obtained, but you know me, Lex, I always want more." He smiles up at me as he reaches out to briefly touch my hand. "It's good to see you."

"Thanks."

"What?" His smile grows wider, his arms opening in kind. "It's not good to see me?"

"It's good to see you, Dad," I comment and lean down to embrace him in a hug, laughing a little at how important it is for him to get confirmation now, given how our relationship began. It wasn't until I was prepubescent that he started to make an effort, when he realized taking care of a child financially was important but unexclusive. Emotional well-being is half the battle in childhood health.

To this day, I credit much of his maturation in our current relationship to my stepmom Charlotte.

Charlotte is warm and kind, and ironically enough, she used to be my uncle Remy's fiancée many, *many* years ago—a long chapter in a different book and an entire story of its own, let me tell you.

Now, she's an accepted and welcome part of my life, and before she and my dad moved to Germany for a year, it wasn't uncommon for her to meet me for lunch near campus every two weeks or so. Some who know the whole story think it's weird.

But it's all par for the course, in my opinion. The path to a father-daughter relationship hasn't necessarily been smooth or without complications, but we're in a good place now.

It took a lot of years for him to gain both my mom's and Wes's trust, but I can't blame them for that either.

I know his status in my life always used to cause my mom a lot of stress. She felt I deserved better, that I deserved an active father figure, but I always felt like I had everything I needed with her. Honestly, I probably don't tell her enough how good of a mother she is.

I really need to do better. I'm trying to do better. But things like that—emotions—are not easy for someone like me.

"So, Lex, tell me, how are you doing?" my dad asks as I head over to the leather sofa in the corner of his office and sit down.

"I'm good."

"And your doctoral dissertation?"

"Already finished."

"Oh man." His laugh is hearty, but there's also a sentiment of pride mixed into each chuckle that leaves his lungs. "I should've known you'd have it done well ahead of the end-of-summer deadline. And has my brilliant daughter decided on a career path?" His smile turns knowing. "Because I know a certain profession that could use a mind like yours."

"I'm not going to med school, Dad." I roll my eyes. "Financially speaking, med school would be a step backward. I'd lose money and miss out on opportunities. I already have over ten companies making offers for some of the software and apps I've created this past year."

He smirks. "You going to sell?"

"I don't know." I shrug. "I guess if I think one of them is the right fit and will utilize what I've created in the way I intended, then I wouldn't be opposed."

"Interesting." He nods slowly, steepling his hands under his chin. "And outside of school and your career, how's everything else?"

"What else is there?" I ask with a snort, defaulting to my factory settings for a moment or two.

"I don't know. New friends?" He pauses, a teasing grin spreading across his face. "Boyfriends?"

Immediately, Blake's face flashes in my mind—his crooked smile, the way he says my name, the way he's been asking me to stop keeping him a secret. My stomach tightens, and I focus hard on my hands, clasped tightly in my lap, but whatever's written on my face isn't lost on my dad.

"Wait…does my daughter have a man in her life?" he asks, leaning forward slightly, his attention sharp and unwavering. His eyes search mine like he's solving one of his Sunday crossword puzzles, and it feels like the walls of his office are closing in. My shoulders stiffen, and I shift in my seat, trying to shake the mounting pressure.

"No," I say quickly, but the word feels foreign, like my tongue doesn't belong to me. It's not quite a lie, but it's definitely not the truth, and it sits there like a pebble I can't swallow.

"Are you sure?" he presses, his curiosity only growing, but just as I start scrambling for an answer, the door swings open. Finn and Scottie come in, their voices cutting through the tension like a lifeline, and my dad's focus snaps to them.

I release a quiet, tangled breath, sinking back into the couch as relief washes over me. I'm not ready to explain my feelings—I don't yet understand them fully myself.

"Dr. Raines?" Scottie asks, and my dad stands up from his chair to greet her at the door.

"You must be Scottie," he says and holds out his hand to shake hers. He does the same with Finn, who currently stands behind Scottie's wheelchair.

"Finn Hayes," Finn introduces himself.

"He's my boyfriend and all-around super support system," Scottie adds, flashing a smile up at Finn.

"That goes both ways, babe," he tells her before my dad gestures for them to come inside. Finn eases Scottie's chair the rest of the way into the office and parks it right in front of his desk.

"Hey, Lex," Scottie greets when she meets my eyes, and I offer her a little wave and smile back. Finn's exchange is a little more curt, just a simple nod—exactly what I'd expect from him.

"Scottie, I've reviewed all of the tests and labs I requested your medical team to do," my dad begins. "I've also spoken at length with your physicians and your physical therapists to get a stronger understanding of your baseline status after your injury. And while I never like to make promises, I do want you to know that I am incredibly optimistic that you might be a candidate for a few options. Though, I would definitely need to run additional tests that will give me a more in-depth look at nerve function before we could move forward with any kind of real optimism."

"Okay." Scottie nods, her eyes fluttering between Finn and Nick and me. "But that's kind of good news, right?" she asks. "I mean, you're not telling me all hope is lost, so I'm assuming that means there's a chance?"

"There's definitely a chance," my dad answers with a soft smile. Scottie's hand shoots out to grab Finn's wrist and squeezes. His skin mottles white with the pressure, but he doesn't flinch.

"And how much would all of this cost?" Finn chimes in. "Because Scottie and I—"

"Oh no, Finn," my dad cuts him off. "This is all pro bono."

"Pro bono?" Scottie asks, her voice a whisper.

"No cost," my dad explains—though, I don't think it was the technical definition Scottie was having trouble with. To offer this level of services and care at no cost is at a great financial risk to the giver. My father is well-off, but this is still a huge deal.

Scottie's response is a mix of outright shock and awe, the shake in her sweet voice giving her away. "I don't know if I can accept that. I mean, I—"

"Any friend of Lexi's is a friend of mine," my dad states definitively, solidifying his redemption arc status in his villain origin story entirely.

Scottie looks over at me, and the emotion that sits behind her eyes makes my throat feel like it's closing in on itself. Finn's normally stoic face crumpling with overwhelm doesn't help.

I look down at the floor and blink rapidly, willing my tears to stay at bay.

"So, how about we get started?" my dad questions, a smile on his lips as he turns his laptop screen toward Finn and Scottie. "Scottie, I want to first show you what I'm seeing from all your tests. Basically, give you an overview of the current state of your injury. And then, I want to tell you about some of the treatment possibilities I see as options and the tests I'd need you to undergo in order to get final confirmation that you're a true candidate."

"Okay," Scottie says, her eyes fixated on the screen of his laptop where an MRI of her spine is showcased.

But just as my dad starts to discuss where her spinal injury is located and what that means in terms of daily function, my phone vibrates in the pocket of my jean shorts.

I pull it out to find a single text.

Blake Boden: I'm coming to your place tonight.

Me: Bossy much?

Blake Boden: Not bossy. Just desperate to see you.

Me: You saw me last night.

Blake Boden: So?

I can feel my mouth threatening to form a smile, but I suck my lips into my mouth and try to keep a neutral expression on my face. Though, I do find myself texting him back.

Me: Fine. But I'll probably be hungry, and I'm not eating pizza from that dude's dorm again. As in, NEVER AGAIN.

Two nights ago, Blake talked me into getting the definitely-against-health-code pizza for the second time. It was good. I won't deny it. But I'm one hundred percent certain the risk for salmonella outweighs the taste, and the anxiety about it had me in the bathroom half the night, just in case.

Blake Boden: I'll get takeout from Zip's.

Me: Perfect. 8:15?

Blake Boden: See you at 8:15, Lexi Lou. Can't wait.

Another night, another secret sleepover with Blake.

I pause, my fingers hovering over my phone as a realization sneaks up on me. *You've created quite the routine this summer. Blake Boden is basically a part of your life now...*

The thought stops me cold.

No fitting him into my routine anymore—he's a *part* of it.

34

Blake

I finish off my burger and start to collect Lex's and my takeout containers from her coffee table. She's already curled up on the couch with a blanket, scrolling through Netflix for something to watch.

Last night, we watched a documentary called *Trust Machine*, and it was all about cryptocurrency, how currencies like Bitcoin and Ethereum were developed, and the possible global implications for the future.

I didn't know ninety-nine percent of the information, but Lexi did. For all I know, she's already created her own form of cryptocurrency.

"Hey, Lex?"

"Yeah?"

"Do you know how to create cryptocurrency?"

"Yeah."

I drop our containers into the trash and walk back into the living room. But I stop right in front of where she's perched on the couch, still scrolling through streaming possibilities. "What do you mean, *yeah?* Like, you know the basic logistics of it, or if I asked you to create a coin named Biscuits, you'd have it done by the morning?"

She glances at the time on her phone. "It's almost ten, Blake. I'd need at least sixteen hours. Possibly twenty-four."

My jaw hits the floor. "You're serious."

She just stares at me.

"Lexi, you mean to tell me, that big, beautiful brain of yours could create me a cryptocurrency named Biscuits?"

"Honestly, Blake, I think Biscuits would be a horrible name if you actually want it to succeed."

I laugh. *Fuck. This girl. She's endlessly intriguing to me.*

"Why are you laughing?"

"Because…" *Because I love you. Because you're everything.* "You're funny."

"I wasn't trying to be funny."

"I know. But sometimes the funniest things are when they're meant to be serious."

She quirks her brow. "That's so contradictory."

"That's life, baby."

She smiles at that.

My phone vibrates from its spot on her coffee table, and I grab it to find a few missed texts in my group chat with Ace and Finn.

> *Ace: BLAKE*

> *Ace: BLAAAAKE*

> *Finn: Blake, this is Ace's annoying way of telling you to come out with us tonight. There's a party on Frat Row. The Sigma house.*

> *Ace: Fuck, Finn. You ruined my whole spiel.*

> *Finn: Zero fucks given, bro.*

> *Ace: What do ya say, Golden Boy? You going to meet up with us tonight? Or are you going to keep being a recluse in your apartment bc football is making your wittle baby muscles sore.*

"You feel like doing something tonight?" I question, and Lex meets my eyes.

"You mean go out?"

"Yeah. Ace and Finn said there's a party."

Lexi furrows her brow. "Blake, I can't do that. *We* can't do that."

"Why not?"

"Because everyone would think we're together."

"Hey, coincidence…we *are* together." She levels me with a look, so I clarify. "Ohhh. You mean, everyone would *know* about us."

"Yeah." She snorts. "That's exactly what I mean."

If I know anything about Lexi, I know that delving deep into the giant pink elephant of a conversation that rears its head every two to three business days is the last thing she wants to do right now, but I also know if I don't bring it up, she won't either.

If I'm ever going to get anywhere, I have to keep nudging her outside of her comfort zone. And I *have* to get somewhere. The need for the security of a real relationship with this amazing woman is eating me alive.

I pause to take a breath and sit down on the couch beside her, willing myself to take the harder road. I could easily let it go—settle in and enjoy her body and mine together over and over again. But the longer I let this conversation go, the harder it gets to have. "Lex, maybe people knowing wouldn't be such a bad thing. *Maybe* it would be the best thing." I pull her hand into mine, gripping it gently between my palms while my heart starts to pound erratically inside my chest. "I need it to be *the* thing."

She tilts her head to the side. "What do you mean?"

"I mean, I love you, Lexi." I tell her my truth, compelled to lay it all on the line. "I'm *in love* with you. I love everything about us, and I want to love it openly and outwardly all the fucking time."

"Blake, I…" She stares at me, her mouth setting in a firm line as her eyes flit away from mine. "I don't know what to say."

"Just tell me how you feel." I squeeze her hand. "About me. About us. About what scares you. The two of us can figure out how to handle it together."

She sucks her bottom lip into her mouth and avoids my gaze entirely. "I don't think I'm the right girl for this, Blake."

"Right girl? Lex, you're the *only* girl for me."

"No, Blake." She shakes her head. "I'm not good with relationships, and I don't fall in love. You want me to tap into my emotions and tell you how I feel, and the truth is, I *don't* feel. Not like you. Not at the surface for everyone to see. I don't think I'm capable of that, Blake. I'm just…different."

"I think you're looking at this all wrong," I tell her, but she pulls her hand away from mine.

"No," she snaps, sitting up with piercing eyes. "I think *you're* looking at this all wrong."

"How?" I question. "How is it wrong that I love you and want to be with you? How is it *so* wrong that I want other people to know how I feel about you?"

"Blake, this isn't how it was supposed to go. This was supposed to be…" She pauses, alarm in her eyes now, and I try my best to calm her as panic seizes my thudding heart.

"I know this wasn't your plan, but sometimes things just happen, you know?" I say. "And this summer, something happened between us. Something strong and fucking special and real. I don't want women to think they can approach me like they used to. I want them to know I belong to you."

She shakes her head several more times, her whole body overcome. She shoves off the couch and stands, pacing in a panic.

"This isn't how this was supposed to go. This is… You were supposed to have fun. You were supposed to be *fun*."

"Lex—"

"I have no intention of making any public announcement about us because I don't see a future beyond the summer." Her mouth is a gun, and her words are bullets striking straight into my fucking chest. Each shot hits the target that's my heart, stinging like a motherfucker. "I think this is a sign we need to stop doing what we're doing," she continues until all the hope inside me withers and dies. "Otherwise, I think someone is going to get hurt."

"*Going* to get hurt?" I laugh, but there's no humor. "Pretty sure it's a little too fucking late for that."

"I'm sorry, Blake," she says, but her voice is barely above a whisper.

"You want to know what I think?"

She turns to meet my eyes as I stand from the couch.

"I think you're being obtuse, and you're too smart to be doing it without purpose. This—what happened between us—isn't something you can write off as research or statistics, and you know it. We're talking about emotions here. And whether you want to face it or not, you *do* have feelings for me, and if you push me away now, you're going to regret it."

Her bottom lip quivers. But she schools her face so quickly, I almost question if I even saw that in the first place. "I think you need to leave."

"So, that's it?" I question, but she makes a point to grab my duffel bag that sits by her kitchen island and hand it to me.

"Goodbye, Blake."

"Goodbye for tonight, or goodbye forever?"

"Goodbye…forever."

I shut my eyes and have to force myself to breathe through the pain. When I feel like my lungs are made of something slightly less dense than lead, I lean forward to press a kiss to her forehead.

"When I said I love you, I meant it," I whisper. "One day, you're going to admit to yourself you feel the same. I just hope it's not too late."

And then, I leave.

Walking away hurts like a motherfucker, but my dignity is all I have left.

With Lexi Winslow, there's no forcing the issue. The only option…is to wait.

Saturday, August 2nd

Lexi

My morning alarm is the equivalent of someone running their nails down a chalkboard, and I reach out to slam my hand down on my phone, desperate to end the noise trauma. Instantly, the sweet sounds of silence fill my bedroom, but the sun decides it's the perfect time to peek in through my window and add an extra blanket of warmth to my skin.

I groan and drag my pillow over my face, my usual routine of getting out of bed at the first sounds of my alarm clearly not happening.

But as I turn over to my side and open my eyes, my vision slowly adjusting from the darkness of my lids to the brightness of the morning, I fixate on the empty spot on my mattress beside me.

For the past few weeks, that spot hasn't been empty at all. It's been filled with the larger-than-life man I kicked out of my apartment last night.

He told me he loved me. And I didn't say anything at all.

He told me he wanted to be with me. And I asked him to leave.

I can't even begin to explain or understand my reaction to his words. All I know is that my physiological reaction was intense. My heart pounded inside my chest and my ears rang and my feet felt like they had been cemented to the floor.

And the hurt I saw on his face reminded me so much of how I've felt after causing tears in my mom's eyes.

I know I'm the problem. I just don't know how to fix it.

I turn back over onto my side and snag my phone from the nightstand, my fingers instantly unlocking the screen and opening up my ongoing text chat with Blake.

Are you okay? I type, but my finger hovers over the send button, hanging precariously in the air as I try to decide what to do.

I want to send it, but upon analysis, I have no idea where I'd go if he were to answer.

I delete the three words and lock the screen of my phone.

I don't want to hurt him, but I don't know how to be anything else but me. And one of the hardest parts about being me is that I don't feel things the same way most people do.

Love is abstract. It defies the logical processes my mind utilizes, and the idea of things like soul mates or finding the man of your dreams has always sounded like an unrealistic notion to me.

But Blake *believes* in those things—believes he's found them in me; that much is clear.

Everything between Blake and me was supposed to be for fun. It was never supposed to end in *I love you.*

I wouldn't have agreed to that.

Love and I are a cosmic mix of oil and water. It's emotion and I'm science. We can't go together.

Right?

Eventually, I force myself out of bed and head into my bathroom. My head is pounding and my body aches, and I silently wonder if I'm starting to come down with one of those summer colds my brother Wes always tends to get this time of year.

After I brush my teeth and pull my hair up into a ponytail, I walk back into my bedroom, only a bra and underwear covering my body, and for reasons my mind can't fathom, I end up grabbing Blake's oversized T-shirt that I stole from his place a few weeks ago and tossing it over my head.

Instantly, I bury my nose into the neckline, allowing the scent of vanilla to fill my head. Vanilla is known to be a comforting scent that causes a physiological response of relaxation and calm, and I find that's exactly what it is right now, too. *It's just for comfort. Doesn't mean anything but that.*

Phone in hand, I head into the kitchen and snag a bottle of water out of the fridge, hoping that a little hydration will ease my headache. I even take two ibuprofen for good measure.

But given the fact that Blake's cologne is now following me around, my mind can't stop thinking about him. *What is he doing right now? Is he engaging in his normal routine of brushing his teeth and watching ESPN while he eats breakfast? Is he eating his usual protein-fueled breakfast of eggs, or has he chosen to give in to his favorite guilty pleasure of Lucky Charms?*

Is he mad at me? Does he hate me?

The mere idea of Blake hating me doesn't make me feel good, and I grab my phone off my kitchen counter. But just before I can rewrite my *Are you okay?* text, my phone starts ringing in my hands.

Incoming Call Doctor Dad, flashes on the screen, and I answer it by the second ring.

"Hey, Dad."

"Lex, I have some big news," he says. "I think I can help Scottie. Actually, I know I can."

"Help her, how?" I ask. "You think you can assist in her getting more nerve and muscle control?"

"More than that, Lex. I think I can help Scottie walk again."

I stand there, stunned.

"Let me guess, you're intrigued," he says, and I don't miss the confident but teasing tone in his voice.

"Incredibly so."

He chuckles. "You got some free time today? Scottie will be coming in to discuss her case and treatment options at ten."

"I can be there in an hour."

Science. It's comfortable. It's what I know. The rest is much harder to figure out.

36

Sunday, August 3rd
Blake

Zip's Diner is pretty slow for the Sunday lunch crowd, but that's probably because most kids are still off campus. This place won't start experiencing its normal hustle and bustle until classes begin at the end of the month.

Finn, Ace, and I sit at a booth in the back corner and start to dig into our meals of burgers and fries after Zip drops them off with his usual jolly grin.

Ace snags the ketchup bottle from the center of the table and squirts an ungodly amount onto the top of his burger. It's so much fucking ketchup that when he smashes the bun on top, red liquid flows down the sides and onto his plate.

And when he takes a big-ass bite, ketchup drips onto his hands and face.

"Dude," I say on a laugh. "That's foul."

"What?" Ace asks through a big smile, grabbing a napkin to swipe across his face as he does. "You got a problem with my love for ketchup?"

"Yeah," I retort. "I do."

Finn laughs when I mime gagging, and Ace just picks up the bottle of ketchup and proceeds to squirt a shitload of it onto my fries.

"You're such a dick," I say, but Ace gives zero fucks. Instead, he just shrugs and takes another bite of his gross burger.

Only a brief moment of silence lasts while we eat before Ace is opening up his pie hole again, half-masticated bite and all. "All right, Finnley. I think it's time you tell us why you wanted this little Sunday lunch. I mean, I don't mind it one bit, but it's not exactly within your God-given role as the group grumpy ass."

Finn smiles despite the insult. "I have news."

But he doesn't give the news, and I know it's on purpose because he loves teasing the hell out of Ace. Normally, I find it charming and amusing. Right now, I hate it. But I also hate the air, water, wind, and sea, despite their lack of sentiency, so my loathing isn't an impugnment of my friends' personalities, but rather, my own.

I've been little more than a miserable human being since Friday.

"And?" Ace questions, his eyes practically bugging out of his head. "Are you going to tell us the news, or do I gotta fucking guess, man?"

Finn's responding smile is sly. "Do you want to guess?"

"No," Ace snaps. "I want you to fucking tell me."

"You sure you don't want to guess, Acer?"

"For fuck's sake, man. Just tell us."

"Calm your tits." Finn laughs. "I'll tell you, but first, I want to finish eating my burger."

"What the fuck?" Ace questions, and God, I wish my chest didn't ache this badly so I could laugh.

"Okay. Okay." Finn gestures a hand in the air. "You can untwist your panties, bro."

Ace lets out an annoyed sigh, but to his benefit, Finn finally starts to explain.

"Scottie had her follow-up with Dr. Raines yesterday afternoon. And he thinks he has treatment options for her."

The mere mention of Lexi's dad is salt in an already painful wound, but I swallow the discomfort and focus on my friend. News of treatment options for my paralyzed friend trump any and all personal crises—quite frankly, it would change her entire life.

"Treatment options?" I ask. "What does that mean?"

"He wants her to do some kind of nerve graft surgery along

with a course of medication that is supposed to help the damaged nerves of her spinal cord regenerate and heal," Finn explains. "He's been doing heavy research with these very treatments while he was in Germany and feels really confident about it. Though, there are some risks involved."

"What would the treatment achieve?" Ace asks.

"He thinks he can fucking heal her. He thinks he can make Scottie walk again."

Both Ace's and my mouths gape widely, and I feel the first tingle of tears as they sting the backs of my eyes. It's joy and pain and hope and despair all in one. The genius of Lexi's paternal DNA is a brilliant, vibrant display for Scottie's healing—and a brutal reminder of the remarkable woman who won't admit she loves me back.

"What?" Ace shouts, so loudly that even Zip glances over at us in confusion. "He thinks he can make her *walk again?*"

"Yeah." Finn nods, clearly understanding the dramatic reaction. I mean, *holy fucking shit*, I'm literally about to cry.

For Finn, though, there's no "about to" about it. He wipes furiously at his face, and neither Ace nor I mentions it. "I know, man. It's *incredible*." His mouth curves up as he gets control of the tears. "Scottie…" He pauses. "She… It would have been okay, you know? Both of us have come to terms, and I love her no matter the state of her body. But to get this hope back…" He shakes his head. "It's *everything*. She's practically freaking sparkling, she's so happy."

Ace reaches out and clamps a hand on Finn's shoulder, squeezing and shaking him slowly. The air is so charged around Finn right now, the whole diner can feel it.

"She's happy. You're happy. And I'm happy. In fact, I'm so fucking happy, I could kiss Nick motherfucking Raines on the mouth," Ace says, and for the first time at this lunch, all three of us laugh.

Finn nods. "Lexi was there, and even her emotionless poker face slipped for a full thirty seconds."

Emotionless poker face. Boy, do I know what he means by that. But I also know why Lexi is the way she is and all the ways that makes her special. I *know* it. And yet…it's the reason we're not together anymore, too. And that fucking sucks.

"Is she going to do it?" Ace questions, and I make myself pay attention to the conversation, even though my mind just wants to loop on thoughts of Lexi and how much I fucking miss her.

"I don't know." Finn shrugs. "She's talking it over with her dad and sister."

"Do you want her to do it?" I ask.

"I don't know that either," Finn answers. "I mean, it's ultimately up to her. I'll support whatever she decides, but I can't deny that the risks of the surgery are scary. I just want her to be safe, you know? I don't know how I'd cope if anything happened to her."

Ace's eyebrows rise subtly, and I nod. We both know how Finn would cope—with an inordinate number of fists in faces.

He loves her for her—a love that, at its core, is one of ultimate acceptance and embracing another person for everything they are— their strengths, their weaknesses, their flaws, their everything. He doesn't give a shit if she is going to be in a wheelchair for the rest of her life. He just wants her to be there, beside him, forever.

And that's how you love Lexi too.

The thought is a steel-toed boot in my gut. I love Lexi for everything that she is. Hell, even the quirkiest things about her are utterly endearing to me.

I love the way she thinks. I love the way she responds. I love *everything* about her—even the parts of her that make me hurt like this waiting for her to figure out she feels the same.

Ace and Finn continue to talk about Scottie's possible surgery, and while I want to give my friend all my attention—I know I should—I can't stop myself from pulling my phone out of my pocket and sending Lexi a message.

We haven't spoken since Friday night, but I'll be damned if I'm just going to walk away from her without a fucking fight.

Me: I don't like how things ended on Friday, Lex. When you're ready, we need to talk.

I guess I shouldn't be shocked when, a minute later, no response comes. And after another five minutes and ten minutes and fifteen minutes pass by, I still haven't heard a peep from her.

But I'll wait. That's what love does.

For the next two weeks, I'll be fully immersed in Dragons' football anyway, on the practice field or in the weight room for at least eight hours a day until August 19th. And after that, we'll be balls deep into preparing for our first game of the season on August 30th against Georgia.

I'll barely have time to sleep, much less eat.

It'll be the perfect distraction. I've walked away and waited for Lexi before. I can do it again.

Right?

Ha. Good luck with that.

37

Lexi

offee in hand, I head toward my home-away-from-home, my favorite lab on campus. But just before I can swipe my keycard to enter the building, my phone vibrates in the pocket of my jean shorts.

> **Blake Boden: I can't tell you how many times I've stopped myself from calling or texting you. Stopped myself from going to your apartment. Stopped myself from doing a lot of things. But fuck, Lexi. I miss you. I really fucking miss you.**

I have to shut my eyes for a brief moment, my mind racing with a million different thoughts and my heart thrumming unsteadily inside my chest.

He misses me. And, if I'm honest, I miss going to bed with him at night and waking up to him in the morning more than I care to admit. I had gotten so used to his comforting presence in my life that the abrupt change has been hard for me to adjust to.

But I've never really been good with change. My brain prefers schedules and mapped-out plans, so it shouldn't be a surprise that something like this would cause me internal anxiety.

There's a part of me that wants to text him back. That wants to tell him that I do miss him too. But there's another part of me that feels so unsure about all of it. So, I simply shove my phone back into my pocket and swipe my keycard to enter the lab.

Blake is still at the forefront of my mind, but I sit down and get myself set up, hoping that, eventually, I'll find my usual studious and focused rhythm.

The lab is empty, and I'm honestly relieved Ginger isn't here. Because if she were, I fear she might ask me about Blake, and I honestly don't know how I'd react to that.

I input my updated data on statistical chances for AI-technology errors into the diagnostic test app I created for my own personal use in finalizing my dissertation. The updated data shows zero change from what I had originally entered prior to finishing my dissertation, but still, I never go off assumptions.

The internal results show no major differential change, and for some reason, I feel annoyed that I don't need to make any last-minute updates to my dissertation.

A sigh escapes my lungs, the opposite reaction one should have when they realize there are zero errors with the final milestone of their graduate school career.

And it's not long before my phone is back in my hands and I'm staring down at the last text Blake sent me. The words *I miss you* standing out the most of them all.

"What are you doing?" a familiar voice grabs my attention, and I look up to find Connor walking into the lab.

"Oh, nothing," I answer, clearing my throat and putting my phone back on the table facedown. "But I think the bigger question is, why are you here? You never come over to Ferris."

"It's the homestretch, Lex. I have exactly one week to finish my thesis or else I can kiss my doctorate goodbye. And I guess I needed a little change of pace."

I tilt my head to the side. "Finish it? As in, you're still working on it?"

"Not all of us are übergeniuses, you know," he retorts with a smile as he sits down across from me.

"You got a perfect score on your SAT, Connor." I snort. "And you're currently in one of the hardest engineering doctorate programs in the country. You're smart."

"But I'm not *Lexi* smart."

I roll my eyes, and he just laughs.

I've known Connor for what feels like my whole life. He was my first boyfriend when I was thirteen, and we were in a relationship for most of my high school career. He's always been a good friend and a challenging academic partner. But as he starts to open his laptop and dive into whatever he needs to achieve today, I can't stop myself from asking him the one question that rolls around inside my head.

"What was it like to date me?"

His head jerks back, and his eyes snap to mine. "Excuse me?"

"What was it like to date me?" I repeat.

He searches my eyes carefully. "You want me to tell you what it was like for me to have you as my girlfriend?"

I nod. "Yeah."

"It was uh…fine," he answers. But his voice wavers a little as he adds, "It was good."

I've never been good at catching social cues—it's always a huge challenge for me—but there's something in the way his voice sounds that makes me feel like he's not giving me an honest answer.

"Are you telling me the truth?"

Connor just stares at me.

"Connor, did you just lie to me?"

"Shit." He lets out a confusing laugh. "I mean, yeah, I guess I did a little."

I narrow my eyes.

"I mean…" He pauses and runs a hand through his hair. "I mean… Do you really want me to answer your question honestly?"

"I wouldn't ask it if I didn't want an accurate answer. I wouldn't waste that time."

He searches my eyes for a long moment, but eventually, he lets out a deep exhale and says, "It wasn't easy, Lex. I really liked you, and you hurt me pretty badly. You were my first girlfriend, and I think I loved you back then. And when you broke up with me, it was like, one day, you just decided it was done. No real reason. No emotions. Just done. It took me a while to get over you."

"But you said you were fine with being friends after... Why would you want to be my friend if I hurt you?"

"I don't know. I just did," he responds with a shrug. "I guess I thought, deep down, you might eventually want to be my girlfriend again, but when that didn't happen, I decided to make the best of it. Now, I'm happy I did that. I love the friendship we have. You'll always be important to me."

All this time, I never really thought about what Connor felt during or after our relationship. I didn't know until now that I'd hurt him because I never even considered the possibility. And man, does that suck.

"I'm...sorry, Connor," I apologize. "I'm really sorry I hurt you."

"It's okay, Lex," he says with a smile and a laugh. "While I do appreciate the apology, that's way in the past. We're good, okay?"

I nod.

"Now, if you don't mind, I'm going to put my AirPods in and get to work." He flashes a wink in my direction and does just that.

I, on the other hand, am the human form of stagnation—at least, I am bodily. A cataclysmic event is hard at work in my mind. The fact that I hurt someone I really do care about and didn't even realize it isn't an easy pill to swallow, and it isn't the first time I've had to try. My mom, my little brother, my stepdad, my dad—I've hurt them all at one time or another, just by being me.

And I've most definitely hurt Blake. With the way he looked when I told him to leave my apartment on Friday, I know I have. Unlike with Connor, I knew right then.

And I did it anyway.

I don't like the adjectives I'd use to describe a person who would do that. And I don't want to hurt him any more than I already have.

So, I do the one thing I do have control over.

> *Me: Blake, I really enjoyed what we had over this summer. I've had a lot of fun with you. I care about you. But our paths are not aligned. You have football and college, and I'm getting ready to head into the real world and start my career. I think it's time we both move on.*

Telling him what we had was nothing was a lie and a dirty trick. But if he thinks we can be together anymore without me hurting him again, I'll need to keep my distance to make sure I don't.

Even if it hurts me.

38

Blake

The sun has set, and the day has transformed into night, only the moon and stars residing in the sky. I'm sweaty and my legs feel like my shoes are carrying an extra ten pounds each as I stride into Lexi's apartment building.

I've spent all day at football conditioning—running drills and doing agility training and suffering so much through full-field sprints in the summer heat that three guys on the team threw up their lunch. It's been a fucking grueling day, and I know I should be at my apartment taking a hot shower and getting my ass into bed, because tomorrow will be much of the same.

But I can't. Not after that text Lexi sent me this morning.

I haven't stopped thinking about it, and if I'm honest, I'm angry about it. I have so many questions that are unanswered, and I won't be able to sleep until I talk to her.

See her.

Try to figure out why she said, *I think it's time we both move on.*

I don't waste any time in the lobby, heading straight for the elevator, and it only takes a few minutes before I'm on her floor.

My heart races inside my chest as I lift my knuckles to rap against the wood of her door.

As footsteps sound on the other side, it only makes my heart pound faster.

The door swings open, and there she is, my beautiful Lexi Lou, standing on the other side. Her blond hair is up in one of her cute ponytails, and she's already dressed for bed in her favorite sleep shorts and tank top.

She looks beautiful. But that's no surprise. Lexi always looks beautiful.

"Blake?" she questions, and her nose scrunches up in confusion. "What are you doing here?"

"I'm here because of this." I take my phone out of my pocket and pull up the last text she sent me. "Is this for real?"

Her head jerks back, and her eyes flit to the floor for a long moment, fixated on her bare feet.

"Lexi? What does this mean?"

She brings her gaze back up to mine. "Blake, it means exactly what I said. It's time for us both to move on."

"Move on?" I repeat her words—stupid words that I do not agree with. Words that feel so wrong when they leave my tongue, I can barely say them. "After everything, you just want to walk away?"

"We're on different paths, Blake."

"Who gives a shit about paths?" I counter. "We've spent this whole summer together while our paths aren't exactly the same, and it was the best fucking summer I've ever had, Lex. We're so good together. Why can't you see that?"

"I know we have fun together," she says. "But that doesn't equal a relationship. It doesn't equal a future."

"We've had more than fun, and you know that," I challenge. "More than just *sex*, Lexi. You *know* it. I love you, and if you'd let yourself, you love me back."

She averts her eyes from me again, and I don't hesitate to step forward and pull her into my arms. She goes willingly, melting against my body, and I hug her tightly to my chest, desperate to make her realize this love isn't one-sided.

"I love you," I tell her again. "I want to be with you. You're the only girl I want to be with."

I slip my hand under her chin and pull her gaze to mine. I

search her eyes. They're hesitant and unsure, and I press my lips to hers.

Our kiss is soft and slow at first, but eventually, she slides her hands up my back and into my hair. She feels so good and perfect in my arms, and I don't ever want this moment to end. I want it to continue forever and fucking ever.

But in an instant, she pulls away, planting both of her hands on my chest and putting distance between us. "We can't, Blake." She shakes her head. "I'm sorry. But we can't do this anymore."

"Lexi—"

"No," she cuts me off before I can say anything else. "I'm sorry. I *don't* love you. I care about you, but I don't *love* you. I don't even know how to love." Her eyes unfocus briefly before a quick shake of her head. "I'm sorry, Blake. This just isn't going to work."

Her words cut me open.

I don't love you.

The pain is acute and damn near takes my breath away. It's one thing for someone not to say "I love you" back, but it's entirely another for them to say they *don't*. It removes the excuse of omission completely.

"So, that's it," I mutter, my voice a scratchy version of its normal timbre. "You're done. We're done."

"I'm sorry."

I can't even look at her. It's too fucking painful.

All I can do is turn on my heel and walk right back through her door, slamming it behind me. I lick my lips and clench my fists, fighting the urge to punch several holes in the wall of her hall on the way out and bang into the stairwell instead. I jog down the stairs, dropping shattered pieces of my heart on each and every level.

Move on from Lexi Winslow? Fucking impossible.

39

Lexi

"I'd like to propose a toast to the smartest girl in the family," Uncle Jude says, lifting his glass of champagne in the air with a big smile. "Lexi, I know everyone in this room is incredibly proud of you and everything you've accomplished. And we're all kind of hoping you're going to carry the torch for the Winslow family and finally prove to the world that we're not a bunch of idiots."

"Jude!" my grandma Wendy chastises, but she also laughs, along with everyone else in the room.

My mom is rolling her eyes at her youngest brother, and my stepdad Wes is pretty much doing the same, though his face is filled with far less annoyance. And I take the time to look around the room, savoring all the faces smiling in my direction of some of the most important people in my life, all gathered here in my grandma's brownstone to celebrate my big milestone of defending my final dissertation of my doctoral career.

I'm officially done with college, and while I feel excited, I also feel a growing sense of anxiety about all the life changes coming my way.

My schedule is going to be different. My life will be different. I'll no longer be spending most of my days at my favorite Dickson lab, but instead, living in the fast lane of adulthood in the real world.

My uncle Remy walks over to give me a big hug, and my aunt Maria does the same. Both telling me how proud they are of me and offering big congratulations on all that I've achieved. And they start a sort of assembly line of family and friends doing much of the same.

My grandma and Howard. My other uncles Flynn and Ty and their wives. My mom and stepdad Wes and brother Wes Jr. My dad Nick and my stepmom Charlotte. My parents' best friends, Thatch and Cassie and Kline and Georgia. All of my cousins— Hawk, Meadow, Emily, Izzy, Carmen, Roman, and Ryder. Even Ace and Julia—and their respective brother and sister—and Finn and Scottie are here, along with Finn's mom Helen and his siblings Reece, Travis, Jack, and Willow.

The house is packed fuller than a can of sardines, everyone basically having to climb over one another in the dining room to get to me, but they all manage to give me big hugs and heartfelt wishes as I prepare to take my next big life journey.

It's clear I've never been an emotional kind of girl, but something about this moment is urging this strange combination of happiness and something akin to melancholy. The happiness makes complete sense, but the glum shadow is something I don't quite understand.

"So, Lex," Ace asks with a big smile. "What's the next big move?"

"Big move?" I question. "As in, where am I going to live?"

"No." He chuckles. "Where does a big-brained girl like Lexi end up working?"

"Yeah, Lex." Uncle Remy joins in. "Have you decided what you're going to do?"

Truthfully, no. I have options. Lots of options that most men and women my age would quite literally sacrifice a lot of things to obtain. But I still haven't decided what I want to do.

I shrug. "I'm still mulling it all over."

"As in, my sister has created an exhaustive spreadsheet of pros and cons and statistical analysis of each job choice," my brother chimes in with a sarcastic grin. "She'll probably need to create a personalized app that can compute all of her data before she can come to her final decision."

"You're a smartass, you know that?" I toss back to him, and he just laughs.

"Does it help that Mom told me I needed to tell you I'm really proud of you?" he questions, and my mom sighs.

"Wesley, leave your sister alone."

"Yeah," my stepdad Wes chimes in. "With that pathetic GPA you've got going on right now, you should maybe consider trying to learn a thing or two from Lex."

My brother snorts. "Whatever."

"Lexi, honey, what are your current choices?" my grandma Wendy asks, and the pressure of having everyone's attention on me is starting to make my skin feel a little itchy.

It's not that I don't like the attention or that I'm not thankful for it, but it's just a little overwhelming. I swallow against my discomfort and start to answer my grandma's question, but my brother starts talking before I can.

"Grandma, I think the easier question would be, what aren't your current choices?" he says and flashes a smile toward me that looks a hell of a lot like a little brother who is actually proud of his big sister. "Pretty much everyone and everything wants Lexi. Google. Apple. Fucking NASA."

"Wesley!" my mom exclaims and reaches out to tap him on the back of the head.

"What?" he asks, rubbing at the spot she hit. "I'm just speaking straight facts, Mom."

"I think your mother is referring to the giant f-bomb you dropped in the middle of the dining room," Thatcher Kelly retorts on a laugh.

"Wait…NASA?" Ace questions with wide eyes. "Fucking NASA wants you, Lex? Holy shit!"

His mom Cassie sighs. "Sometimes I wonder if it was a good idea to combine and unleash our genes into the world," she mutters to her husband Thatch.

But Ace ignores his parents completely and stays focused on me. "Are you seriously going to work for NASA, Lex? Like, am I actually going to be able to tell people I know a rocket scientist?"

"Doubtful." I shake my head. "NASA isn't at the top of my list."

"NASA offered you a job, and they're not at the top of your list?" Ace retorts on a laugh. "What else you got going on?"

Julia laughs at his joke and shoves his shoulder—a normal inter-action for the two—but Ace's gaze jerks to her hand, lingering long after it leaves. Blake was right about him spiraling over his newfound discovery that he's been obsessed with Julia Brooks his whole life. I've known him since I was a kid, and I've never seen him like this.

I shrug. "A few things."

"Technically, it's a fucking ton of things," my brother corrects, and everyone in the room chuckles. Well, everyone besides our mom.

Frankly, he's not wrong. I mean, besides the offers from major corporations to be on their payroll, I have a big medical company that's offered me eight figures to sell them an app I created that uti-lizes AI to analyze patient medical data to generate potential health risks, along with important proactive measures that can be taken to improve overall well-being outcomes.

Though, I don't know if I want to sell it to them. My fear is that they'll end up employing it in other ways that might include increasing financial strain on patients. Which is the last thing I want to occur.

I'd like to make the world a better place, thank you very much. And in order to do that, I need to help people, not hurt them.

And what about Blake? Was he just collateral damage?

The fact that his name pops into my brain makes my chest grow tight with discomfort. I don't know why I'm thinking about him, but it's like my mind hasn't fully moved on from him. I chalk it up to just needing to adjust to not having his presence in my life.

Surely that takes a little time.

"Okay, that's enough badgering Lexi," my grandma announces as she carries a giant buffet-sized tray of spaghetti into the dining room. "It's time to eat!"

Everyone listens to her demands, most of the women heading into the kitchen to help carry more of the food out into the din-ing room.

But just before I can sit down at the table, Ace pats my shoulder, a sneaky smile on his lips.

"You're coming out with us tonight."

I quirk a brow. "What do you mean?"

"I mean exactly what I said, Lex. You're coming out with us tonight to enjoy your last college party."

I sigh. "I don't know, Ace. I—"

"Uh-uh," he cuts me off. "Consider this a metaphor for you passing the torch to me." He waggles his brows, and I roll my eyes at how he might think he's being discreet. In fact, he's so obvious, if anyone in the room were paying attention to us instead of filling their plates with food, they might start asking questions.

"Fine," I answer, mostly focused on just shutting him up rather than asking him the most likely important questions of what going out entails. For all I know, he's taking me to some illegal party in someone's dorm.

Surprise dorm pizza is risky enough, let alone some party with mystery punch in the communal bathroom.

As fast as that thought comes in, I shove it right back out of my head, focusing on Ace instead. "I'll go, but you have to stop talking about anything related to parties for the rest of the night."

"You got it." He pretends to lock his lips and throw away the key.

And I work to mentally prepare myself to let Ace Kelly take me to my last college party.

Pray for me.

"You want anything to drink, babe?" Finn asks Scottie, his voice just barely rising above the din of laughter and music and boozed-up college co-eds who litter the frat house Ace dragged us all to.

"Just a water," Scottie says with a smile.

Finn presses a kiss to her forehead and meets my eyes for a brief moment.

"I'll stay here," I tell him, and he nods, clearly grateful, and pushes his way through a crowd of twerking girls to head toward the back of the house where the kitchen is located.

It's taken me a long time to be able to pick up on social cues or unspoken words, but the quiet exchange with my technical half uncle makes me feel confident in the progress I've made. I still have a lot of work to do and I know I'll never be perfect, but my evolution is certainly trending upward.

"Do you think I should be scared?" Scottie asks, and I look down to where she sits in her wheelchair, her eyes solely fixated on my face.

"Scared?" I question as I kneel down to get closer to her. "Of what exactly?"

"The surgery."

Oh. The surgery. As in, Scottie has decided to move forward with the surgical and medical treatment plan my father wants to do. It's a complicated surgery that involves nerve grafting, and the follow-up medication will require months of treatments.

"Are you scared?" I ask her, and she shrugs.

"Sometimes I am," she answers and shrugs again. "And sometimes I'm excited for what this could all mean for me. But then, having that kind of excitement and knowing that nothing is a certainty scares me too. Would you be scared?"

"I don't know," I answer honestly. "It's hard for me to place myself in your shoes and know exactly how I'd feel, but I think I'd probably be feeling like you are. A mix of lots of things."

"Really?" she questions, her eyes going wide and a smile cresting her lips.

"You're surprised by that?"

"Um, yeah." She nods several times. "You're Lexi Winslow. You're, like, the strongest, most brilliant, powerful girl I know."

My head jerks back at her words. "Well, thanks, I guess?"

"It's definitely an accomplishment," she adds and reaches out to touch my forearm. "I wish I had your poker face."

My poker face. As in, my face that almost never shows emotion, even though, on the inside, I have plenty of emotions rolling through me. I know she also means that as a compliment, but it makes me feel this strange sense of vulnerability. Like I'm in the middle of one of those dreams where I forgot to put on clothes and I'm stuck in a public place.

Finn appears through the crowd, a bottle of water in one hand and a red Solo cup in another. He hands the bottle to Scottie. "People are fucking insane," he mutters, and Scottie just laughs.

"Holy shit!" a boisterous voice exclaims, and I know without even turning around the culprit is the guy who dragged us here. Ace barrels into our little group, wraps his arm around Finn's shoulders, and tugs him to his side. "Is Finnley Hayes enjoying an alcoholic beverage tonight?" he asks, looking down at Finn's red Solo cup.

Finn rolls his eyes. "It's Mountain Dew."

"Fuck me." Ace groans. "And I thought you weren't going to be lame for once."

"Stop being a dick, Acer." Julia shoves Ace in the chest on a laugh. "You're like one of those bullies on an afterschool special, trying to get everyone to drink his parents' booze."

Ace cracks up. "Damn, Jules. Don't hold back."

She just offers him a sweet smile, and he proceeds to let go of Finn's shoulders and take hold of Julia's, his arm comfortably wrapped around her. She rolls her eyes like she's annoyed, but her body easily falls into place against his side. And I don't miss the way Ace's mouth morphs into this soft, gentle smile as he gazes down at her.

Ace is in love with Julia. It's quite literally written all over his face. But Julia still appears oblivious to the way he's looking at her or the way he always seems to find a way to touch her, hug her, hold her.

Ace starts to regale us with a story about how he and Julia got drunk off her dad's favorite scotch when they were sophomores in high school, and since I've already heard this story, I let myself look around the room, taking in all the partygoers who are celebrating the start of another college year.

Some of the faces, I recognize as people who are in Double C, but most, I don't know at all. I can imagine some of the kids here are a new generation of freshmen, just starting their college journey at Dickson.

But my gaze comes to a screeching halt when I spot the familiar strawberry-blond hair of a guy I've thought about way too often since I made the decision that we needed to move on from each other. Blake stands in the middle of a small group, his face etched into a smile as he chats with another guy I know is a running back on the football team. He has a bottle of water in his hand, and he's dressed in jeans and a black T-shirt.

I can't stop myself from wondering how everything is going for him. Wondering what football training has been like and if he thinks the team is ready for their first big game against Georgia next Saturday.

But all of my wondering stops abruptly when a girl with red hair and a flirty smile sidles up beside him and wraps her arm around his waist. He smiles down at her, and a shock of excruciating pain rolls through my chest so intensely that I look down to make sure a knife isn't actually lodged in it.

The girl is laughing at something he says, and not once does he try to remove her arm from his waist. Is he with her?

Of course he's with her. You told him to move on. So that's what he's doing…moving on.

Obviously, Blake is a popular guy on campus, and there's a whole slew of girls who are desperate to have his attention. Moving on to someone new wouldn't be a hard thing for him to achieve.

A rock of something I don't understand forms at the base of my throat, and I swallow several times to try to clear it. But when my bottom lip starts to tremble and a sheen of tears coats my eyes, my vision goes hazy.

And I realize that all I want to do right now is cry.

40

Blake

"It's so good to see you, Blake," Carla says, her red-painted lips morphing into a flirtatious smile as she looks up at me. Her arm is wrapped around my waist, and I can literally feel her breast against my side.

Since she's a SoCal native like me, I've known Carla since I was a fourteen-year-old boy. We went to high school together, even dated a little during our sophomore year, and despite the fact that we've both been at Dickson since we left California over two years ago, I rarely see her on campus.

But that's most likely because we run in different social circles. I know she's in a sorority, but I can't for the life of me remember which one. I also know that she's spent a lot of time fixated on most of the guys on the water polo team.

Word on the street is that she's dated—*bagged*—nearly half of them.

"Good to see you too, Carla," I say, my voice as kind as possible as I purposefully remove her arm from my waist. "How have things been for you at Dickson?"

"Oh my God," she says, a purr to her words as her hand finds my bicep. "Life in New York is so different from back home, right?"

I nod.

She squeezes my arm. "But, like, good different." Her smile takes on a seductive edge. "Lots more freedom. And things to do. Don't you think?"

"New York is great, but I wouldn't know about the whole

concept of freedom," I retort with a shrug. "I'm too busy on the field ninety-nine percent of the time."

Her eyes take on the same doe-eyed look I've seen so many times on college girls who love getting the attention of star athletes on campus. "You know what I think that means, Blake?"

I quirk an eyebrow. "What?"

"I think that means you should," she whispers, leaning closer to me so her lips are near my ear, "have more *fun*."

Her words are harmless, but the way in which she says them has evidence of propositions of hookups and sex.

"I'm here at this party, aren't I?"

"Oh, Blake." She giggles, and her hand is back on my bicep again. "I didn't mean fun like a party. I meant fun like with me."

Apparently, there's no more beating around the bush. Carla has chosen to make her advances clear as fucking day.

"You want to get out of here?" she asks, and just before I can find a way to let her down gently, my eyes catch sight of something across the room.

Actually, *someone* across the room.

Lexi.

She stands beside Ace and Julia and Finn and Scottie, and I'm shocked that she's even here, at this frat party. Ace is dramatically telling a story with his usual outlandish hand gestures, and Julia is giggling and rolling her eyes. Finn and Scottie listen on with smiles on their faces. But Lexi isn't engaged in anything that Ace is saying.

Her eyes are focused toward *me*.

Our gazes lock, and for the longest moment, I try to somehow gain the powers of telepathy to read her mind's thoughts from across the room as I search her eyes for any inkling of what she's thinking or feeling right now.

Her mouth is set in a firm line until she sucks her bottom lip into her mouth and digs her top teeth into it. Something's off with her normally gorgeous eyes, and I rapidly realize by the hunched shape of her shoulders and the discomfort within her gaze that she's upset.

Her eyes flit to the girl standing beside me, and I don't miss how they home in on the way Carla's hand is still gripping my bicep.

I look down at Carla and back at Lexi, and it only takes my brain a hot second to put the pieces of the puzzle together—Lexi thinks I'm here with the redhead.

Truth be told, I came to this party by myself. And even that took a Herculean effort. Ever since Lexi told me I needed to move on, I've had a hell of a time getting my ass out of bed and to practice, much less finding the desire to socialize with a bunch of rambunctious college co-eds.

My heart isn't even close to mended, and just looking at her causes the most acute, intense, terrorizing pain to spread throughout my chest. *I miss her. I love her.* But she made it clear she doesn't want to be with me.

But despite how she broke my fucking heart, seeing her here, standing across the room with an expression on her face that makes her look as if she's moments away from crying, the only thing I want to do is go to her. Pull her into my arms. And tell her everything is going to be okay.

She's the first to break eye contact, averting her gaze from mine with a snapping whip of her head. But shortly after that, she turns on her heel and starts heading for the door. Ace is still rambling on about something, and Julia and Scottie and Finn are none the wiser, but I don't miss the fact that Lexi is leaving this party.

And it sure feels a hell of a lot like she's leaving this party because of me.

Fuck. I feel like the worst kind of asshole. She probably thinks I've moved on and done it so easily. Which is absolutely absurd. I've been pining over Lexi Winslow ever since I first met her at Double C a year ago. And I've spent this entire summer trying to make her mine.

Quickly, I remove my bicep from Carla's grip, and she looks up at me with confusion on her face. But I could give two shits about this chick. No offense, but there's only one girl I want, and she just left this party.

I don't even bother giving Carla an excuse. Instead, I turn on my heel and head straight for the path Lexi just took. But once I step out the door and onto the pavement, I move my head back and forth erratically, searching up and down the sidewalk for Lexi's pretty blond hair.

Fuck.

I don't know which direction she went, and I pull my cell out of my pocket, a large part of me tempted to text her.

But when my eyes catch sight of the last message she sent me, the very one that grew hands, reached inside my chest, and ripped my heart out, a deep sigh escapes my lungs.

She's made it clear she doesn't want to be with me, and yet, here I am, still trying to chase her down.

"Boden!" someone exclaims from behind me, and I turn around to find a few guys from my team walking toward me.

"What the fuck you doing out here?" Ron asks, wrapping an arm around my shoulders.

"Just catching a little fresh air," I mutter, but my eyes are still glancing around the sidewalk and the street in search of the girl who got away.

"Pfft." Ricky laughs. "Let's get you back inside, QB. We've got some partying to do! Coach gave us tomorrow off, and I'm going to make damn sure we have a good time."

He doesn't even give me a moment to respond. Instead, he pretty much drags me back toward the front door, and before I know it, I'm inside the building.

The music is still pounding from the DJ's speakers at the back of the house. And everyone in the place is laughing and chatting and dancing and partying. They're carefree and happy and living up the notorious college experience with everything they have.

And everything inside me wants to go to Lexi. Wants to talk to her. Wants to get on my fucking knees and beg her to realize how goddamn good we are together.

My phone is still in my hand, and the urge to text her, to check on her, is too strong to deny. I want to say a million things. But I settle on the simplest option.

> *Me: Are you okay?*
>
> *Lexi: Yeah.*

Her response is succinct, but it feels like complete bullshit.

> *Me: You didn't seem okay, Lex. You seemed upset. I'm worried about you. And I fucking miss you like crazy.*
>
> *Lexi: Blake, I'm sorry to say this, but you need to stop texting me. I've moved on, and you need to move on too.*

There it is again. She wants me to move on.

And I'm going to have to learn how to do just that with the giant hole inside my chest I fear will never heal.

41

Lexi

I stare down at my phone, my last text to Blake the final entry in our chat. I wait for him to respond. I wait for him to call me out on my bullshit.

I wait and I wait, and it's all useless because I'm the one who just completely pushed him away.

I reread my words, and I hate how cruel and unemotional I sound. It's the worst form of irony to tell someone to move on when you're sitting on the subway with tears streaming down your cheeks because of the fact that you just witnessed them moving on right in front of your face.

Blake told me he missed me. And I'd be the ultimate liar if I didn't admit that I miss him too.

I miss his laugh and his smile, and I miss the way he makes me feel whenever we're together. I miss his cheesy jokes and the way his face always brightens the room, and I miss how comforting it feels to be in his arms.

I miss our late-night chats and our documentary binges and how he's probably the only person who could get me to eat pizza that was made in some dude's dorm.

More tears stream down my cheeks, and even though I'm not alone on the subway, I'm silently thankful that I live in a busy, fast-paced city like New York so that I can blubber in peace without some random stranger asking me what's wrong.

That's the thing about New Yorkers; they can certainly be kind, but for the most part, they mind their own business. They don't even blink an eye if someone decides to take their clothes off in the middle of a busy street and start shouting about the world ending. They simply go about their day and let that person do their thing.

There's beauty in that. But there's also pain. Because what I need now more than anything is the exact opposite of what I'd expect or normally want.

Existing as someone with a propensity for being a loner doesn't bode well during times like these. I'm stuck inside my own head, aimlessly walking through my thoughts and replaying every single moment I've spent with Blake over the summer.

I think about all of our conversations and our special moments, and it feels like the worst kind of torture mentally reliving all the highs when I'm currently sitting at what feels like the rock bottom of my lows.

I've never felt this sad or confused or upset. And the fact that I don't have control over my emotions, that I can't analyze my way out of my feelings, is the biggest kick in the ass. It makes me angry and scared and anxious, and the mere idea of going back to my apartment so I can just sit in my current state of misery by myself is the very last thing I want to do.

There's only one stop that makes sense for me to even be on the subway, and I stay rooted to my seat, my eyes downturned to my lap, until I get there.

Fifteen minutes later, I'm walking toward the brownstone I used to call home and pulling my spare key out of my purse. I unlock the door, and when I step inside, the sounds of the security alarm start to give a warning ding. I quickly head to the keypad and shut it off before dropping my purse and keys on the small catch-all table in the entryway.

I slip off my shoes and walk on bare feet down the hallway, taking the stairs that lead to the bedrooms on the second and third floors.

And when I reach my mom's room, I carefully push open the

door and find her lying in her bed by herself, completely asleep and unaware of the rest of the world.

I know my stepdad Wes is on some business trip related to the Mavericks, and he won't be home for another two days. And while I normally love his presence, tonight, I'm silently thankful that my mom is the only one in her bed right now.

Without delay, I slide into the empty spot to her left and wrap my arms around her back, cuddling my body close to her warmth. Instantly, she stirs, turning over onto her side with groggy eyes, and she tries to focus on my face.

"Lexi?" she asks and reaches out to smooth some of my blond hair out of my face. "What are you doing here, honey?"

The softness of her voice and her gentle, motherly touch break something inside me, and I just start crying. I press my head into her shoulder, and she hugs me tightly as I let the uncontrollable tears fall down my cheeks.

"Aw, honey," she whispers, gently rubbing my back with her hand. "Tell me what's wrong."

"Everything," I whisper back, my voice strangled around my emotion.

She lets me cry, tenderly rubbing my back the entire time, and I don't know how much time passes, but eventually, a sort of numbness washes over me, and I find the strength to pull away from the safety of her embrace and meet her eyes.

"I messed up, Mom," I admit. "And I don't know what to do or how to fix it."

"How about we go downstairs and I make us some hot cocoa, and we can try to sort it all out together?"

I have so many memories of my mom doing exactly this when I was a little girl. Being on the spectrum isn't an easy thing in general, but being on the spectrum when you're in middle school and trying to understand how to socialize and make friends is really freaking hard.

If it weren't for my mom and our many hot cocoa chats, I don't know how I would've survived my adolescence.

I nod. Grateful. "Sounds perfect."

———

My half-drunk cup of hot cocoa sits in front of me, my hands still clutching the mug like a lifeline as I continue to tell my mom all about my summer with Blake.

I've told her how it all started and about my stupid research project and how, at some point, it was like I was spending all my waking moments with him.

I've told her about how thoughtful he is and how much fun he is, and without giving her too many details, I've told her about how I've never felt so intimately connected to another person.

I've told her pretty much the whole trajectory of what went down between us, and she's mostly just listened, only occasionally interrupting me to ask a question to clarify.

"I told him to move on," I explain. "He wanted to be together, and he wanted our relationship to be out in the open where everyone would know that we're together. He told me he loved me, and I honestly don't know if I'm capable of loving someone like that. I don't know if I'm capable of loving someone in the same way that you love Wes."

My mom nods and takes a drink of cocoa, silently encouraging me to continue.

"But tonight, I saw him at a party. That dumb party Ace talked me into going to after dinner," I explain. "And Blake was there, but he was with another girl. A redhead who was pretty much fawning all over him, and it made me feel…terrible. But I know that's not fair because I told him to move on, you know? He wanted to be with me, and I told him I didn't want to be with him."

"Is he with that girl now?"

"I don't know." I shrug. "I didn't hang around long enough

to find out. It was like I couldn't hold back the urge to cry, and I just had to get out of there before I sobbed in front of a bunch of drunk college kids. But he did text me."

"What did he say?"

I slide my phone across the table and let her read the last few messages between us.

"He was worried about you, Lex," my mom says, lifting her eyes to meet mine.

"Yeah."

"But I don't think you actually mean what you said here," she says, searching my eyes carefully. "I don't think you want him to move on."

"Why do you think that?"

"Because what you felt at that party when you saw him with that girl was jealousy, honey," she says, and even though, deep down, I know that to be true, I'm still having a hard time processing the fact that someone as logical and rational as me could be jealous about anything or anyone.

Admitting that I was jealous feels worse and just as productive as swallowing a handful of nails.

"I have no reason to be jealous," I respond, and she smiles softly at me.

"No, you don't," she answers. "But we can't always help how we feel."

A deep sigh escapes my lungs, and I have to avert my eyes for a long moment as my mind tries to process it all. But when my mom gently reaches out her hand to touch mine, I meet her eyes again.

"Lexi, honey, it's okay that you were jealous. We all do that sometimes. It's normal," she says. "And you're capable of loving someone like I love Wes and Wes loves me. You're very much capable of that and being in a relationship, and I think your summer with Blake proves that."

I know she's right. I know she's right, but that doesn't make it any easier to confront the undeniable truth that's staring me down. The whole idea of love is such a complicated thing for a girl like me. Being in love equates to being out of control. And that's the one thing I always try to avoid.

I want to be in control of everything. Of data and statistics and routine and schedule. And I most certainly want to be in control of my emotions.

But when it comes to Blake, I haven't been in control of anything, especially not of how deeply my feelings have grown for him.

"I'm in love with him," I say, but my words are so quiet that I almost can't even hear them myself. So, I force myself to say it again. "I love him, Mom. I really love him. And I want to be with him."

A soft, knowing smile crests her lips.

"But I guess you already figured all that out, huh?" I question, and a little laugh leaves her lungs.

"I had a hunch," she says, still smiling. "But ultimately, you needed to be the one to decide."

"I feel like I've messed everything up with him. And I know I hurt him. Really bad."

"No, sweetheart." She shakes her head and reaches out to hold my hand. "Don't think like that. We all make mistakes. We all do things we regret. I think you just need to tell him how you feel. Tell him the truth, even the ugly parts of it. I think if you tell him all the things you just told me, he'll understand."

I have no idea if Blake will want to hear what I have to say. I have no idea if he'll forgive me for all the things I've put him through over these past few weeks. It's all an unknown, and while the fear of the unknown is something I absolutely loathe, I'm determined to suck it up and face it head on.

I have to. Plain and simple. Blake deserves that much from me.

He deserves everything, because time and time again, that's exactly what he's given me.

Instantly, I get an idea and grab my phone to send a text.

> **Me: Are you busy tomorrow? I need your help with something.**

Her text comes in a moment later.

> **Scottie: Name the time and place, and I'll be there.**

I don't know if Blake still wants to be with me, but I know I want to be with him.

And I'm going to do everything I can to show him just how much.

42

"This is our house! This is our year! And Georgia is the first stop on the road to our championship! Let's do this!" Coach Gordan shouts at the top of his lungs, finishing his speech off with a bang.

The locker room goes wild, most of my teammates jumping up and down and hooting and hollering as they high-five and chest-bump one another. And I grab my mouthpiece and helmet from my locker and give myself a mental pep talk.

Focus, you motherfucker. It's game time.

The coaching staff leads our team toward the tunnel, and I follow like a dutiful soldier.

For the last week, all my mind has wanted to think about is a certain beautiful blond girl who broke my goddamn heart. It's taken every ounce of willpower I have not to reach out to her. Not to text her or call her. Not to show up at her apartment. Hell, even though I know for a fact that she's officially done with her doctorate program, I've been so tempted to make a pit stop at the Ferris Research Lab between my classes and practices just to see if she's in there.

But I've managed to survive another seven days without her.

I've managed to eat and sleep and go to practice and classes.

I've managed it all, but I wouldn't say I've done it well.

My head was in my asshole pretty much every practice, so much so that Coach Gordan asked me to come into his office after practice on Thursday to have an impromptu heart-to-heart. I didn't have the balls to tell him I'm a fucking love-sick fool who is missing the girl of his goddamn dreams because she told him to move on.

Instead, I made some excuse of having issues with migraines, but I tried to lift his spirits by telling him I'm feeling a lot better. He made me see our team physician, and once I got the all clear, Coach Gordan didn't look like someone pissed in his Cheerios anymore.

And even though, on the inside, I feel like absolute dog shit, I refuse to drag my teammates to the depths of hell with me. They deserve better than that. They deserve for me to stay focused and have the kind of mental clarity that wins football games.

And this game is an important one.

Today marks the official kickoff of the Dragons' football season. And while I haven't officially set foot in the stadium yet, with the roars and cheers from the crowd echoing inside the tunnel that leads to the field, I'm certain we're dealing with a full house.

Georgia is one of our biggest rivals, and while they aren't the team we lost the championship to last year—fuck you, Buffalo— we need to win if we want to stand a chance at another championship opportunity.

And fuck, I want another opportunity. In fact, I refuse to accept anything less this year.

Then get your head out of your ass and focus on the win.

I might have my future plans set on playing in the NFL, but right now, my sights are set on leading the Dickson Dragons to a championship.

My helmet sits on top of my head, and I shake the tension out of my arms and hands as we sit and wait to be announced to the field. It's a decades-long university tradition that the first game of the season includes a ceremony of sorts where each football player walks out onto the field with one of the Dickson cheerleaders for good luck.

Personally, I think it's a little fucking stupid, but I refuse to bring the vibes down. A good quarterback, a good leader, doesn't bitch and moan about petty shit.

And trust me, I know, complaining about something like this is top-tier petty.

"You ready, Boden?" Drake asks. His helmet is already over his face, but I don't miss the pirate's smile on his lips.

Drake Martin has always been a crazy motherfucker, and anyone who's seen his running game would know he's reckless in a good way. The man takes tackles like he doesn't feel pain and gets a thrill out of taking on a three-hundred-pound linebacker. He's nuts and lives and eats football just like I always have.

"Of course I'm ready." I reach out to slap the top of his helmet. "Let's fucking go!"

"Hell yeah, BB!" he agrees and then raises his voice so every one of our teammates waiting in the tunnel can hear him. *"Let's fucking go!"*

The response is several shouts and cheers that eventually turn into, "Dragons! Dragons! Dragons!" Followed by "Eat shit, Georgia!"

Seeing as that last part technically goes against the Dragons Football code of ethics, I know Coach Gordan has to be rolling his eyes over it, but he's also not saying anything. The more amped up we are, the better.

"Ladies and gentlemen, please stand up from your seats!" the announcer exclaims. "And get ready to welcome this year's Dickson Dragons to the field!"

The crowd bursts into excitement. And the student section doesn't disappoint when they start shouting, *"BBE! BBE!"*

Yes, it's a play on BDE—otherwise known as Big Dick Energy—and yes, they are utilizing my initials. It's something that started halfway through my freshman season and caught on.

In front of me, each of my teammates starts to walk out of the tunnel, meeting up with their Dragons' cheerleader match, and walking onto the field with her arm tucked within theirs.

It's tradition that the quarterback is the last one to exit the tunnel, and it's a first-game-of-the-season tradition that the quarterback walks onto the field with the captain of this year's Dickson cheerleaders.

I can't for the life of me remember which cheerleader was named captain this year, and there's a small part of me that's annoyed it's not Scottie Bardeaux. But I swallow it down and force a smile to my lips when I reach the end of the tunnel.

Instantly, my eyes look out toward the packed stadium, taking in the gold-and-navy crowd of excited fans. *Fuck, this is why I'm here. This is what I love. This is what I live for.*

Once Drake Martin is announced and he makes it to the center of the field with Kayla—a cheerleader who is one of Scottie's best friends—I look to my right and hold out my hand for the captain of the cheerleading squad.

But when I meet familiar blue eyes, I have to blink several times to try to make the fucking mirage disappear.

It doesn't work, though.

Instead, Lexi is still there, dressed in a Dragons' cheerleader uniform with a shy but adorable smile on her lips. Her mouth is painted red just like the rest of the squad normally sports on game days, and her blond hair is in this high ponytail with a big gold bow at the top.

What the fuck is happening right now?

"Hi, Blake," she says, and I just stare at her, my voice mute and my eyes practically wider than my face. "Mind escorting me out onto the field?" she asks, tucking her arm into my still-outstretched one.

If it weren't for a chick with a headset and wild eyes waving me toward the center of the field, I don't know if I'd even move.

But somehow, I do. Though, my legs feel like they're made of a terrible combination of lead and wood. Each step I take is stiff and heavy.

And by the time we make it to the center of the field, the entire stadium is on their feet, clapping their hands with excitement as the announcer encourages their applause. But my eyes are now fixated on Lexi's face. At first, she's looking out toward the crowd, but eventually, she locks her gaze with mine.

"What is going on right now?" I whisper toward her. "Am I dreaming, or are you really dressed in a Dragons' cheerleader uniform?"

"No, Blake, you're not dreaming." She smiles. Shakes her head. "I am, in fact, wearing a cheerleader uniform."

"H-how? Why?"

"It was a combination of help from Scottie and a Double C invite to McKenzie."

"McKenzie?"

"The captain of the squad," she explains with a shrug.

"Okay…" I blink several times, my brain trying to process this insane situation. "But why are you here?"

"Isn't it obvious?" she asks, but just before I can tell her, no, it's not fucking obvious, the announcer tells the crowd to quiet down for the national anthem.

Some chick with auburn hair steps up to the microphone that sits right in front of us and starts to give her best Whitney Houston impression of our country's most famous song.

She's good, truthfully, but all I care about right now is trying to understand why Lexi is even here.

"Lexi," I whisper toward her, and she meets my eyes again. "Seriously. What is going on?"

"Oh, you mean you want to know why I'm here?"

I nod. "That'd be nice."

She searches my eyes for a long moment before averting them completely to stare at her feet. And the chick at the microphone is halfway through the song before Lexi locks her gaze with mine again, a hard swallow making her throat vibrate at her neck. "Blake, I'm sorry for everything," she whispers. "I'm sorry for the way I treated you. I'm sorry for hurting you. And mostly, I'm sorry that I was so scared to let myself feel what you make me feel that I chose to destroy us instead of face my feelings for you head on."

She pauses and digs her teeth into her bottom lip, and I just stand there, her arm still tucked within mine.

"I love you," she says, but it's so quiet, and the girl singing the national anthem is starting to really bring it home, hitting some seriously high notes, that I almost think my ears make it up entirely. But then, she says it again, this time turning her body toward mine and grabbing both of my hands into hers. "Blake, I love you. And I know I was slow on the uptake in letting myself realize that, but in my defense, I've never been good at emotional stuff. It's a serious weak point for me and, clearly, a learning curve. This whole summer, I tried to convince myself that you and I were just playing games, just having fun. But in the end, it wasn't a game at all to me because I fell in love with you. I *am* in love with you. And I'm here, standing in the middle of this packed stadium, wearing a freaking cheerleader uniform, because I wanted to show you that I'm ready to be together. Out in the open. No secrets anymore."

"You want to be with me?" I ask her, my gaze searching hers for any sign of fear or hesitancy or doubt, but all I see are determination and confidence and her heart.

"I want to be with you. More than anything. Because I love you."

"I love you too," I tell her just as the national anthem comes to a close, and the crowd claps their hands reverently. But I hardly notice any of it because the girl of my dreams is standing in front of me and she's saying words I only dreamed of hearing her say.

Words I thought I'd never hear her say.

She loves me. She wants to be with me.

I don't hesitate. I don't hold back. And between one breath and the next, I pull Lexi into my arms, lift her up so that we're face-to-face, and kiss her.

I fucking kiss her.

She tastes like everything I remembered. She tastes like love. She tastes like mine.

She kisses me right back, wrapping her hands around my neck

as she melds her mouth with mine. But our kiss is cut a little short when the sounds of the crowd booming with applause and cheers and wolf whistles start to echo inside my ears.

I pull back, and when I see Lexi's eyes move to the jumbotron to the right of us, I follow their lead and find out that we're currently the center of attention.

"Oh my God," Lexi mutters through a half giggle, half groan.

"Too much?" I ask, smiling at her. "I mean, you said you wanted to be out in the open, so…"

Her giggle turns into an outright laugh. "No, Blake. It's not too much. But it's certainly something I'm going to have to get used to, huh? Dating the star quarterback and all that."

It's my turn to laugh. But I cut off my own laughter by kissing her again.

But she only lets me do it for a few seconds before she pulls away with a big smile.

"I love you, Blake," she says and climbs out of my arms and back to her feet. "But now, it's time for you to get your head in the game." She reaches up to pull my helmet the rest of the way down my head, and she grips the face mask with her petite hand. "And if you win, you can spend the night at my place."

"And if I lose?"

"You won't lose."

"You're right." I wink. "I won't."

There's not a chance in the world I'm walking away from this game with anything but a win and *my* Lexi on my arm.

43

Lexi

Friends and family stand outside the Dragons' locker room, everyone vibrating with excitement from the game.

The Dragons won, just like I knew they would. And Blake is undoubtedly the MVP of the game, with twenty-four of twenty-five completed passes, four touchdowns, 360 passing yards, and zero interceptions.

He was a beast and, statistically, showcased a game that will have ESPN commentators recalling it for years to come.

And this game was most certainly on ESPN. I know this because I've received so many phone calls and texts from my family about the infamous kiss between Blake and me that I could hardly keep up.

I'm so happy for you, honey. And more than that, I'm proud of you, was the text from my mom.

Tell me I didn't just see you kissing Blake Boden, was the message from my stepdad Wes.

Fucking gross, Lexi! came from my brother.

Quinn Bailey sent me an *I told you so!* Followed by *Proud of you, Lexi Lou.*

But the most entertaining of them all was Ace's dad Thatch, who sent me a video message that included him blubbering like a fool and telling me how he was all up in his feels over Blake's and my love story.

I haven't heard from my dad Nick, but that's probably because he spends most of his time at the hospital instead of watching Saturday college football.

And I haven't had time to go through the messages from my aunts and uncles, but I'm sure I'll get an earful at the next Winslow family dinner.

But all of that can wait, because right now, there's only one person I want to see, and he's currently walking out of the locker room with a big smile on his face. Blake's hair is wet from a fresh shower, and he's sporting his favorite pair of jeans and a Dragons Football T-shirt. He looks big and strong and so damn handsome I simply let myself enjoy the view that is *my* guy.

He doesn't see me at first, but when he does, the widest smile appears on his lips, and he doesn't waste any time pushing through the crowd to get to me.

And before I know it, I'm being lifted off my feet and into his arms.

"Good game," I tell him, and he leans back to meet my eyes.

"And what's your official analysis of my stats?"

"No doubt, you'll be all over ESPN for the next week," I say with a grin.

"That's nice, but there's only one person I wanted to impress," he says and brushes his lips against mine. "Did I manage to impress her?"

"You did more than impress her." I speak my truth. "You made her fall in love."

"You love me?"

"Yeah." I nod. "But I'm pretty sure we already established that before the game when I was wearing that ridiculous cheerleading uniform."

He smirks, but then he sets me on my feet. And I scrunch up my nose in confusion when he gets down on one knee in front of me.

"Blake?"

"Relax," he says, smiling up at me. "Lexi Lou Winslow, I would like to officially ask you to be my girlfriend."

I laugh. "Oh my God."

"So, will you be my girlfriend?"

I roll my eyes, but I also say, "Yes."

"Hell yeah, Blakey!"

"Get it, BB!"

Several hoots and hollers fill my ears, and I realize that half of his team is watching this ridiculous scene, but Blake doesn't care. And you know, the craziest thing of all, I don't care either. My eyes are solely fixated on Blake. The rest of the world might as well not exist.

He's smiling proudly as he rises to his feet and pulls me back into his arms. "I love you," he says and presses a soft and sweet kiss to my lips. "Thank you for doing what you did today. Thank you for thinking I'm worthy of you putting yourself out there like you did," he whispers directly into my ear. "I know it wasn't easy. So, I just want you to know I'm proud of you, Lexi. I'm proud of you, and I love you."

"I love you too, Blake," I whisper back, squeezing my arms around his neck and burying my face into his shoulder. "Thank you for being patient with me. Thank you for understanding me. And mostly, thank you for loving me exactly the way I am."

"Always," he says and presses another kiss to my lips. "And that's a guarantee."

"What do you say we get out of here?" I eventually ask, and he meets my eyes again.

"As in, go to one of the many after parties we've been invited to tonight?"

I shake my head. "I was thinking something a little more private…"

"Thank fuck," he says, but he doesn't even bother setting me on my feet. Instead, he tosses me over his shoulder and just starts carrying me toward the hallway that leads to the exit of the stadium.

"Blake! What the hell?"

"Relax, Lex. I'll have us back at my place in no time."

I giggle. "You're insane!"

"No, babe. I'm just a man in love with his girlfriend!"

And I'm just a girl who is in love with Blake Boden. A football player.

God help me, the universe sure has a sense of humor.

EPILOGUE

PART 1

Friday, September 6th
Blake

I step out of the shower and dry off with one of the fluffy tow-els Lexi was adamant about buying and keeping at my place. Apparently, my flimsy towels weren't cutting it.

I smile to myself as I think about the conversation that trans-pired on that topic.

I told her my towels were just fine, and she responded by div-ing into a ten-minute discussion about how our skin is the largest organ of our body and having good towels is imperative to the del-icate nature of the human biome.

Hence, how I ended up with new, fancy-as-fuck towels in my apartment.

I can't deny they feel a hell of a lot better on my skin, but no way in hell am I going to admit that to Lex. Even though she's the smartest person I know, the smartest person in every room she steps into, I prefer to keep my girl on her toes every once in a while. If that means telling secret white lies about how I don't notice a dif-ference with the new towels—even though they are the epitome of luxury—so be it.

Once I'm dried off and dressed for the day, I brush my teeth and run a comb through my hair before heading into the kitchen.

Lexi is sitting at the small island across from the fridge, her lap-top out and her fingers busy at work. The cutest little wrinkle mars the space between her eyebrows, and she's so focused on whatever she's doing that she doesn't even notice my presence at first.

I gently press a kiss to her forehead as I pass her, but other than that, I let her be. I know Lexi well enough to know when an interruption is a good thing or a bad thing. Right now, it'd be a bad thing. But she'll come around to me in due time.

By the time I have a cup of coffee poured and my preferred sugar and creamer mixed in, I feel two petite arms wrap around my waist. I turn around to find Lexi standing there, her blue eyes bright and her smile beautiful.

"Mornin', Lex," I say and set my cup of coffee back on the counter to wrap my arms around her for a suitable good-morning hug.

"Morning," she says, resting her chin on my chest as I gently sway us back and forth.

We've only officially been together for a little over a week, and I still can't get over how much things have changed. We aren't living together, but we've resumed the routine of staying at each other's places nearly every night. Last night, she stayed at my place. And the two nights before that, I was at hers.

"So…it's decided, then," I say, a big smile on my lips as I think about our quiet conversation in bed last night after I made Lexi come three times—two while she rode my face, and the big finale was when I got to witness her riding my cock like my favorite rodeo queen. It was fucking fantastic, but it pales in comparison to the conversation that occurred after.

"It's decided." Lexi's smile matches mine. "We're moving in together."

"Are you sure you want to live with your football-playing boyfriend who comes home sweaty ninety-nine percent of the time and has horrible taste in towels?"

"I've already fixed the towel situation," she says with a wink. "And I don't mind the sweat."

I reach down to squeeze her ass playfully. "Good."

"But don't jump the gun on this, okay?" she requests, standing on her tippy-toes to press a kiss to my lips. "I still have a few more buildings to scout, and the ideal location for our apartment provides easy commutes for both of us."

Despite her numerous job offers all over the country—from incredible companies and organizations that pretty much everyone in the world knows—Lexi has decided she wants to stay in New York. She's also decided that she doesn't want to work for someone else. She wants to work for herself.

"I'm pretty sure your mind is already set on one specific location in Lower Manhattan, but I will wait patiently for the official go-ahead."

"Perfect." She steps out of my embrace when her phone starts ringing from the spot beside her laptop. She answers it on the second ring, even tapping the button so it's on speaker while she sits back down to finish up whatever she is working on.

And I head over to the stove to start making us some eggs.

"Lexi!" her lawyer Caplin Hawkins greets jovially into the receiver. "I have some news."

"Okay…"

"Do you want to hear the news?" he asks, a hint of teasing in his tone. Lexi rolls her eyes.

"If it's about the contract you're working on for me, clearly, I want to hear the news."

"That's great to hear because I have some news," he says, but he doesn't pussyfoot around. "Medivanta upped their offer. Thirty-two million."

"And what about the provisions?"

"That is still being negotiated."

"Negotiated?" Lexi retorts as I crack a few eggs into a pan. "There's no negotiating, Cap. I refuse to sell this software to a medical company that will then sell it off to insurance companies so they can pinpoint patients who are at an increased risk for chronic disease and raise their premiums. If Medivanta can't sign on the dotted line with those provisions, I'll find someone else who will."

Her lawyer laughs, which might seem odd for a lawyer to do,

but this is Caplin Hawkins. He's best friends with Lexi's stepdad and Thatcher Kelly and almost never takes anything too seriously. Well, besides his client's contracts.

"Love the spunk, Lex," he eventually says. "And I hear you loud and clear. I have your back on this, okay? We're on the same page. And I can't guarantee Medivanta will agree, but if they don't, I'll help you finalize a contract with a company that will. Sound like a plan?"

"Yep."

"Okay then, Lexi. We'll talk later."

The call ends shortly after that, and I shut off the burner as I fill two plates with eggs and a few slices of a banana. I slide one plate over to her, and she offers me a grateful smile.

"You're the best."

I waggle my brows. "You know, you told me that last night too, while I had my mouth on your pussy."

"Blake!" she giggles around a mouthful of eggs.

"What? It's true. You did. You said, *You're the best, Blake! Oh my God, you're the best!*" I smile at her. "It was really sweet."

She rolls her eyes. "I cannot be held accountable for anything I say in the heat of the moment."

I just smile at her, my mind already going back to the conversation she just had with her lawyer and how fucking huge of a deal it all is. I mean, thirty-two million dollars for something she developed while she was in college? Holy fucking shit.

"You're going to be the next Iron Man but better. Smarter. More successful." I smile at my beautiful, intelligent girlfriend. "Damn, I can't wait to watch you take on the world, Iron Woman."

"Speak for yourself, Mr. Star Quarterback," Lexi retorts with a knowing grin. "Your future is bright with endorsement deals and multimillion-dollar contracts."

And while her vision for my future is certainly one I can get on board with, I realize I need to head out so I'm not late for class. I drop my plate into the sink and walk over to Lexi to pull her off the barstool and give her a big hug.

"What are your plans tonight, Iron Woman?"

"I have a very important cloak-and-dagger sort of ceremony thing."

I grin. "Sounds very 'If I tell you, I'll have to kill you.'"

"Oh, it is."

"And when are you going to be done?"

"Probably in time for you to grab that awesome Chinese take-out and meet me back here to eat dinner together."

"Okay, okay. I'm loving the sound of this so far…"

"So far?" she asks. "As in, you're expecting more?"

"I don't know." I lift one shoulder. "I was kind of hoping your pussy was on the menu too."

Lexi giggles, and I lean forward to kiss her lips.

"Love you," I whisper against her lips. "Have a nice day at work, honey."

"Have a nice day at school, sweetheart," she teases.

"Damn, I love being with an older woman. It's hot." I tell her between playful kisses. "Oh, by the way, maybe you should see if Medivanta or, you know, another bigwig company is interested in your *Polarize* app too?" I purposefully overenunciate the word Polarize. "Surely that might be something they're interested in…" I pause while Lexi pointedly leans back to meet my eyes.

"I never should've told you about that app."

Three nights ago, Lexi revealed the truth of her secret little Blake Boden Experiment to me *and* the app she created with me in mind. By the timid way she delivered the details, I think there was a part of her that was worried I'd be upset about it. Quite the contrary, though. Pretty sure it made my love for Lexi—and my ego—grow a hundred times in size.

I mean, my dream girl created an app, and I was the inspiration? *Hell fucking yes.*

"You're wrong, Lex." I waggle my brows. "You should've told me about it. Though, I'm still waiting for you to let me play around with it."

"You want to find out if you're compatible with Blake Boden?" She quirks a teasing brow at me, and I just squeeze her cute little ass and lift her up into my arms.

"Fuck that Blake Boden guy," I say, pressing a soft kiss to her lips. "The only person I want to be compatible with is Lexi Lou Winslow. Always and forever, baby."

And then, I press several more playful kisses to her lips and her nose and her forehead and each of her cheeks.

She giggles, and I spend another five minutes kissing her some more. Because that's what you do when Lexi Lou Winslow is your girlfriend—you fucking *kiss* her.

Even if you end up having to sprint across campus to make it to class on time.

PART 2

Lexi

I've spent so much of my college career at the Nash Mathematics Center that I can name every floor, every lecture hall, every professor and where their office is located. I know that there are a total of ten bathrooms scattered across all the floors, centrally located near the elevators and stairs. And I know that this building hosts one of the creepiest basements you'll ever enter.

It's only a little after six in the evening and the sun still hasn't made its full descent into the horizon, but the main hallway of the basement is dark as I walk down it. I've been in this basement a total of twenty-two times. Hosted eight Double C events here. Ironically enough, the last Double C event I hosted here was the first time I met Blake.

It was also the night that I watched Finn kick an ex-UFC fighter's ass and walked out with an extra three hundred bucks in my pocket.

My phone buzzes in my hand, breaking my train of thought.

I glance at the screen, and a smile tugs at my lips when I see the sender.

> Ginger: *Guess who has an interview with Apple?*

> Me: *Tim Cook's long-lost niece?*

> Ginger: *Close. Ginger Lewis, soon-to-be Queen of Code. Silicon Valley better roll out the red carpet.*

> Me: *When's the big coronation?*

> Ginger: *Thursday at 10 a.m. Let's all pray that I don't blow it.*

> Me: *You won't.*

> Ginger: *You're right. I won't. And then I'll be so freaking happy! And you'll be happy too, because your favorite Ferris pal can send you free swag.*

> Me: *I'll take a Macbook. Thanks.*

> Ginger: *You'll be happy with Apple stickers and, like, a pen or two. Oh! By the way, I saw that ESPN footage, making the rounds again on TikTok...*

> Me: *Don't remind me.*

> Ginger: *Don't remind you? Lex, that footage is ICONIC. Your studly football star boyfriend kissed you on the mouth in the middle of the field and was looking down at you like you're the love of his life because, well, you are. Sheesh. I'm still swooning over here, you lucky bitch. Also, it did remind me of something very important...*

> Me: *And that important thing would be?*

> Ginger: *You still owe me lunch. And a full-fledged rundown*

of everything that's happened between you and Mr. Football Star. I'm talking alllll the details.

Me: How about next Friday? Then, you can tell me all about the big interview.

Ginger: Oh honey, count me in. I'll text you next week to harass you about a time and a place.

I laugh and tuck my phone back into my bag just as a voice calls out behind me.

"Lex!"

I glance over my shoulder to find Connor jogging to catch up with me. I slow my steps until he's at my side, and he doesn't hesitate to hand me the deep navy velvet cloak I was given the night I was initiated as the president of Double C with Connor as my VP, surrounded by candles and darkness and four of the fifteen Dickson alumni who make up the chairpersons of the board for Computare Caterva.

Pretty official for a secret society, I know, but when it was formed in the early 1900s, only a few years after Dickson University was established, formality was at the center of everything, and that history that runs deep. Historical figures, political figures, celebrities, professional athletes—there's a whole slew of big names who have been a part of Double C.

Though, I can't speak of those names. No one can. That rule is one of the pillars of the society.

The farther we get into the basement hallway, the darker it gets. A dingy, metallic smell settles inside my nose as we reach the door that leads into the very same room where we once hosted an underground fight club for the night, and Connor unlocks it, utilizing the stack of keys that gives us entry into every single building and room on campus.

A set of keys that is about to be handed off to someone else.

He holds the door open for me, and I step inside, pulling my cloak over my body as I do. I lift my hood, covering my hair, and spot the two chairs that will be running tonight's torch-passing ceremony.

Candles are already lit around the room, and a single gold velvet throne sits in the center. And it's exactly how I remember it from when Connor and I were initiated into our head Double C positions five years ago.

But now that we've closed the college chapters in our lives, both of us heading into the real world of adulthood and careers, it's time to move on.

Both of the chair members have their backs turned to us, their gold cloaks covering their bodies. And while I don't know who will be handling tonight's ceremony, I do know who the next sitting president of Double C will be, and it wouldn't feel right if one chair, in particular, weren't here to witness the passing of the torch.

"This is wild," Connor whispers toward me. "I can't believe we're done with college. Done with Double C."

I look over at him and smile. My emotions are a mix of excitement and nostalgia. "I know. We've had some good times with Double C, haven't we?"

He grins. "Too many."

My phone vibrates in the pocket of my jeans, and I reach beneath my cloak to grab it. Seeing as the ceremony hasn't officially started, I discreetly pull it out to check the screen.

I'm expecting it to be Blake, sending me something funny or sexy or a combination of both, but my brow furrows when I see it's from my lawyer.

> *Caplin Hawkins: Medivanta agreed to all provisions. Their legal team is signing the contract now. And while this is off the record and completely out of character for your very professional—and incredibly talented—lawyer to say, as your Uncle Cappy, I have to say it. I'm so fucking proud of you. Congratulations.*

Oh my God. I stare down at my phone, my eyes wide with

surprise and elation and all the myriad emotions that come with finding out the news. This is huge. So huge that I'm not sure I'm going to be able to fully process it all until I see Blake's reaction when I tell him later tonight.

I just sold something I made for thirty-two million dollars.

And now, I can officially start my own company and continue to do what I love—creating software and apps and technological advancements.

Lexi Winslow, CEO and owner of LexLink. Soon, that's going to be me.

Holy hell.

I look over at Connor, my mind desperate to tell someone the good news, but just before I can open my mouth, I clamp it shut. It doesn't feel right telling anyone but Blake first. He's…my person.

I guess that's what happens when you love someone. I never understood what my mom would mean when she'd say that about Wes, but now, I get it.

It's not scientific. It's not logical. But it is fact.

Blake is my person. He's my lover and my favorite confidant and my biggest support and my loudest cheerleader. He's my best friend. I don't know how one person can play all those roles at the same time, but that's what he does for me.

One of the chairs walks toward the secret door at the back of the massive room, and I slide my phone back into my pocket, forcing myself to focus on the ceremony that's about to start.

I can't make out the chair's face as they guide Double C's next sitting president out of the secret room that I know from Connor's early text confirmation, he's been waiting in for a good forty-five minutes.

His face is blindfolded, but a perpetual full-toothed smile is etched on his lips. Fucking kidnapped with little to no explanation and the bastard is still smiling—I swear, only him.

When the chair guides him to sit in the gold velvet throne in the center of the room, her hood shifts a little, and I spot her familiar dark-brown hair and pretty eyes and her proud but mischievous smile.

Oh man, the family's all here. *This is going to be good.*

"Ace Tobias Kelly, I'd like to welcome you here tonight," the other chair—whom I recognize as a very well-known billionaire who was once on a mainstream television show that allowed everyday people to pitch their company in front of a board to try to get investments—starts to announce, walking around where Ace still sits blindfolded on the velvet throne. "This is going to be one of the most important nights of your life. Are you ready to take on the challenge?"

"I'm ready," Ace chatters excitedly. "I'm so ready."

Connor and I stay put in the corner of the space, but both chairs step directly in front of Ace's perched spot on the throne. They drop the hoods of their cloaks, revealing their faces, and the male chair—aka the billionaire—steps forward to remove Ace's blindfold.

Ace blinks several times, working to adjust his vision to the change from darkness to candlelight, but I can tell the instant everything comes into focus.

"Mom?" he questions, his eyes wide and pointed directly at the female chair I've known for most of my life.

Cassie Kelly is a Dickson alum and secret chair of Double C. She's the whole reason I put up with Ace's bullshit all last year of inviting new people to our secret society without permission. She was, after all, one of the chairs who initiated both Connor and me into Double C.

Trust me, it was a shock, but it was also a pleasant surprise.

"Hi, Acer," Cassie says, and even though I can't see her face, I can hear the smile in her voice.

"What are you doing here?" Ace questions, looking around the room.

"Surprise, motherfucker," she says without hesitation. "Your clearly very cool mom is one of the secret chairs of Double C."

Ace's eyes are so big, they look like they could consume his entire face.

The male chair nods toward Connor and me, and we both move forward, dropping the hoods of our cloaks to reveal our faces and stepping up to where Ace still sits in shock.

"Tonight, we are gathered here for the ceremony of your initiation," I state, and Ace searches my eyes. His gaze is silently questioning if I knew about his mom's secret society secret, and I just offer him a brief, knowing smile.

"Tonight, you will be initiated as the current sitting president of Computare Caterva," Connor instructs. "Are you ready to take the oath, Ace Tobias Kelly?"

Ace looks at me and then looks at his mom, and then the biggest smile forms on his face. "I'm ready."

"Julia won't be mad?" Cassie hedges, making Ace's smile fall for the briefest of moments before he picks it up again.

He shakes his head. "She will. But that's why we have the fifteen-minute rule. It's saved my ass more than once, and it'll save it again. I'm ready."

I raise my eyebrows with interest. *A fifteen-minute rule?*

I guess that's a question for another time because, right now, we've got a ceremony to perform.

Look out, world. There's a new Double C president in town, and his name is Ace Kelly.

PART 3

Saturday, September 7th

Blake

This afternoon, the Dickson Dragons beat Pennington, one of our biggest rivals, keeping our winning streak going with a blazing win of thirty-two to fourteen.

And right now, I'm out celebrating with my closest friends in the middle of a dusty basement in the psychology building. The only thing that would make this better is if my girl Lexi were here, but she was adamant that I didn't want to miss tonight's first official Double C event of the year.

I don't know much, but from what little Lexi revealed to me last night in bed after we had celebration sex over her big contract with Medivanta, since she's officially done with college, the torch has been passed to someone else. And while she is still considered a chair within the society, her role no longer includes attending the actual events.

Not to mention, Ace has sent exactly one thousand text messages today, even while I was in the middle of a fucking football game, telling me I had to be there tonight.

I have no idea what is on the agenda for tonight, but I know my friends haven't stopped smiling since the moment we walked inside these doors.

Ace, well, I think he's just fucking pumped to be back on campus and getting all the attention he loves so much from Dickson's social scene. And Julia is most likely just vibing off him.

But Finn and Scottie are happy for a completely different reason. Yesterday, Lexi's dad, Dr. Raines, confirmed that Scottie has the official green light for the surgery and treatment plan he believes will make her walk again.

And she's going to do it. Her surgery is set for the end of this month.

"It's kind of weird not seeing Lexi here, running the show," Scottie says, looking up at me with a smile. "Though, I guess it's not that weird for you now, huh, Blake? You see your girl all the time."

"Damn straight," I say with a big smile. "I see *my girl* all the time."

Finn laughs. "Man, I still can't believe, over a year ago, I thought you had lost your fucking marbles when you said you were going to marry the girl who didn't give you the time of day. And now, look at you."

"When you know, you know." I give his shoulder a hearty pat. "Right, Finn?"

He looks down at Scottie and gently squeezes her shoulder. "Right."

"I wonder what tonight's big event is going to be," Julia muses, but before she can say anything else, Ace squeezes her shoulders playfully and looks at all of us.

"I'll be right back, okay?"

"Okay, weirdo," Julia says, rolling her eyes and laughing at the same time.

But when Ace walks away from our little friend group that's gathered in the center of the rest of the Double C society, I don't miss the fact that he doesn't head to the dingy bathroom near the entrance or to the center of the crowd to chat with all the people he knows.

Instead, he makes a beeline for the makeshift stage at the front.

And then, he hops onto the stage and grabs the microphone.

What is he doing?

"What the fuck?" Finn questions.

But the answer comes from the smiling man with the mic. "I'd like to welcome everyone here tonight. This is our first official Double C event of the year, and while I think we can all agree that filling our previous president Lexi's shoes is quite the big responsibility, the secret chairs of our even secreter society have chosen me to take on that role."

Several hoots and hollers come from the crowd at his announcement.

"They made a good choice, right?" Ace muses into the mic. "I mean, if there's one person who knows how to have some fucking fun, it's me."

"Hell yeah!"

"President Acer!"

"This is going to be a good fucking year!"

It's clear he has the approval of the crowd, and I swear I can see his ego grow right along with his smile.

"Holy shit," Finn mutters. "Ace Kelly is president of Double C."

"This is awesome!" Scottie says through several amused laughs.

And I can't disagree with her. If there's one guy who should be running a secret society, it's Ace Kelly. Though, I'm a little scared to think about the events he's going to be tossing our way. Fingers crossed, none of us ends up in handcuffs.

Ace continues to schmooze his constituents with jokes and commentary, and as I look around the room, taking in all the smiling, entertained faces, I'm shocked to find Julia standing there with a furrowed brow and her lips set into a firm line.

She's not smiling or laughing or enjoying the fact that her best friend is standing on that stage. Instead, she looks…upset.

"You good, Jules?" I ask her, and when she meets my eyes, the smile that follows on her lips feels off. It feels forced.

"Of course," she says, clearing her throat. "Just surprised, you know?"

"You didn't know about this?"

"Nope." She shakes her head, and her throat bobs a little as she swallows. "I just found out right now…with everyone."

Of all the people in the world Ace talks to, Julia Brooks is his go-to girl. They've been best friends their whole lives, and even in college, they're basically attached at the hip.

But maybe he couldn't tell her? Maybe there's some kind of rule against it?

I don't know.

Scottie asks Julia to go the bathroom with her, and Julia doesn't hesitate to take hold of Scottie's wheelchair and guide her toward the entrance doors behind us.

Ace is still working the crowd, and I just sit back and enjoy the show, reveling in one of my best friends living his moment in the sun.

Though, my attention gets diverted pretty quick when my phone vibrates in my pocket, and I find a text message from Lexi.

Lexi: You shocked?

Immediately, I know what she's referring to.

Me: Completely. But also, not at all. It makes sense.

Lexi: Yeah, I thought so too.

Me: What are you doing right now?

Lexi: Watching a documentary on YouTube in bed.

Me: And what are you wearing?

Lexi: Does it matter?

Me: Yes, it matters. I need a visual, babe.

Lexi: Just one of your T-shirts.

Me: Let me get this straight. You're in my bed, and you're only wearing my T-shirt? No bra? No panties?

Lexi: That is correct.

Me: I'll be there in fifteen minutes.

Lexi: Oh my God, you're insane. Stay with your friends. I'll be here all night.

Ha. Like I want to stay out when I have Lexi in my bed?

Me: Make it eight minutes. I can run.

Thirty seconds later, I'm out the entrance doors after giving Finn a lame excuse of needing to go home. Two minutes after that, I'm running across campus, straight in the direction of my apartment. By the time I'm walking through my door, I'm a little sweaty and out of breath, but the fact that I shaved a minute off my estimated time makes it all worth it.

I don't waste another minute slipping off my shoes at the door and heading straight for my bedroom.

Though, when I get there, I find a completely naked Lexi in my bed.

She offers me a little wave. "Hi, honey. I'm so glad you're home."

"Yeah. I made the right choice," I say and start to remove my own clothes. "I mean, it was cool seeing Ace running the show—a little odd that it wasn't you—but I'm happy for him." My jeans and T-shirt hit the floor. "Though, not going to lie, it kind of felt like Julia was mad or something," I update as I slide off my boxer briefs and crawl onto the bed. "Which is weird, right? I would've thought Julia would've been happy for him."

"Blake?"

"Yeah?" I question, my mouth already busy kissing a trail up her legs.

"How about we continue this whole conversation a little later?" Lexi says with a smile as she sits on her knees and pushes me back into the mattress. "You know, after I make you come."

"Damn, I'm one lucky son of a bitch," I say, looking up at this beautiful woman in awe as she straddles my hips.

"Yeah, you are." She smiles. "But I'm lucky too."

I wrap my arms around her and pull her tight against my chest, burying my face into her neck as I kiss the tender skin below her ear. "We both are," I tell her.

"One day, I think I'm going to marry you," Lexi whispers into my ear, and her words slip under my skin until they find their way to my heart. It pounds excitedly in my chest, and I lean back to meet her eyes.

"Oh, Lexi Lou Winslow, that's a certainty I've known since the first moment I saw you at that Double C event."

She snorts. "You're lying."

"No." I shake my head, just barely brushing my lips against hers. "I'm not. I actually said those words aloud. *I'm going to marry that girl.* Ask Finn. He heard it."

Lexi leans forward and presses a slow and seductive kiss to my lips. "I'd like to make a plan."

"A plan?"

"A five-year plan."

"And what does this five-year plan entail?"

"Both of us succeeding in our careers and getting married."

"I'm in," I exclaim and wrap my arms around her as I flip her onto her back. My gaze locked with hers, I reach up to brush a few strands of her pretty blond hair out of her eyes. "I'm fucking in. Call your lawyer and have him start the paperwork. I want to sign my name in blood just to make sure it sticks."

Lexi bursts into laughter. "No contract or blood oath needed. You have my word."

"And you have mine."

Lexi and me together forever. That's my plan, and I'm sticking to it.

This isn't the end of Dickson University, it's just the beginning.

Preorder Ace and Julia's book!

The next book in the highly addictive Dickson University Series, featuring Ace and Julia and their blind love for one another, *The Fifteen-Minute Rule*, is coming soon!

Preorder **The Fifteen-Minute Rule** today!

Haven't read Finn and Scottie's book yet?

Start reading *Learning Curve* today!

Sign up for our newsletter, and we'll keep you up-to-date on any **Dickson University Series** news, AND a lot of times, we share fun teasers and excerpts!

www.authormaxmonroe.com/newsletter

Plus, our newsletter is hilarious! Character conversations about royal babies, parenting woes, embarrassing moments, and shitty horoscopes are just the beginning! If you're already signed up, consider sending us a message to tell us how much you love us. We really like that. ;)

Need EVEN MORE Max Monroe before our next release?

Never fear, we have a list of nearly FIFTY other titles to keep you busy for as long as your little reading heart desires!

Check out our Suggested Reading Order on our website!

www.authormaxmonroe.com/max-monroe-suggested-reading-order

Follow us online here:

Facebook: www.facebook.com/authormaxmonroe

Reader Group: www.facebook.com/groups/1561640154166388

Twitter: www.twitter.com/authormaxmonroe

Instagram: www.instagram.com/authormaxmonroe

TikTok: m.tiktok.com/ZMe1jv5kQ

Goodreads: goo.gl/8VUIz2

ACKNOWLEDGMENTS

To all of the most important people in our lives.

You know who you are.

We couldn't do this without you.

We love you.

To all of our reader friends, THANK YOU FOR READING. You're the best.

XOXO,
Max & Monroe

Printed in Great Britain
by Amazon

59255989R00179